PENGUIN

DEATH AT THE PRESIDENT'S LODGING

Michael Innes was the pseudonym of J. I. M. Stewart, who was a Student of Christ Church, Oxford, from 1949 until his retirement in 1973. He was born in 1906 and was educated at Edinburgh Academy and Oriel College, Oxford. He was lecturer in English at the University of Leeds from 1930 to 1935, Jury Professor of English at the University of Adelaide, South Australia, from 1935 to 1945, and lecturer in Queen's University, Belfast, between 1946 and 1948. J. I. M. Stewart died in November 1994.

He published many novels – including the quintet *A Staircase in Surrey* (*The Gaudy*, *Young Pattullo*, *A Memorial Service*, *The Madonna of the Astrolabe* and *Full Term*) – several volumes of short stories, as well as books of criticism and essays, under his own name. His *Eight Modern Writers* appeared in 1963 as the final volume of *The Oxford History of English Literature*, and he was also the author of *Rudyard Kipling* (1966) and *Joseph Conrad* (1968). His other books include *Andrew and Tobias* (1981), *The Bridge at Arta and Other Stories* (1981), *A Villa in France* (1982), *My Aunt Christine and Other Stories* (1983), *An Open Prison* (1984), *The Naylors* (1985), and *Parlour 4 and Other Stories* (1986).

Under the pseudonym of Michael Innes he wrote broadcast scripts and many crime novels including *Appleby's End* (1945), *The Bloody Wood* (1966), *An Awkward Lie* (1971), *The Open House* (1972), *Appleby's Answer* (1973), *Appleby's Other Story* (1974), *The Appleby File* (1975) *The Gay Phoenix* (1976), *Honeybath's Haven* (1977), *The Ampersand Papers* (1978), *Going It Alone* (1980), *Lord Mullion's Secret* (1981), *Sheiks and Adders* (1982), *Appleby and Honeybath* (1983), *Carson's Conspiracy* (1984) and *Appleby and the Ospreys* (1986). Several of these are published in Penguin.

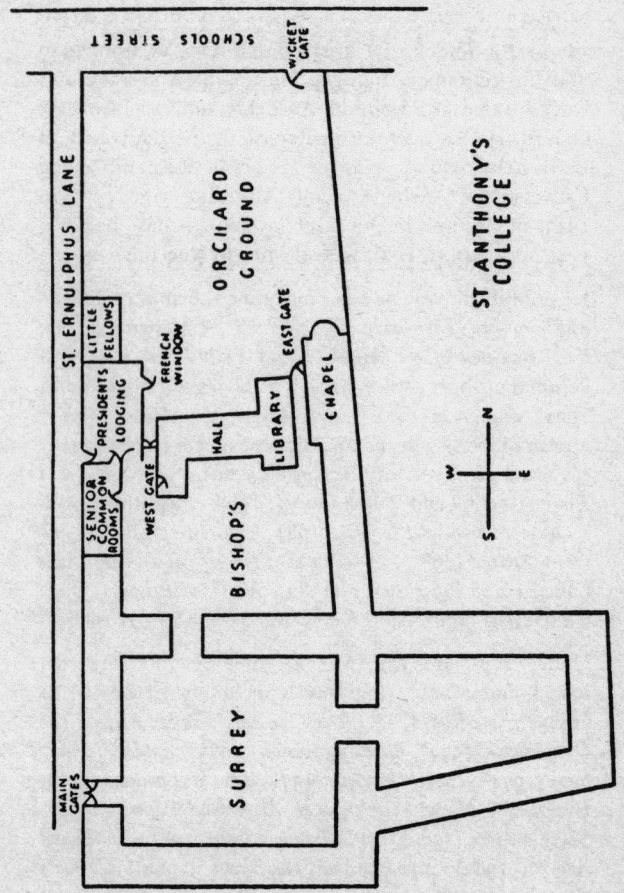

DEATH AT THE PRESIDENT'S LODGING

BY

MICHAEL INNES

PENGUIN BOOKS

PENGUIN BOOKS

Published by the Penguin Group
Penguin Books Ltd, 27 Wrights Lane, London W8 5TZ, England
Penguin Putnam Inc., 375 Hudson Street, New York, New York 10014, USA
Penguin Books Australia Ltd, Ringwood, Victoria, Australia
Penguin Books Canada Ltd, 10 Alcorn Avenue, Toronto, Ontario, Canada M4V 3B2
Penguin Books (NZ) Ltd, Private Bag 102902, NSMC, Auckland, New Zealand

Penguin Books Ltd, Registered Offices: Harmondsworth, Middlesex, England

First published in Great Britain under the title
Death at the President's Lodging 1936
First published in the United States of America by
Dodd, Mead & Company, Inc. 1937
Published in Penguin Books in Great Britain 1958
Published in Penguin Books in the
United States of America under the title *Seven Suspects* 1984
Published in Penguin Books in Great Britain under the title
Death at the President's Lodging 1988
7 9 10 8

Copyright 1936 by J. I. M. Stewart
Copyright 1937 by Dodd, Mead and Company, Inc.
Copyright © renewed
John Innes Mackintosh Stewart, 1965
All rights reserved

Printed in England by Clays Ltd, St Ives plc
Set in Baskerville

Except in the United States of America, this book is sold subject
to the condition that it shall not, by way of trade or otherwise, be lent,
re-sold, hired out, or otherwise circulated without the publisher's
prior consent in any form of binding or cover other than that in
which it is published and without a similar condition including this
condition being imposed on the subsequent purchaser

NOTE

THE SENIOR MEMBERS of Oxford and Cambridge colleges are undoubtedly among the most moral and level-headed of men. They do nothing aberrant; they do nothing rashly or in haste. Their conventional associations are with learning, unworldliness, absence of mind, and endearing and always innocent foible. They are, as Ben Jonson would have said, persons such as comedy would choose; it is much easier to give them a shove into the humorous than a twist into the melodramatic; they prove peculiarly resistive to the slightly rummy psychology that most detective-stories require. And this is a pity if only because their habitat—the material structure in which they talk, eat and sleep—offers such a capital frame for the quiddities and wiliebeguilies of the craft.

Fortunately, there is one spot of English ground on which these reasonable and virtuous men go sadly to pieces—on which they exhibit all those symptoms of irritability, impatience, passion and uncharitableness which make smooth the path of the novelist. It is notorious that when your Oxford or Cambridge man goes not "up" nor "down" but "across"—when he goes, in fact, from Oxford to Cambridge or from Cambridge to Oxford—he must traverse a region strangely antipathetic to the true academic calm. This region is situated, by a mysterious dispensation, almost half-way between the two ancient seats of learning—hard by the otherwise blameless environs of Bletchley. The more facile type of scientific mind, accustomed to canvass immediately obvious physical circumstances, has formerly pointed by way of explanation of this fact to certain deficiencies in the economy of *Bletchley Junction*. One had to wait there so long (in effect the argument ran) and with so little of solid material comfort—that who wouldn't be a bit upset?

But all that is of the past; when I last sped through the Junction it seemed a little paradise; and, anyway, my literary temper is for more metaphysical explanations. I prefer to think that midway between the strong polarities of Athens and Thebes the ether is troubled; the air, to a scholar, nothing sweet and nimble. And I have fancied that if those Oxford clerks who centuries ago attempted a secession had gone to Bletchley there might have arisen the university—or at least the college—I wanted for this story. . . Anyone who takes down a map when reading Chapter X will see that I have acted on my fancy. St. Anthony's, a fictitious college, is part too of a fictitious university. And its Fellows are fantasy all—without substance and without (forbearing Literary reader!) any mantle of imaginative truth to cover their nakedness. Here are ghosts; here is a purely speculative scene of things.

DEATH AT
THE PRESIDENT'S
LODGING

CHAPTER I

I

AN academic life, Dr. Johnson observed, puts one little in the way of extraordinary casualties. This was not the experience of the Fellows and scholars of St. Anthony's College when they awoke one raw November morning to find their President, Josiah Umpleby, murdered in the night. The crime was at once intriguing and bizarre, efficient and theatrical. It was efficient because nobody knew who had committed it. And it was theatrical because of a macabre and unnecessary act of fantasy with which the criminal, it was quickly rumoured, had accompanied his deed.

The college hummed. If Dr. Umpleby had shot himself, decent manners would have demanded reticence and the suppression of overt curiosity all round. But murder, and mysterious murder at that, was felt almost at once to license open excitement and speculation. By ten o'clock on the morning following the event it would have been obvious to the most abstracted don, accustomed to amble through the courts with his eye turned in upon the problem of the historical Socrates, that the quiet of St. Anthony's had been rudely upset. The great gates of the college were shut; all who came or went suffered the unfamiliar ordeal of scrutiny by the senior porter and a uniformed sergeant of police. From the north window of the library another uniformed figure could be glimpsed guarding the closely curtained windows of the President's study. The many staircases by which the mediæval university contrived to postpone the institution of the corridor were lively with the athletic tread of undergraduates, bounding up and down to discuss the catastrophe with friends. Shortly before eleven o'clock a sheet of notepaper—unobtrusive, but displayed contrary to custom outside the college—informed undergraduates from elsewhere that no lectures would be held in St. Anthony's that day. By noon the local papers had their posters on the streets—and in no other town would they have read as discreetly as they did: *Sudden Death of the President of St. Anthony's.* For in the papers themselves the fact was stated: Dr. Umpleby had been shot—it was suspected deliberately and by an unknown hand. Throughout the afternoon a little knot of lounging townsfolk, idly gathered on the further side of St. Ernulphus Lane, satisfied their curiosity by staring up at the long row of grey-mullioned, flat-arched Tudor windows behind which so intriguing a local tragedy lay. And local tragedy meanwhile was becoming national news. By four-thirty hundreds of thousands of people in Pimlico, in Bow, in Clerkenwell, in the mushroom suburbs of outer London and the hidden warrens of Westminster, were adding a new name to their knowledge of a very remote university town. The later editions put this public on a level with the local loungers, for the same long line of Tudor windows stretched in photographic perspective across the front page. By seven o'clock quadruple supplies of these metropolitanly-keyed news-sheets were being feverishly unloaded within hail of St. Anthony's itself. The cloistral repose of the college was shattered indeed.

But it is a troubled quiet that much of the university enjoys in the twentieth century. Day and night the vast aggregation of London, sixty miles away, clamours for supplies; day and night it sends out products of its own. And day and night the venerable streets, up and down which so many generations of scholars and poets have sauntered in meditative calm, re-echo to the roar of modern transport. By day the city is itself a chief offender; local buses and innumerable undergraduate-driven cars jam and eddy in the narrow streets. But by night the place becomes an artery only; regularly, remorselessly, with just interval enough to allow uneasy expectation, the heavy night-travelling lorries and pantechnicons of modern commerce rumble and thunder through the town. And day and night as the ceaseless stream goes by, the grey and fretted stone, sweeping in its gentle curve from bridge to bridge, shudders and breathes, as at the stroke of a great hammer upon the earth.

St. Anthony's is fortunate amid all this. Alone among the colleges that front the worst of the hubbub, it presents on this aspect a spacious garden, the famous Orchard Ground. Behind the privacy of a twelve-foot wall, topped by lofty ornamental railings, a spreading lawn thickly set with apple trees runs back to meet the first and most massive group of college buildings: the chapel, the library and the hall. Beyond the great screen of these, in Bishop's Court, the hum of traffic scarcely penetrates. And beyond that again the oldest part of the college, the mediæval Surrey Court, with its high Early English archway and main gates giving on St. Ernulphus Lane, almost touches the inviolate calm of King Alfred's Meadows. The ancient town has its haunts for the dreamer still.

But the great garden of Orchard Ground had proved from time to time the haunt of anything but quiet activities. The St. Anthony's undergraduates had rioted in it, hunted a real fox in it, smuggled into it under cover of darkness a very sizeable sow on the verge of parturition. Orchard Ground, therefore, had long been locked up at night; junior members of the college had no access to it after ten-fifteen. The senior members, the Fellows, could use a key: for four of them who lodged in Orchard Ground a key was essential. . . . And upon Orchard Ground, thus peculiarly insulated at night, opened the French windows of the study in which Dr. Umpleby's body had been found.

II

It had been a quarter past two when the great yellow Bentley swung out of New Scotland Yard; it drew up outside St. Anthony's just as four o'clock was chiming from a score of bells. Seldom, Inspector John Appleby reflected, had he been so expeditiously dispatched to investigate a case of presumed murder beyond the metropolitan area. And indeed, his arrival in the Yard's most resplendent vehicle was sign and symbol of august forces having been at work: that morning the Dean of St. Anthony's had hastily seen the Vice-Chancellor; the Vice-Chancellor had no less hastily telephoned to the Lord Chancellor of England, High Steward of the university; the Lord Chancellor had communicated quite briskly with the Home Secretary. . . . It was not unlikely, Appleby thought as he jumped out of the car, that local authority might feel central authority to have been pitched somewhat abruptly at its head. He was therefore relieved when, on being shown by a frightened parlourmaid into the deceased President's dining-room, he discovered local authority incarnated in no more formidable shape than that of an old acquaintance, Inspector Dodd.

These two men offered an interesting contrast—the contrast not so much of two generations (although Appleby was by full twenty years the younger) as of two epochs of English life. Dodd, heavy, slow, simply bred, and speaking with such a dialectical purity that a philologist might have named the parish in which he was born, suggested an England fundamentally rural still—and an England in which crime, when it occurred, was clear and brutal, calling less for science and detective skill than for vigorous physical action. He had learned a routine, but he was essentially untrained and unspecialized, relying upon a pithy if uncertain native shrewdness, retaining something strong and individual in his mental, as in his linguistic, idiom. Beside him, Appleby's personality seemed at first thin, part effaced by some long discipline of study, like a surgeon whose individuality has concentrated itself within the channels of a unique operative technique. For Appleby was the efficient product of a more "developed" age than Dodd's; of an age in which our civilization, multiplying its elements by division, has produced, amid innumerable highly-specialized products, the highly-specialized criminal and the highly-specialized detector of crime. Nevertheless, there was something more in Appleby than the intensely taught product of a modern police college. A contemplative habit and a tentative mind, poise as well as force, reserve rather than wariness—these were the tokens perhaps of some underlying, more liberal education. It was a schooled but still free intelligence that was finally formidable in Appleby, just as it was something of tradition and of the soil that was finally formidable in Dodd.

The two men were likely enough to clash; with a little goodwill they were equally likely to combine. And now Dodd, for all his fifteen stone and an uncommon tiredness (he had been working on the case since early morning), sprang up with decent cordiality to welcome his colleague. "The detective arrives," he said with a deep chuckle when greetings had been exchanged, "and the village policeman hands over the body with all the misunderstood clues to date." As he spoke, Dodd turned towards the table, on which a pile of papers evinced his industry during the day. They were flanked on the one hand by a hastily-made but sufficiently clear ground-plan of the college and on the other by the remains of bread and cheese, and beer in stout academic pewter—refreshments which it had occurred to Dr. Umpleby's servants, round about three o'clock, that the inspector might stand a little in need of. "The St. Anthony's beer," Dodd said, "is a good feature of the case. The village policeman is baffled, but he gets his pint."

Appleby smiled. "The village policeman has notably mastered his facts," he replied, "at least if he's the same policeman I knew a couple of years ago. The Yard still talks about your check-up on those motor-thieves . . . you remember?"

Dodd's acknowledgment of the compliment in the reminiscence took the form of wasting no time now. Drawing up a chair for Appleby he placed the pile of papers between them. "I've been going a bit fast today," he said abruptly, "and what I've got here is limited by going fast. It's short all round but it gives us bearings. There has been ground enough to cover, and first on the spot must get quickly over all, you'll agree. I've taken dozens of statements in a hasty way. Any one of them might have put me direct on somebody making out of the country. But none of them has. It's a mystery right enough, Appleby. In other words, it looks like one of your cases, not mine."

Dodd's handsome speech was sincere but not wholly disinterested. Fortified by the St. Anthony's ale, he had been spending the last hour thinking, and the more he had thought the less he had liked the results. His mind, indeed, had begun to stray, shying from this case on which he could see no beginning to another case of which he hoped soon to see the end. For some time he had been working on an extensive series of burglaries in the suburbs and this baffling matter of Dr. Umpleby, obviously urgent, had come to interrupt his personal control of a round-up from which he saw himself as likely to gain a good deal of credit. He put his position to Appleby now and it was agreed that the latter should, for the time being, take over the St. Anthony's mystery as completely as possible. As soon as they had come to an understanding on this, Dodd placed the plan of the college in front of Appleby and proceeded to outline the facts as he knew them.

"Dr. Umpleby was shot dead at eleven o'clock last night. That's the first of several things that make his death something like the story-books. You know the murdered squire's house in the middle of the snowstorm? And all the fancy changes rung on that—liners on the ocean, submarines, balloons in the air, locked rooms with never a chimney? St. Anthony's or any other college, you see, is something like that from half-past nine every night. Here's your submarine." As he spoke, Dodd took up the ground-plan and ran a large finger aggressively round the perimeter of the St. Anthony's buildings. "But in this college," he went on, "there's more to it than that." This time his finger ran round a lesser circuit. "In this college there's submarine *within* submarine. At half-past nine they shut off the college as a whole from the world. And then later, at ten-fifteen, they shut off one bit of the college from the rest. That is almost a pure story-book situation now, isn't it? Nobody gets in or out of the college after half-past nine that the porter doesn't know of—*with certain exceptions*. Nobody got in or out from half-past nine last night to this present moment that we don't know of—*with the same possible exceptions*. And after ten-fifteen, nobody can go to and fro between the main body of the college (submarine) and this additionally shut-off Orchard Ground (submarine within submarine) with, again, *the same possible exceptions*. Only"—and here Inspector Dodd suddenly spoke with a vigorous irritation—"none of the exceptions appears to be a homicidal lunatic! And therefore the lunatic who did *that*"—and here Dodd jerked his thumb in the direction of the next room—"ought still to be on the premises. *I* haven't found him, Appleby. Every man alive in this college is saner and more blameless than the rest."

"Why necessarily look for a lunatic?" Appleby asked.

"I don't," responded Dodd soberly. "That hanky-panky through there rattled me for a moment," and again he motioned towards the next room. "You'll see what I mean presently," he continued a little grimly, "but the point I have to make now is about these exceptions. The exceptions, as you may guess, are certain of the Fellows of the college —not by any means all of them. They have keys—double-purpose keys. They can enter or leave the college with them through this little door on Schools Street. And you see where—if they're coming in—that lands them. It lands them straight in the submarine within a submarine, Orchard Ground. They can then use the same key to get them out of Orchard Ground into the rest of the college. And when I give you the facts of the case in a minute you'll see that the murderer of Dr. Umpleby appears to have had one of those keys. Which is no doubt," the inspector added dryly, "why *you* have been sent for in such a hurry."

"I see the suggested situation, anyway," Appleby replied, after a brief scrutiny of the ground-plan. "Whereas in a normal college a nocturnal murder would probably be physically within the power of anyone within the college, *this* college is so arranged that *this* murder could apparently be carried out only by quite a few people—people who had, or who could get hold of, a key to this Orchard Ground. For the keys—you are maintaining, are you not? —gave the particular sort of access to Dr. Umpleby that the circumstances seem to require."

Dodd nodded. "You've got it," he said, "and you can understand the perturbation of St. Anthony's."

"There is the obvious fact that keys are treacherous things. They're easier to steal usually than a cheque-book—and far easier to copy than a signature."

Dodd shook his head. "Yes, but you'll see presently that there's more to it than that. The topography of the business really is uncommonly odd."

Both men looked at the plan in silence for a moment. "Well," said Appleby at length, "here is our stage setting. Now let us have the characters and events."

III

"I'll begin with characters," Dodd said, "indeed I'll begin where I had to begin this morning; with a list of names." As he spoke, the inspector rummaged among his papers as if looking for a memorandum. Then, apparently thinking better of it, he squared his shoulders, wrinkled his brow in concentration and continued with his eyes fixed upon his own large boots.

"Here are the Fellows who were dining in college last night. In addition to the President there was the Dean; he's called the Reverend the Honourable Tracy Deighton-Clerk." (There was an indefinable salt in the inspector's mode of conveying this information.) "And there were Mr. Lambrick, Professor Empson, Mr. Haveland, Mr. Titlow, Dr. Pownall, Dr. Gott, Mr. Campbell, Professor Curtis, Mr. Chalmers-Paton and Dr. Barocho."

Appleby nodded. "Deighton-Clerk," he repeated, "Lambrick, Empson, Haveland, Titlow, Pownall, Gott, Campbell, Curtis, Chalmers-Paton—and a foreigner who just beats me. Go on."

"Barocho," said Dodd. "And only one Fellow, as it happens, was absent. He's called Ransome and at the moment he's said to be digging up some learned stuff in central

Asia." Dodd's tone again conveyed some hint of the feeling that Dr. Umpleby's death had landed him among queer fish. "Not that I've any proof," he continued suspiciously, "of where this Ransome is. That's just what they all say."

Appleby smiled. "The submarine seems well officered," he said. "If you're going on to extract a list of a couple of hundred or so undergraduates from those boots of yours I think I'd certainly prefer the baronet's country house. Or the balloon in the stratosphere—that generally holds about two." But his eyes as he spoke were on the plan in front of him and in a moment he added: "But the point seems to be that the undergraduates don't come in?"

"I don't think they do," replied Dodd; "at least it's *likely* they don't, just as it's likely the college servants and so on don't—and, as you've gathered, for simple topographical reasons. So the list I've given you may be important. And now, after the scene and the persons, I suppose, events and times. Here is the time-scheme of the thing as far as I've got it into my head.

"Dinner was over by about eight o'clock—as far as the proceedings in hall were concerned. But all the people at the high table—the President, Dean and Fellows, that is— went across in a body as usual to their common-rooms. They sat in the smaller common-room for about half an hour, having a little extra, I gather, in the way of port and dessert. Then at about half-past eight they made another move —still in a body—to the larger common-room next door. They had coffee and cigarettes there—all according to the day's routine still—and talked till about nine o'clock. Dr. Umpleby was the first to leave: he went off through a door that gives directly into his own house. And if we're to believe what we're told, that was the last time any of his colleagues saw him alive.

"Well, the common-room began to break up after that,

and by half-past nine everybody was gone. Lambrick, Campbell, Chalmers-Paton are married men and by half-past nine they were off to their homes. The others all went to their rooms about the college. All, that is, with the exception of Gott, who is Junior Proctor and went out patrolling the streets.

"At nine-thirty the locking up began. The porter locked the main gates. That is the moment, you may say, at which the submarine submerged: from that moment to this nobody can have got in or out of St. Anthony's without observation—*unless he had a key.*"

Appleby shook his head in mild protest. "I incline to distrust those keys from the start," he said, "and I distrust your submarine. A great rambling building like this may have half a dozen irregular entrances—or exits."

But Dodd's reply was confident. "The submarine may sound as if I've been reading novels, but I believe it's near the mark. It's something we have to know in a quiet way—and we could surprise some colleges by pointing out a good many smart dodges. But I've overhauled St. Anthony's today, and it's *watertight.*"

Appleby nodded his provisional acceptance of the point. "Well," he said, "the President is in his Lodging, the dons are in their rooms, the undergraduates are in theirs, and the great world is effectively locked out. What next?"

"More locking out—or in," Dodd promptly replied. "The President's butler locked three doors. He locked the front door of the Lodging giving on Bishop's Court, he locked the back door giving on St. Ernulphus Lane, and he locked the door between the Lodging and the common-rooms—the one, that is, the President had used a little before. That was about ten o'clock. At ten-fifteen came the final locking-up. The porter locked the gates to Orchard Ground. . . ."

Dodd had so far been delivering himself of this scheme of things without book. Now he paused and handed Appleby a sheaf of notes. "I'd go over that again, if I were you," he said; "it takes a little getting clear."

Appleby went slowly over the notes and observed, with something of the admiration that was intended, that Dodd had apparently let no discrepancy creep into his oral account. He looked up when he had digested the names and times, and Dodd went on to the crisis of his narrative.

"When Dr. Umpleby left the common-room he went straight to his study. At half-past ten his butler, Slotwiner, took in some sort of drink—it was the regular routine apparently—and then retired to his pantry off the hall. Slotwiner more or less had his eye on the hall during the next half-hour and nobody, he says, entered the study that way, and nobody came out. In other words, there was only one way into—or out of—the study during that period—by way of the French windows that give on Orchard Ground."

"The so-securely locked Orchard Ground," murmured Appleby.

Dodd took up the implications of the other's tone perceptively enough. "Exactly. I suppose our first clue is just that—that we have to deal, from the outset, with so obviously artificial a situation. But here meantime is this butler, Slotwiner, in his pantry. The pantry is a mere nook of a place and normally he would have gone downstairs to where he has a room of his own beside the kitchens. But apparently on this night of the week, Mr. Titlow—that's the senior Fellow—has been in the habit of calling on the President for a short talk on college business. He comes regularly just on eleven—pretty late, it seems to me, for a call, but the idea was that each could get in a couple of hours' work after the usual common-room convivialities were over. I believe, you know, that these folk do quite an amount of work in their own way. Well, Slotwiner waited upstairs to let Titlow in. He had to unlock the front door—this one opening on Bishop's Court—because, as you remember, he had locked it along with the other two doors at ten o'clock, following the rule in Umpleby's household. Titlow turned up as usual on the stroke of eleven and he and Slotwiner were just exchanging a word in the hall when they heard the shot."

"The shot coming, no doubt," said Appleby, "from the study where Umpleby was supposed to be sitting *solus?*"

"Exactly so. And he was *solus*—or rather his corpse was —when Titlow and Slotwiner rushed into the room. Umpleby was shot; there was—if we are to believe these two— no weapon; but the French windows giving on Orchard Ground were ajar. Well, Titlow and Slotwiner (or one of them—I don't know which) tumbled to the situation surprisingly quickly. They saw it was murder and they saw the significance of Orchard Ground. If the murderer had escaped that way he was there still, unless—what didn't occur to them—he had the key to those gates."

The inspector picked up a pencil this time and ran it over the plan. Very laboriously, once more, he made his cardinal point. "You'll see how certain that is," he said, "when you get out there. On these three sides Orchard Ground is bounded either by an exceedingly high wall or by an arrangement of combined wall and railings that is higher still. The fourth side has the President's Lodging here at one end and the college chapel at the other, with the hall and library in between. These make a line of buildings that separated Orchard Ground from Bishop's Court, and there are just two passages through: one between chapel and library and the other between hall and President's Lodging. The only other exit from Orchard Ground is by a little wicket gate opening on Schools Street. And all three exits were, of course, locked. Escape from Orchard Ground without the key was impossible.

"So you see Titlow and Slotwiner decided they'd got the murderer safe. They didn't think he could get out because they didn't think he could have the key to those three gates. And they didn't think he could have a key because it didn't occur to them to think of a Fellow of the college.

"I suspect Slotwiner of taking the initiative. He's an old soldier and would be up to an emergency, whereas Titlow seems a dreamy soul enough. But Titlow's got guts. The look of that room was pretty surprising, but he stuck there guarding the window while Slotwiner ran to the telephone in the hall and got the porters across, called a doctor and got on to us. I was at the station late working at reports of my own case and I got enough from Slotwiner to be along with every man I could muster in ten minutes. Slotwiner and Titlow were in the study still with a porter to help them keep guard. We went through everything on the orchard side of those gates as if we were looking for a black cat. We worked on a cordon basis from one end to the other, ransacked the chapel and the little block of Fellows' buildings opposite and climbed every tree. Apart from three of the four Fellows (Titlow is the fourth) who live in Orchard Ground and were there undisturbed in their rooms, we found no one. We searched again by daylight, of course, and the gates are guarded still."

Dodd paused for a moment and Appleby asked a question: "There is no trace of any sort of robbery?"

"None at all. Money, watch and so on still on the corpse. There is one point, though, that might conceivably be relevant." Dodd picked up a small object wrapped in tissue-paper and tossed it down in front of his colleague. "Umpleby's pocket-diary—and found in his pocket all right.

Plenty of entries for you to study—until you come just up to date. The leaf for the last two days, and the leaf for today and tomorrow, have been torn out. . . . And now come along."

IV

The two men left the dead President's dining-room and crossed the hall to where, at the end of a narrow corridor, a stalwart constable stood guard over the study door. He stood aside with a salute and a frank provincial stare at Appleby, while Dodd, taking a key from his pocket, unlocked the door and pushed it open with something of a restrained dramatic gesture.

The study was a long, well-proportioned room, with a deep open fireplace opposite the single door and with windows at each end: to the left (and barred like all the ground-floor outer windows of the college), a row of small windows giving on St. Ernulphus Lane; to the right, rather narrow French windows, now heavily curtained, but giving, as Appleby knew, upon Orchard Ground. The sombrely-furnished, book-lined apartment was lit partly by the dull light of the November evening and partly by a single electric standard lamp. Half-way between the French windows and the fireplace, sprawled upon its back, lay the body of a man—tall, spare, dinner-jacketed. So much, and so much only, was visible, for round the head there was swathed, as if in gross burlesque of the common offices of death, the dull black stuff of an academic gown.

But it was not at this sight that Appleby started a little as he entered the room. If Dodd had spoken of a lunatic he now saw why. From the dull dark-oak panels over the fireplace, roughly scrawled in chalk, a couple of grinning death's heads stared out upon the room. Just beside the

President's grotesquely muffled head lay a human skull. And over the surrounding area of the floor were scattered little piles of human bones.

For a long moment Appleby paused on the spectacle; then he moved over to the French windows and pulled back the curtain. Dusk was falling and the trim college orchard seemed to hold all the mystery of a forest. Only close to him on the right, breaking the illusion, was the grey line of hall and library, stone upon buttressed stone, fading, far above, into the darkness of stained-glass windows. Directly in front, in uncertain silhouette against a lustreless Eastern sky, loomed the boldly arabesqued gables of the Caroline chapel. An exhalation neither wholly mist nor wholly fog was beginning to glide over the immemorial turf, to curl round the trees, to dissolve in insubstantial pageantry the fading lines of archway and wall. And echoing over the college and the city, muted as if in requiem for what lay within, was the age-old melody of vesper bells.

CHAPTER II

I

For some minutes Appleby continued to stare out upon the fast thickening shadows. Then, without turning round and almost as if in soliloquy, he began to feel for his own grip on the case.

"At ten-fifteen this court, Orchard Ground, was locked up. After that, anyone who was in it could get out, or who was out could get in, in one of two ways. The one way was by means of the key possessed by certain of the Fellows: with that one could pass either between the orchard and the rest of the college by one of the two gates giving on Bishop's Court; or between the orchard and the outer world by means of the little gate that gives on Schools Street. The other way was through these French windows, through this study and out by one of the doors in the President's hall— the front door giving on Bishop's Court, the common-room door giving indirectly on the same quarter, or the back door giving on St. Ernulphus Lane and, again, the outer world.

"At ten-thirty Umpleby, according to the butler, was alive. From then until eleven o'clock, according to the butler, no one passed from the study through the hall to Bishop's Court or St. Ernulphus Lane—or conversely.

"At eleven o'clock, according to the butler and Titlow, there was a shot from the study. They went in at once and found Umpleby dead. They then claim to have had the route through the study under continuous observation until they handed over to you. And you had it under observation until you had searched study, Orchard Ground and all the buildings in Orchard Ground thoroughly.

"Accepting these appearances we have a fairly clear situation. If Umpleby was shot when we think he was and where we think he was and other than by himself, then his assailant was *either* one of the three people discovered by you during your search *or* a fourth person having a key. That fourth person, again, might be *either* another of the persons legitimately possessed of keys *or* an unknown person in wrongful possession of one. It follows that there are two preliminary issues: first, the movements of the persons legitimately possessed of keys and, as an extension of that, the relations of such persons to Umpleby; secondly, the provenance of the existing keys—the history of each, with the likelihood of its having been abstracted and copied in the recent past."

Appleby, as he worked out this concise and knotty résumé of the facts, spoke with a shade of reluctance. He was less ready than Dodd for anything savouring of a conventional mystery, and he was inclined to distrust inference from the oddly precise conditions under which Umpleby had apparently been murdered. As Dodd had shrewdly remarked, the affair was obtrusively artificial, as if the criminal had gone out of his way to sign himself both ingenious and grotesque, calculating and whimsical. Within an hour of his arrival at St. Anthony's, Appleby was finding a particular line of action imposed upon him—a line demanding minute and probably laborious investigation into the conduct and dispositions of a small, clearly-marked group of people. He saw that he was confronted, actually, with two propositions. The first was simple: "The circumstances are such that I must concentrate on so-and-so." The second was less simple: "The circumstances *have been so contrived as to suggest* that I must concentrate on so-and-so." In pursuing the first proposition he must, at least, not lose sight of the second.

Appleby checked surmise and turned once more to Dodd for information. "Which of the Fellows lodge in Orchard Ground?" he asked. "Which of them have keys? How far have you traced their movements after the break-up in the common-room last night?"

"The four that lodge in Orchard Ground," Dodd replied, "are Empson, Pownall, Titlow and Haveland. They're in a building next to, but not communicating with, this Lodging. It's just through here"—and Dodd tapped his finger stolidly on one of the scrawled death's heads above the dead man's fireplace. "The block is called Little Fellows'. There are two sets of rooms on each side of a staircase," he continued with precision, "and the men live like this." And with a quick rummage Dodd produced another of his industriously prepared papers.

Upper floor	Empson	Titlow
Ground floor	Pownall	Haveland

"We found Empson, Pownall, Haveland each in his own room; Pownall in bed, the others working. About Titlow's movements you know. Now about the keys; with them we come to the really extraordinary factor. These four people lodging in Orchard Ground all have keys. Being shut off from the rest of the college they naturally have to. And you would expect that for convenience of getting at them, as well as to get in and out of the college by the wicket without rousing the porter, all their colleagues would have keys as well. But they haven't. You know, they're an unpractical lot."

Appleby smiled a little grimly. "There may be one among them," he said, "who is—efficient."

"Well, for that matter most of them are efficient after a

particular fashion. They're not vague, for instance. They're keen and precise, really. Only it's a preciseness, I reckon, that has all run to things a long way off or a long time back. For instance, there's Professor Curtis. He lodges in Surrey Court. I asked him if he had a key to the gates. 'Gates, Mr. Inspector,' he said, 'gates?' 'The gates between this and Orchard Ground,' I explained. 'Yes, to be sure,' he said, 'there's a story they came from Cordova. The college had them from the third earl of Blackwood; he served in Sidmouth's second ministry.' 'But have you a key?' I asked again. 'I relinquished my key,' he replied at once, 'at the end of April, 1911.' 'End of April, 1911,' I repeated a bit blankly. 'Yes,' he said, 'at the end of April, 1911. Empson won both Cornwalls that year, you know, and we elected him to his Fellowship at once. He's done nothing since, either. He'll make an admirable President, no doubt. You did say poor Dr. Umpleby was quite dead, did you not?' 'Quite dead,' I answered, '—and you're quite sure you haven't had a key since 1911?' 'Quite sure,' he said; 'I gave up my key to Empson. I remember reflecting what an excellent thing a locked gate between colleagues might be. If you want a key, Inspector, the porter will no doubt lend you his.' "

As Dodd concluded this remarkable feat of witness-box memory, he produced yet another paper. "Here," he added impressively, "is a table." And he laid it before Appleby.

x Deighton-Clerk	Bishop's
x Empson	Orchard Ground
x Haveland	Orchard Ground
x Pownall	Orchard Ground
x Titlow	Orchard Ground
Barocho	Bishop's
Campbell	*married;* Schools Street
Chalmers-Paton	*married;* suburb

Curtis	Surrey
x Gott	Surrey
x Lambrick	*married;* suburb

"I've put a cross," said Dodd, "against the people who have keys. There seems to be no system in it. For instance, Lambrick, who is married and lives out of college, keeps a key, but Campbell and Chalmers-Paton, who are in just the same position, get along without one. Gott and the Dean live in college and have keys; Curtis and Barocho also live in college and have not. So much for how the keys are distributed. And now for their history." At this point Dodd broke into an unaccountable chuckle. "You know, I was reading a story the other day which turned on keys—the provenance of keys, as you call it in your learned London way. It was the key of a safe that it was all about, and it couldn't have been stolen—had literally never been in unauthorized hands. And yet it had been copied. Do you know how?"

Appleby laughed. "I could give a good guess, I think. But we don't know we have to search for any fancy tricks here. A key might very easily have been stolen and returned in the recent past."

"Yes," Dodd replied; "recent past is the word." And he looked almost slyly at Appleby as he spoke. For with a nice sense of the dramatic he had delayed the climax of his narration. *"The keys were all changed yesterday morning!"*

Appleby whistled. Dodd when he had heard the same news had sworn. It was the final and overwhelming touch of that topsy-turvy precision that seemed to mark the St. Anthony's case.

Briefly Dodd explained. No one had taken much care of his key. A key is not at all the same thing to a scholar that it is to a banker, a doctor or a business man. The possessions of the learned classes are locked up for the most part in their heads and to a don a key is more often than not something that he discovers himself to have lost when he wants to open a suitcase. And those Fellows of St. Anthony's who possessed keys to the gates which had suddenly become so tragically important had for long been careless enough with them without anybody worrying. But recently there had been a scandal. An undergraduate had got into serious trouble during an illicit nocturnal expedition, and the mystery of how he had made his way in and out of St. Anthony's had not been satisfactorily cleared up. The President had decided that a key had been copied. He had ordered fresh locks and keys for the three vital gates—and the locks had been fitted, and the keys distributed to the people concerned, only the morning before he met his death.

It was Dodd's view that this circumstance, though extraordinary in itself, introduced a welcome simplification into the case. It seemed likely to save an enormous amount of laborious and difficult inquiry—for nothing, as he had found in the interviews he had already conducted that morning, could well be more difficult, delicate and tedious than pursuing a number of academic persons with minute questions as to their material possessions. Moreover, the circle of possible suspects seemed at once to be narrowed in the most definite way. If Dodd at that moment had been called upon to write a formal report on the progress of the investigation he would have risked a categorical assertion. Dr. Umpleby could have been murdered only by one of a small group of persons definitely known.

And Appleby, as he reviewed the situation while pacing restlessly but observantly round the fantastic death-chamber, had also reached one definite conclusion. Mystery stories were popular in universities—and even among the police. Dodd, who still kept so much of an English country-side that read Bunyan and the Bible, and who was, besides, a monument of efficient but unimaginative police routine, was a case in point. His native shrewdness had at once led him to note the artificiality of the present circumstances. But (and such, Appleby reflected, is the extraordinary power of the Word) he was half-prepared to accept the artificial, the strikingly *fictive*, as normal. And he seemed in danger, as a consequence, of missing that most important *Why* in the case: *Why* had Umpleby met his death in a story-book manner? For that his death had been set in an elaborately contrived frame seemed now clear: the circumstance of the changing of the locks made this evident almost to the point of demonstration. Umpleby had died amid circumstances of elaborate ingenuity. He had died in a literary context; indeed, he had in a manner of speaking died amid a confusion of literary contexts. For in the network of physical circumscriptions implicitly pointing (as Appleby had put it to himself) to *so-and-so* there was contrivance in a literary tradition deriving from all the progeny of Sherlock Holmes, while in the fantasy of the bones there was something of the incongruous tradition of the "shocker." Somewhere in the case, it seemed, there was a mind thinking in terms both of inference and of the macabre. . . . A mind, one might say, thinking in terms of Edgar Allan Poe. Poe, come to think of it, was a present intellectual fashion, and St. Anthony's was an intellectual place. . . .

An intellectual place. That was, of course, a vital fact to remember when proceeding a step further—when attempting to answer the question of which Dodd was perhaps insufficiently aware: *Why* had Umpleby met his death like a baronet in a snowstorm? There were two tentative answers: (1) because, for some reason, it was *useful* that way; (2) because it was intellectually amusing that way. . . . Intelligence, after all, had its morbid manifestations.

Appleby caught himself up. He was trying somewhat wildly, he saw, to find an approach to his problem on a human or psychological plane. He knew it to be at once his strength and his weakness as a detective that he was happier on that plane than on the plane of doors and windows and purloined keys. The materials of the criminologist, he used to declare in theoretical moments to colleagues at Scotland Yard, are not finger-prints and cigarette-ends but the human mind as exposed for study in human behaviour. And of human behaviour he had as yet had nothing in the present case. He had been met, so far, not with human actors, but with a set of circumstances—once more the story-book approach, he told himself.

With an odd effect of thought-reading Dodd spoke. "You'll be beginning to look for some of the livestock." And as Appleby, startled by the odd ring of the phrase in the presence of what had been Josiah Umpleby, turned back from the window through which he had been staring, his colleague crossed the room to ring the bell. "We'll have in a witness," he said. And the two men adjourned again to the dining-room.

II

Mr. Harold Tapp had been waiting for half an hour to be interviewed in connexion with a murder, but he was not in the least nervous as a result. He was a sharp, confident little person; he had all the appearance of being reliable and, according to Dodd, he enjoyed the reputation of being an excellent locksmith. Very little prompting was necessary to get him to give a tolerably connected account of his recent dealings with St. Anthony's. His statement was impressively recorded by a sad and portly sergeant summoned for the purpose.

"The late Dr. Humpleby," said Mr. Tapp, "sent for me a week ago today. To be exack—which is what *you* want, you know—the late Dr. Humpleby gave me a ring-hup."

"To be more exact still," said Appleby, "did Dr. Umpleby ring through to you direct, can you tell, or did somebody else make the call before Dr. Umpleby spoke?"

The question found Tapp decided—the only point it was designed to test. Umpleby himself had summoned the locksmith, who had immediately presented himself at the President's Lodging. "You see," said Tapp, "the late Dr. Humpleby was in a nurry. He was in a nurry and a flurry about them locks. I don't think flurry's too strong to describe his 'urry: he was hanxious for the change. He explained the why and wherefore of it too—a nundergrad having been getting hout and all. Hanxious was the late Dr. Humpleby."

Appleby was regarding Mr. Tapp with more interest than he had expected to feel.

"Well, you see," continued the locksmith, "it weren't what you'd call a big job nor it weren't rightly what you'd call a little 'un. So I fixed yesterday morning for fitting, and the late Doctor said it would serve so. Very interested he was in the way of the work too, and particular over the keys. Very proper notions over keys had the late Doctor. Ten keys there were to be and all going to him direck. And ten he got yesterday morning as soon as the locks were fitted and tested by myself."

"Just how did he get them," asked Dodd; "and just how safe had you been keeping them?"

"Well, you see, I'd been on them all week myself and done all the assembling and finishing. And the drawing was in the safe, and the locks and keys in the safe, as often as they weren't in my 'ands. All that's a nabit, you see, with a nigh-class locksmith. Not that all my business is 'igh-class, you know. Still, this was—and treated accordingly. I fitted the locks yesterday morning and then I saw Dr. Humpleby 'imself and gave him the ten keys as required. And from the moment I set file to them to the moment I 'anded them hover every one of them keys 'ad been treated like a bag of golden sovereigns. And they're not a thing you often see nowadays," Mr. Tapp concluded somewhat irrelevantly.

A little questioning substantiated the fact that the new locks and keys had been prepared under completely thief-proof conditions. Appleby's problem of "provenance" was proving very simple indeed. He turned to the point in Tapp's statement which had particularly arrested his interest. "You say that Dr. Umpleby appeared anxious about the keys and gave you a reason—something about an undergraduate? Just how anxious was he? Would you describe him as agitated—really worried about the matter?"

Tapp answered at once. "Hagitated, sir, I wouldn't nor couldn't rightly say. But he was in a nurry and a flurry—and that I *do* say."

Appleby was patient. "Not really agitated, but flurried. I wonder if you can make that a little clearer? Agitation and flurry seem to me very much the same thing. Perhaps you can give me a clearer idea of what you mean by flurry?"

Tapp reflected for a moment. "Well, you see, sir," he said at length, "by flurry I wouldn't quite mean scurry, and by scurry I *would* mean hagitation. I 'ope that's clear. And certainly Dr. Humpleby was in a *nurry*."

This was as much information as was to be obtained from the locksmith and, after he had signed a correctly aspirated version of it prepared by the lugubrious sergeant, he was dismissed.

"Just how odd is it," asked Appleby, "that Umpleby should give the excellent Tapp *reasons* for changing the locks and keys? I don't see that, Dodd, do you? It strikes me as just a shade queer. It's a queerness that may be nothing more than a minute queerness of character. I may be noticing only a minute way in which Umpleby's behaviour has differed from the dead normal behaviour of a dead average Head of a House—or I may be noticing something much more significant. And the same thing applies to the other interesting point—that Umpleby was in what our friend called a flurry about the business; that he was within some recognizable distance, measured by flurries and scurries, of being agitated."

"There's something strikes me as more significant than that." Dodd was very stolid. *"There was an extra key."*

Appleby gave his second whistle of the afternoon. "Your point again! The Dean, Empson, Gott, Haveland, Lambrick, Pownall, Titlow, one for the head porter. . . . Hullo! That's only eight. Surely there were two extra keys?"

Dodd shook his head. "The head porter got one for his ring and another went as a spare in the safe in his lodge. But one key does remain to be accounted for. And an awkward complication it makes."

"Umpleby himself perhaps kept a key?"

Dodd again made a negative gesture. "I don't think so. At least he never, according to the Dean, used to. He had no need of one. He could walk out of his own Lodging into either Orchard Ground or the main courts. And similarly his own back-door let him out on the street. And, of course, we've found no key in his belongings."

"A missing key," murmured Appleby. "Do you know, I'm rather pleased about the missing key. It represents a screw loose somewhere—and so far your submarine has been screwed down uncomfortably tight." But he was speaking absently, and pacing about as he spoke. Then, with a sudden gesture of impatience, he led the way back to the study.

III

The black gown which had been found swathed round the President's head, and which had been replaced there, following police routine, after the police-surgeon had certified life to be extinct, Appleby now carefully removed. It was caked with blood, but only slightly, and Appleby laid it on a chair. He gazed with some curiosity at the dead President. Umpleby's was a massive and, for the spare-bodied man that he was, a surprisingly heavy head, with bone-structure prominent about the brow and commanding nose—fleshy and heavy-jowled below. The mouth, sagging in death, had been rigid in life; firm to the point perhaps of some suggestion of cruelty; ruthless certainly rather than sensual. The eyes were open, and they were cold and grey; the features were composed—oddly at variance with the tiny but startling hall-mark of violence in the centre of the forehead. And death had brushed away a load of years from the pallid face: it was some moments before Appleby saw clearly that Umpleby had been an old man. At the moment he made no examination but picked up the gown again to do the office of a temporary shroud. As he did so something about it held his attention. "I take it this is not Umpleby's gown?" he asked Dodd.

"No, it's not. And it has no name on it. I haven't, as a matter of fact, questioned people about it so far."

"You needn't, I think, expend much effort on that. It's Dr. Barocho's gown."

A second thought and Dodd had taken the point neatly. "You mean it's some sort of foreign gown, not an English one?"

"Exactly so, and Barocho follows as a good guess. But

I doubt if it will be a case for bringing out the handcuffs. And now what about the movements of all these people? How far, to get back to where we were, have you traced their movements after the break-up of the common-room last night?"

Appleby was prowling round the study again. Dodd rustled among his papers as he answered. "In the course of the day I've taken preliminary statements from everybody who seems concerned—or everybody who seemed concerned until this infernal tenth key started up. Some are apparently checkable as alibi-statements for the time of the shooting; others not. I'm checking up as fast as the three capable men I've got can work—incidentally they're *your* men now for the purposes of the case. Meantime here are the carbons of the different statements. You'd better hold on to them." As he spoke, Dodd put the little pile of flimsies down in front of his colleague with an air that suggested plainly enough the symbolic shifting of responsibility latent in the act. Appleby turned to the first sheet.

Slotwiner, George Frederick (54). Entered the college service as buttery-boy at sixteen. Personal servant to Dr. Umpleby on the latter's becoming Dean of the college in 1910. Has acted as butler since Dr. Umpleby became President in 1921.

10.30 p.m. Took in drinks to study, finding President working at his desk and alone. Thereafter had a full view of the study door from his pantry.

11 p.m. Crossed hall and admitted Mr. Titlow at front door. Titlow still speaking to him when shot heard. Entered study along with Titlow and discovered body. Returned to hall and telephoned doctor, porter and police. Rejoined Titlow in study and kept guard until arrival of porters.

11.10 p.m. Took message from Titlow to Dean.

Corroboration: Titlow.
Titlow, Samuel Still (51). . . .

At this moment there came an interruption in the form of a heavy knocking at the door, and the melancholy sergeant thrust in his head and announced lugubriously: "The valley has a message!"

The valley of the shadow. . . . For a moment in the darkening room with its litter of dead men's bones, the effect of the words was almost startling; a second later they were explained by the appearance of a discreet black-coated figure in the background. A discreet voice remonstrated, "*Butler,* if you please, *constable!*" and added, to the accompaniment of a ghost of a bow to Dodd, "The Dean's compliments, sir, and if the gentleman from London has arrived he would be glad to see him in his rooms at his convenience."

Appleby regarded George Frederick Slotwiner with all the interest due to the first intimate actor in the recent drama to present himself. Slotwiner bore little trace of any period he might have spent in the Army. Slight and sallow, he moved and held himself like a typical upper servant. Apparently somewhat short-sighted, he looked out upon the world through a pair of pince-nez glasses with an effect at once impressive and disconcerting—impressive because they contrived to elevate the mind from butlers to housestewards, and from house-stewards to majordomos and grooms of the chamber; disconcerting because of a sudden doubt that their owner's stiff bearing was less the expression of professional dignity than the result of some chronic balancing feat on his nose. As this thought crossed Appleby's mind Slotwiner, who appeared to have been inwardly debating whether propriety permitted him any direct awareness of the gentleman from London's presence, made the ghost of a bow to him as well and, having effected this judicious compromise, waited impassively for a reply.

Appleby solved Slotwiner's difficulty. "My compliments to the Dean," he said, "and I will be with him in half an hour. When Inspector Dodd rings the bell perhaps you will be good enough to take me across." And as the butler turned to withdraw he suddenly added: "One moment. When did the President last use candles in this room?"

The effect of this question was remarkable. Slotwiner swung round with a most unbutler-like rapidity and stared at Appleby. He was plainly startled and confused—more so even than the odd and abrupt question, pitched at his back across the shrouded body of his employer, could warrant. But in a moment his look gave way to one of bewilderment; a moment more and he was wholly composed.

"The President never used candles, sir. As you will see, the room is very adequately lighted." The man's hand went swiftly out as he spoke and flicked down a switch by the door: the single standard lamp which had been burning was reinforced by half-a-dozen further lamps set high up on the walls and throwing out a brilliant light over the ceiling. Appleby continued his questions. "How did the President usually sit when he was here in the evenings? Did he use all the lights or merely the standard lamp?"

The butler answered now without hesitation. When at his desk, or when sitting in his arm-chair near the fire, Dr. Umpleby had been accustomed to use only the standard lamp. But if he had to move about among his books, or if he had visitors, he would turn on the other lights as well. They worked on a dual control and could be turned on from the fireplace as well as by the door.

"Last night at ten-thirty," Appleby next asked, "how were the lights then?"

"All the lights were on, sir. The President was selecting

books from the far corner there while I was in the room."

"And afterwards, when you broke in with Mr. Titlow?"

"Only the standard lamp was burning."

"Dr. Umpleby would have turned off the others on returning to his desk?"

"I could not say, sir. It is possible."

"Tell me what happened about the lights then."

"Sir?"

"I mean did you, or did Mr. Titlow, at once turn on the other lights when you found the body?"

Slotwiner hesitated. "I can't say, sir," he replied at length. "Not, I mean, with any certainty. I believe I turned them on almost at once myself, but at such a moment the action would be mechanical. I do not positively recollect it. Later certainly all the lights were on."

Slotwiner, feeling now that he was being interrogated in form, was speaking with caution and every appearance of conscientious precision. But Appleby broke off. "I shall want your whole story later," he said. "Only one more question now." He had half turned away, as if what was significant in the interview was over. Suddenly he turned round and looked at the butler searchingly. "I wonder why you were so startled by my question about the candles?"

But this time Slotwiner was perfectly composed. "I'm sure I hardly know, sir," he answered. "If I may say so, the question—*any* question, sir—was a trifle unexpected. But I am unable to account for my reaction—you must have seen that I was quite perturbed. If I may attempt to express my feeling when you spoke, it was one of puzzlement. And I was puzzled as to why I was puzzled." Slotwiner paused to consider. "It was not over the overt content of your question, for I am quite clear that candles are never used in the Lodging. Dr. Umpleby did not care for them, and with so much old panelling around I would certainly not sanction their use among the servants. To be as clear as I can, sir, I would speak a trifle technically and say that your question had a *latent* content. The feeling-tone evoked was decidedly peculiar." And with this triumph of academic statement Slotwiner gave one more ghost of a bow to Appleby and glided—levitated almost, to speak technically—out of the room.

Dodd gave a chuckle which would have been boisterous had his eye not fallen on the object stretched before the fire. "You can see that you've landed among the dons," he said. "If you get that sort of cackle from the butler, what are you likely to get from the Dean, eh?"

But Appleby's smile in reply was thoughtful rather than merry. "The feeling-tone evoked was decidedly peculiar," he quoted. "You know, Dodd, that's an interesting man and he said an interesting thing. By the way"—Appleby glanced innocently at his colleague—"what do you make of the candle business?"

Dodd looked bewildered. "What candle business?" he said; "I had no idea what you were getting at."

Appleby took his colleague's arm for answer and led him to the far side of the room round which he had earlier made what had appeared to be a casual tour. Here the bookcases not only clothed the walls but projected into the room in the form of shallow bays. Islanded in one was a revolving bookcase containing the *Dictionary of National Biography;* in a second similarly was the *New English Dictionary*—the two sets of heavy volumes uniformly bound. But it was to the third of the four bays that Appleby led Dodd. Here was yet a third revolving bookcase—and Dodd found himself confronted by the fourteen bulky volumes of the Argentorati Athenaeus.

"The *Deipnosophists*," Appleby was murmuring; "Schweighaüser's edition . . . takes up a lot of room . . .

```
              ┌─────────────────────────┐
              │                         │
              │    Athenæus □  ┆ SAFE   │
              │                ┆        │
              │                         │
              │   □DNB    NED □         │
              │                         │
              │                         │
              └─────────────────────────┘
```

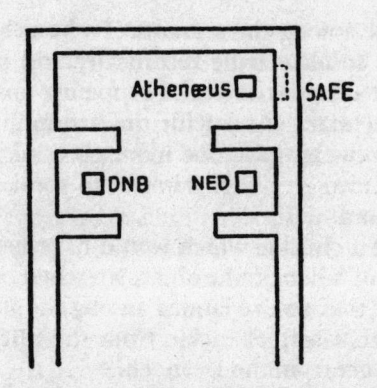

Dindorf's compacter—and there he is." He pointed to the corner of the lower shelf where the same enormous miscellany stood compressed into the three compact volumes of the Leipsic edition. Dodd, somewhat nonplussed before this classical abracadabra, growled suspiciously: "These last three are upside down—is that what you mean?"

"Well, that's a point. How many books do you reckon in this room—eight or nine thousand, perhaps? Just see if you can spot any others upside down. It's not a way scholars often put away their books."

Dodd declined the invitation. "I thought you said something about candles. Is it all a little classical joke?"

Appleby straightened himself from examining the lower shelf and pointed gently to the polished surface, breast high, of the top of the bookcase they were examining. A few inches from the edge farthest into the bay was a small spot, about half an inch in diameter, of what appeared to be candle grease.

"Some cleaning stuff," said Dodd. "Beeswax preparation, perhaps. Careless servant."

"A burglar—an amateur burglar with a candle?" Appleby suggested.

Dodd's response was immediate: he vanished from the room. When he returned, Appleby was on his knees beside the body. "You were right, Appleby," he announced eagerly. "Only some sort of furniture cream is ever used on these bookcases. And they were done yesterday morning. The housemaid swears there wasn't a speck on them then—and she's a most respectable old person." He paused, and seeing that Appleby's inspection of the body seemed over, added: "I've something of my own to show you in that alcove. It made me jump to your suggestion of a burglar at once. We didn't ignore the nine thousand books altogether, you know." He led the way back to the bay and paused, this time not before the revolving bookcase but before the solid shelves of closely packed books behind it. Putting his hand behind what appeared to be a normal row he gave a sharp pull—and the whole swung easily out upon a hinge. "Dodge they sometimes decorate library doors with—isn't it? And look what's behind the dummies." What was behind, sunk in the wall of the room, was a somewhat unusual, drawer-shaped steel safe.

"The sort of burglar who potters about with a candle," remarked Appleby, "wouldn't have much of a chance with that. Difficult to find too, unless he knew about it. Not that I expect you knew about it?"

Dodd had not known. He had found the safe in the course of a thorough search. The thousands of books had not been moved from their shelves, but every one had been pressed back as far as it would go to ensure that no discarded weapon lay anywhere concealed on the shelving between books and wall. He was positive, however, that the searchers were not responsible for turning the smaller Athenaeus. He had examined its particular revolving bookcase himself—missing, he admitted, the candle grease—and had found it unnecessary to take any of the books out. He had also himself inspected the whole bay and had come upon the concealed safe in the process.

Appleby's eye travelled once more along the endless rows of books, rapidly noting the character of the dead man's library. But it was the physical appearance of hundreds of heavy folios on the lower shelves which prompted his next remark. "Lucky he was shot through the head, Dodd. Do you see what a job that has saved us?" And seeing his colleague's puzzled look he went on: "Fancy it this way. Umpleby wants to commit suicide. For this reason or that—just out of devilment, perhaps—he decides to conceal the fact. Well, he takes any one of these books, probably a big one, perhaps quite a small one"—here Appleby tapped a stoutish crown octavo—"and he hollows out a little nest in it—large enough to hold an automatic. He holds it open with his left hand, close by its place on the shelf. Then he places the pistol just where a careful study of anatomy tells him, fires, slips the pistol in the book and the book in its place, staggers across the room and falls—just where you see him!"

Following Appleby's pointing finger, Dodd strode across the room to where the body lay. The small round hole, central in the forehead of the dead man, reassured him—but he glanced with new curiosity nevertheless at the vellum and buckram and morocco rows, gleaming, gilt-tooled, dull, polished, stained—the representative backs of perhaps four centuries of bookbinding. But Appleby, with a gesture as if he had been wasting time, had turned back to consider the concealed safe. "Finger-prints?" he asked.

Dodd shook his head.

"None at all?" pursued Appleby, interested.

But this time Dodd nodded. "Yes," he said, "I'm afraid so. Umpleby's own. No one has been feeling the need of polishing up after himself. It looks as if the safe has been undisturbed. One thing's queer about it all the same—and it's this. Not a soul seems to know anything about it. I asked fishing questions of everyone the least likely—'Do you happen to know where the President kept his valuables?' and that sort of thing. And then I asked outright. Slotwiner, the other servants, the Dean and the rest of the dons—none of them admitted to knowing of its existence. And there's no key. It's a combination lock and a combination lock only—not the kind where the combination opens to show a keyhole. Further than that I haven't had time to follow the thing up."

At the mention of time, Appleby looked at his watch. "I'm due for the Dean," he said, "and you for your supper and a rest. They'll want to take the body now, I expect."

Dodd nodded. "The body goes out to the mortuary," he agreed; "the room's locked up and sealed and you take the key. And it's for you to say when we bring a sack for these blasted bones."

Appleby chuckled. "I see it's the ossuary that really disturbs you. I think it may help a lot." He picked up a fibula as he spoke and wagged it with professionally excusable callousness at Dodd. And with an association of thought which would have been clear to that efficient officer only if he had been a reader of Sir Thomas Browne he murmured: "What song the Sirens sang, or what name Achilles assumed when he hid himself among women. . . ."

The fibula dropped with a little dry rattle on its pile as Appleby broke off to add: "Nor is the other question, I hope, unanswerable."

"*Other* question?"

Appleby had turned to the door. "Who, my dear Dodd, were the proprietaries of these bones? We must consult the Provincial Guardians."

CHAPTER III

I

THE Reverend the Honourable Tracy Deighton-Clerk, Dean of St. Anthony's, contrived, though still in middle age, to suggest the great Victorians. His features were at once wholly strong and wholly benevolent, evoking, even to a hint of side-whisker, the formidable canvases of G. F. Watts. His manner was a degree on the heavy side of courtesy and not at times without that temerarious combination of aloofness and charm which used to be attempted, some two generations ago, by those who had once glimpsed Matthew Arnold. He had a fancy for himself in the role of *ultimus Romanorum;* the last representative of a clerical and leisured university, of an academic society that was not cultured merely but also Polite.

The psychologically-minded Slotwiner (who was said to model himself not a little on Mr. Deighton-Clerk's manner) might have remarked that in the Dean's *persona* the episcopal idea had of late been rapidly developing. Indeed, the episcopal idea was hovering round him now, a comforting penumbra to the disturbing situation which confronted him as he stood, in elegant clerical evening-dress, before the fireplace of his study.

It was a room in marked contrast with the sombre and somewhat oppressive solidity of the dead President's apartment. Round a delicate Aubusson carpet, on which undergraduates instinctively trod as diffidently as if they had been schoolboys still, low white book-shelves enclosed the creamy vellum of the Schoolmen and the Fathers. The panelling was cream, its delicate Caroline carving touched with gold. The ceiling was cross-raftered in oak and from the interstices there gleamed, oddly but harmoniously in blue and silver, the twelve signs of the zodiac. Over the fireplace brooded in austere beauty one of Piero della Francesca's mathematically-minded madonnas, the blue of her gown the same as that amid the rafters above. The whole made a pleasant frame—and the rest of the furnishing was ingeniously unnoticeable. Mr. Deighton-Clerk and the Virgin between them dominated the room.

But at the moment the Dean was feeling in a scarcely dominant mood. He was doubting his own wisdom—a process he disliked and avoided. But he could not but doubt the wisdom of the action he had taken that morning. To insist on bringing down a detective-officer—no doubt a notorious detective-officer—from Scotland Yard because of this appalling affair! This was surely to court the widest publicity—to say the least?

Mr. Deighton-Clerk's gaze went slowly up to the ceiling, as if seeking comfort in his own private astrological heaven. Comfort came to him in some measure as his eye moved from *Cancer* to the taut form of *Sagittarius*. He had taken energetic action. And was it not (but here the thought floated only in the remoter regions of the Dean's brain)—was it not the capacity for energetic action that was called in question when the possible preferment of a mere scholar was canvassed? At this moment the Dean's eye, voyaging still among his rafters, rested on *Aquarius*, "the man who bears the watering-pot," as the rhyme has it. And by processes connected perhaps with the association *cold-douche*, the full mischief of the business was brought home to him more vividly than it had been yet. To be *mixed up* in a scandal under these outrageous circumstances of modern nation-wide publicity! Hardly helpful, he thought grimly;

hardly helpful whatever solution of the business the police achieved. That there would be no sensational domestic revelation—it was for that that he must hope and pray. And it was of that that he had, in the course of the day, almost succeeded in convincing himself. (*Pisces*, as if they had ventured some contradiction, came in for a stern glance here.) In the long run it would not be left in any doubt that the crime (crime in St. Anthony's!) was an outside affair—the purposeless stroke, perhaps, of a madman.

But here *Libra*, the scales, asserted themselves. There was matter to be balanced against that hope. Let this detective be anything but a model of discretion, let him have a taste for amusing the public, and there might be an uncomfortable enough period of startling, if improbable and unprovable, theories blowing about. The unlucky topographical circumstances of the deed, the Dean had realized from the first, set suspicion flowing where it should be fantastic that suspicion should flow. . . . He frowned as he thought of his colleagues under suspicion of murder. How would they stand badgering by policemen, coroners, lawyers? How, for that matter, would he stand it himself? Praise Providence, he and his colleagues were all demonstrably sane.

Those bones! They were mad. Last night, when he had viewed them, he had been annoyed by them. He had at first been more annoyed by the bones (he recollected with some discomfort) than distressed about the tragedy. He had been annoyed because he had been bewildered (Mr. Deighton-Clerk disliked being bewildered—or even slightly puzzled). But later he had felt—somewhat incoherently—a possible blessedness in them: their very irrationality removed the crime somehow from the sinister and calculated to the fantastic. They were a sort of bulwark between the life of the college, in all its measure and reason, and the whole horrid business.

And then—and it was as if *Leo*, *Taurus* and *Aries* had roared, bellowed, butted all in a moment—Mr. Deighton-Clerk realized what a feeble piece of thinking this was. The first thing that this detective would suspect about the bones was that they were some sort of blind or bluff. How obvious; how very, very obvious! Indeed, were the man literate, his mind might run to some notion of the touch of fantasy, the vivid dash of irrationality, that it might please an intellectual and cultivated mind to mingle with a laboriously calculated crime. . . . A mixture, thought Mr. Deighton-Clerk, somewhat in the manner of Poe.

Decidedly, he did not like the bones after all. And suddenly he realized that, subconsciously, they had profoundly disturbed him from the first. Sinister, grisly objects—surely they were striving to connect themselves with . . . something forgotten, suppressed, unconsidered on the borders of his consciousness . . . ? He was nervous. The dock (he heard his own inner voice absurdly exclaim) is yawning open for us all. . . .

Mr. Deighton-Clerk pulled himself up. He was decidedly tired. More than tired, he was unsettled. Indeed it was a terrible, a shocking business. Murder—the human soul hurled all unprepared to Judgment—was equally awful in college or cottage. He had seldom seen eye to eye with Umpleby—but how meaningless their disagreements had been! How absurd this or that estrangement between them in face of abrupt and total severance—the quick and the dead! The Dean looked at his watch. Just half-an-hour to hall, and hall and common-room would be something of an ordeal.

At this moment there came a knock at the door and the announcement: Mr. Appleby.

II

Mystery in the vicinity, the Dean was finding, was productive of irrational annoyances. He was annoyed again now, and it seemed for two most inadequate reasons. The stranger who had just been shown in upon him was remarkably young, and he had all the appearance of being —indeed quite plainly *was*—what Mr. Deighton-Clerk still liked to think of under the designation "genteel." But if both facts were disconcerting both might well be advantageous. In a moment the Dean had advanced and shaken hands. "I am glad to see you, Mr. Appleby," he said. "I am very glad that it has been possible to—ah—detail you for this"—the Dean hesitated—"this investigation. Sit down."

Appleby displayed a suitable awareness of politeness intended and seated himself in the chair which had been indicated—one somewhat uncompromisingly central before the Dean's tidily-arranged desk. It was plain that, in the introductory exchanges at least, Mr. Deighton-Clerk intended to lead the conversation. Tapping the arm of his chair deliberately rather than nervously, he began speaking in an even, rather cold but pleasantly modulated voice.

"You will have seen the extraordinary circumstances in which our President has met his death," he began. "The university, I need hardly say, is very much shocked, and it is the duty of the college to assist in every way what must, it is only too clear, be called the course of justice. As soon as I saw the gravity of what has happened I determined that the college itself, for its own credit, must take . . . energetic action"—Mr. Deighton-Clerk paused meditatively over the phrase—"and so overriding what I suspected might be tardy processes, I took steps to secure assistance from London at once. Nothing could be more satisfactory—more reassuring, indeed—than the promptitude of the response. We look to you, Mr. Appleby, to clear up this terrible affair."

The Dean paused at this, but even as Appleby was framing a reply he continued in the same somewhat formal strain. He had apparently delivered himself merely of a sort of exordium or proem and intended something like a speech. Perhaps, thought Appleby, it was simply the academic habit of sustained utterance; perhaps something more idiosyncratic and revealing. Anyway, he sat tight, with an air of respectful attention.

"I should not like," Mr. Deighton-Clerk continued, "to say that this tragedy has occurred at a particularly unfortunate time. It would be a most improper thought. Nevertheless you will understand me when I tell you that the five hundredth anniversary of the foundation of the college falls to be celebrated in only two months' time. The occasion is to be marked in—ah—various ways. It is known, for instance, that Dr. Umpleby was to have been knighted. That the college must enter upon the sixth century of its history upon the morrow of its President's violent death is, of course, terrible in itself. But it would be yet more deplorable should we have to suffer from prolonged mystery and scandal. And the longer Dr. Umpleby's death is unexplained, the more scandal—shocking though the admission be—will circulate. I know that, Mr. Appleby, only too well. And it is my duty as the acting Head of this House to see that the living are not penalized, either in their peace of mind or in their careers and material interests, by an ounce of avoidable scandal—or suspicion."

Here Mr. Deighton-Clerk made a real stop, conscious perhaps that in a somewhat wandering declaration he had spoken two words more than was discreet. Appleby replied briefly. He was fully aware of the likelihood of extravagant and irresponsible rumour. Searching inquiry in various directions would, perhaps, be unavoidable, but in whatever he did he would endeavour to act with all possible discretion. He hoped he could do something to restrain the exuberance of the Press. . . . Appleby's tactful speech, terminated by an inviting pause, had the effect which was intended. Mr. Deighton-Clerk began again. And this time he advanced from generalities to a specific position. Dr. Umpleby—he declared in fine—had met his death under certain complicated circumstances which the police would interpret. But a valid interpretation must be congruous, not with physical or mechanical facts merely, but with higher psychological probabilities as well. Obviously, a murder in St. Anthony's could not be a domestic matter.

This proposition—put forward with a good deal of complication—Appleby in some measure met. "I agree," he said, "that the physical circumstances of the case are not in any way conclusive. They may be very misleading—deliberately misleading. I recognize that they do not point in any certain way either at any one person or at any group of persons. They are merely factors in a total situation about which as yet I have very insufficient information." Appleby let this sink in and then he added: "There is the queer business of those bones. They may well be thought to point to a wholly irrational element in the affair. I remember something very similar, sir, in a case in Cumberland: homicidal mania accompanied by what is called, I think, obsessional neurosis. A man broke into a totally strange building—a public-house as it happened—and committed a murder. Then he turned everything he could move upside down, chalked up his own name on the wall and went home. They've never been able to discover at the asylum whether he remembers anything about it."

That Mr. Deighton-Clerk, fresh from his recent revelation on the likely official view of the bones, was altogether taken in by this reassuring anecdote is uncertain. But in combination with Appleby's manner it encouraged him to proceed with the train of thought he plainly wished to develop. Dr. Umpleby's death, he agreed, might well be the work of a demented person—indeed he could imagine no other explanation. And that the bones pointed the same way he also thought extremely probable. Not that he considered that a matter of certainty: the bones might be some sort of blind—a point Mr. Appleby had no doubt considered—though the very obviousness of this somewhat discounted the idea. But of one thing the Dean was certain: there existed within St. Anthony's itself no circumstances, no relations, no individual that could, with the slightest psychological probability, be in any way connected up with an attempt on the President's life. The actions and motives of his colleagues and himself might quite properly fall to be scrutinized: he would not, for his part, object for a moment. But with what authority he might possess, and in the interests of a rapid elucidation of the crime, he would again state his simple conviction that, whatever physical circumstances might suggest to the contrary, the problem must be one which lay essentially outside the precincts of St. Anthony's.

Was this gentleman, Appleby wondered, protesting too much? Or was he, in all this declamation, simply pumping up conviction within himself? And he wasn't finished yet. Standing up now with his back to the fire, the Dean looked directly at Appleby and began again. "Mr. Appleby," he said, speaking in more abrupt tones than he had yet permitted himself, "there's another thing. You may find your man, mad or sane, tomorrow. Or you may, as I have said, find it necessary to undertake a laborious investigation among us all. If you do, you may find—you certainly *will* find—disturbing circumstances. It is such circumstances which I suggest, very seriously, are only too likely to delude. In a college like this we have our own manners, and I hope they are the manners of scholars and gentlemen. But superficially—I deliberately use the word—there are jealousies, conflicts—quarrels even—enough. When you come upon them I ask you to do two things: first to weigh the gravity of such learned squabbles carefully against the well-nigh imponderable deed of murder; secondly to give some thought to the possible relevance of each before pursuing it to the point of publicity."

This was Mr. Deighton-Clerk's best speech, and he might have rested on it. But he had something to add and he added it forthrightly enough.

"I will quote an example. Only a few days ago Dr. Umpleby and I had something approaching a personal quarrel —in public. Consider it, and you will find it pretty evidently not the quality of thing men commit murder over. Investigate it further and, while keeping that quality, it will reveal matter of minor scandal—matter which, in the interest of the college, I would not see made public without dismay. And so on. You must know only too well, Mr. Appleby, that in any company of men minute perscrutation of act and motive may have the most miserable consequences. . . . But I am at your disposal for such inquiries as you may think useful—and so, I am sure, are my colleagues. Mr. Appleby, how would you wish to proceed?"

But Appleby, who was inwardly congratulating the Dean on this quite magnificent manner of admitting to a recent quarrel with a murdered man, was given no opportunity to reply. Indeed, the climax of the interview had all the appearance of being timed to the minute: even as Mr. Deighton-Clerk ceased speaking the college bell began to ring.

"That is our dinner-bell, Mr. Appleby," the Dean explained. "I am afraid we must defer further discussion until tomorrow—or later tonight should you choose." And after a moment of apparent hesitation he added: "May I ask what your arrangements are? You will need constant access to the college: would you care, I wonder—would it be regular, if I may so put it—to stay in St. Anthony's? We would be glad to receive you if you should think it convenient, and I can promise you a quiet set of rooms from which to—ah—operate."

Appleby reflected rapidly on this unexpected suggestion. No official objection, he felt sure, would be made to his lodging in the college if he considered it expedient. And it had several obvious advantages—not least that it made him free of the college buildings at any hour of the day or night. He accepted the proposal gratefully, explaining that he had driven straight to St. Anthony's and that his suit-case was at the porter's lodge. He would be glad to sleep in college that night—and for longer should it prove necessary.

Mr. Deighton-Clerk was pleased with himself. Here was more energetic action. It entailed, perhaps, some breach of the minor proprieties—but it was in a crisis in the college's history that justified the action fully. He took another glance at Appleby—the man was indubitably a gentleman—and plunged finally. "Excellent," he said, "a most satisfactory arrangement. And you will of course dine with us now in hall. I only wish you were meeting the hightable on a more auspicious—ah, on a less melancholy occasion."

This was slightly more than Appleby had bargained for and the official in him was moved to demur. But Mr. Deighton-Clerk, having twirled a dial and murmured into an ivory telephone, was enfolding himself in his gown. "Not at all, not at all," he said, meeting what he took to be the reason for Appleby's objection. "There is no need whatever for you to change. A number of the Fellows will not have taken the trouble. Mr. Haveland, for instance, will certainly not be changed. He never does change. It annoys—dear me!—annoyed poor Dr. Umpleby. Indeed, the manciple had to bring him a list every day, and if Haveland and his tweeds were to be in hall the President as often as not stayed away. I fear they detested each other. Mr. Appleby, let me lead the way downstairs."

Appleby followed obediently, feeling that he had gained a point. The Reverend and Honourable the Dean, for the past half-hour so elevated and so correct, had condescended to a fragment of downright gossip.

CHAPTER IV

I

ONE of the nicest of academic fantasies is *Zuleika Dobson,* that pleasing narrative of Max Beerbohm's in which an entire undergraduate population, despairing of its heroine's affection, casts itself into the fatal waters of the Isis. The great touch, it will be remembered, comes at the end. Life goes on undisturbed; that night the dons file into the halls of their several colleges as usual; and at the high-table dinner proceeds, in complete unawareness of the deserted benches where armies of perished undergraduates had sat.

Inspector Appleby had this fable flitting in his head as he entered the hall of St. Anthony's on the morrow of a less comprehensive academic fatality. The college had already assembled as he was guided up to the dais by Mr. Deighton-Clerk. Round the high-table there stood, gowned and for the most part dinner-jacketed, the Fellows—looking grave certainly, but no graver than the ceremonial preprandial moment commonly demanded. Stretching down the length of the hall were the lines of those *in statu pupillari:* two tables of commoners in the oddly diminished, vestigial-looking gowns of their order; an equally long table of more generously-swathed scholars; a short and bunchy table of completely enfolded Bachelors. By a lectern near the high-table, ready to say grace, was the bible-clerk, a blue-eyed cherubic undergraduate, doing his best to disguise an undisguisable constitutional breeziness. The few whispers in the hall died away as the Dean took off his cap and bowed gravely to the cherub—who bowed profoundly, if not exactly gravely, in return and proceeded to deliver himself with miraculous speed of a flood of mediæval latinity. The bible-clerk bowed; the Dean bowed; the Dean sat down; the college—and Appleby with it—did the same; ritual was preserved. But there was no instant babble of voices such as customarily would have arisen. St. Anthony's conversed but conversed sparely and quietly. The high-table set the tone, and the cherub, in occasional brief remarks to his neighbour the senior scholar, seconded. From around the lofty dark-panelled walls the vanished statesmen, divines, poets and philosophers whom St. Anthony's had, in one century or another, produced, looked down on a decorum amply maintained.

Appleby considered his neighbours. A rapid count made one fact evident: all the Fellows of the college had made a point of turning up in hall. Decorum once more, thought Appleby. Decorum too in the fact that nobody seemed to regard him with any curiosity—and decorum finally, he reflected, required that he should not begin a too-curious circumspection himself. He was on the right of the Dean; on his own right there sat, as a murmured introduction had informed him, Mr. Titlow—middle-aged, handsome, with a touch of encroaching flabbiness, nervous. And Titlow's present nervousness, he quickly decided, was something that went with a good deal of chronic irritability or internal excitement. Alone among the diners that night Titlow had the look of an imaginative man—a man, as used to be said, of quick invention. Those long, square fingers, alone preserved from some old portrait, would have suggested just that mobile mouth and lively eye. What they would not have suggested was so negative a nose. If features could be read, Appleby concluded, Titlow was a brilliant but unreliable man.

Directly opposite Appleby was Dr. Barocho, a round,

shining and beaming person, eating heartily and happily. He was a clear specimen of the stage foreigner—the foreigner who remains obstinately foreign. Which by no means prevented him from being an equally clear specimen of the maturest thing in the world—Latin culture. Dr. Barocho, Appleby's considering mind told itself, was master by right of birth of something in which his colleagues were laborious undergraduates still. And his mind would not work like theirs. . . . But of one thing Barocho was plainly not master—his colleagues' language. He was getting into difficulties now in the simple matter of explaining that he had mislaid his gown. (Would he be put off the capital grilled sole, Appleby wondered, if he knew what purpose it was now serving? Probably not.)

"You did not notice it please, Titlow, Empson, Pownall, I beg? You did not see me put the gown down, Pownall, at all—Titlow *no?*"

The appeal was not very politely received. A sardonic person who was to reveal himself as Professor Empson murmured that Barocho might well have mislaid his head, a response which the Spaniard at once contrived to muddle. "Ah, yes, you said our dead Head!"—and he crossed himself and looked solemn over what he apparently took to be some obscure reference to the late Dr. Umpleby. Then a thought seemed to strike him and he turned to Titlow. "One thing I want to ask you. You speak of Heads of Houses and that is university Houses—Colleges—*no?* And then you speak of Safe as Houses, and that is university Houses too, Titlow—*verdad?* You call this House safe?"

Barocho's mind seemed to work not so much differently as weirdly—or it had a whim for appearing to do so. Several people were looking at him with the sort of half-irritated tolerance which one bestows upon a familiar oddity. But one member of the high-table, an impassive featureless person who was to turn out to be Haveland, seemed, to Appleby's eye, to be attending with considerable concentration. The Spaniard was now embarked on random philological speculation and inquiry. For a minute his voice was lost, save to his immediate neighbours, amid such subdued talk as the high-table was allowing itself. And then, in a pause, it rang out in question:

"Do I say, then, that you will be *hanged,* or that you will be *hung?*"

Titlow's glass came down abruptly; equally abruptly Haveland's went to his mouth—it was impossible to tell to which the fantastic question had been addressed. . . . Had the round innocent eyes of Barocho, Appleby wondered, meditatively sought his own in that disturbing moment? The Spaniard, he suspected, was neither witless nor concerned deliberately to give offence. He had simply conducted an experiment. Why?

In an instant Deighton-Clerk had taken charge, subtly but absolutely, of the whole table. He seemed to dictate alike the subdued conversations and the interspersed silences which marked the rest of the meal. He had determined, clearly, that there was to be no further incident—and there was none. Half an hour after dinner had begun, and without allowing a suspicion of haste towards the close, the Dean rose and murmured two words of grace. Chairs were drawn back, caps were handed, the occupants of the high-table filed out through the rows of standing undergraduates. Hall was over.

II

The little file of dons streamed over the narrow neck of Bishop's Court separating hall from common-rooms: Appleby, with his instinct for observation, brought up the rear. Away to the left, and clearly illuminated by a brilliant lamp, was the big, unimpeded archway between Bishop's and Surrey. To the right, close by, but illuminated only accidentally by a light streaming from the open common-room door, were those problematical gates which had been locked at ten-fifteen the night before, and which were locked still now. Through the elaborate iron-work there flowed a velvet blackness, and the faint sighing breeze that must be stirring the mist around the invisible trunks and branches of Orchard Ground. None of the little procession, Appleby saw, looked that way. But through that gate some lurking minion of Dodd's would presently have to admit Empson, Titlow, Pownall and Haveland, if these were to pass the night in their own rooms. . . . It was an awkward arrangement at best, this nightly splitting of the college in two with lock and key. It was a piece of practical awkwardness typical perhaps of the place. Had it been exploited with an equally typical intellectual finesse? This question took Appleby, in the wake of his host, into the smaller of the St. Anthony's common-rooms.

The room had the air of somewhat desiccated luxury characteristic of such places, but it was pleasant enough. A long mahogany table, lit by candles in heavy silver candlesticks, glowed with the ruby and gold of port and sherry, glittered with glass, broke into little rainbows of fruit. The only other light was from a generous fire in a generous fireplace. The walls, covered with innumerable portraits of Fellows dead and gone, swam in and out of shadow, surrounding the living with a company of fleeting ghosts—Victorian ghosts looking like Mr. Deighton-Clerk; eighteenth-century ghosts sitting in libraries, walking in parks, striking postures amid fragments of the Antique; a few seventeenth-century ghosts holding prayer-books. The great of St. Anthony's hung in hall; these were her illustrious obscure, appropriately perpetuated on a miniature scale. It was like a cloud of witnesses.

There was a moment of confusion. As Mr. Deighton-Clerk crossed the threshold of the common-room, his authority—or rather the authority of the dead President now vested in him—was by some inviolable custom suspended. It fell to Mr. Titlow to dispose the company around the table. But Titlow was still plainly in a state of agitation and he showed every sign of making a bad job of it. His gestures were vague and contradictory and there was a generally embarrassed shuffling and shifting before the company was settled down. Appleby found himself oddly placed at the head of the table, facing the single figure of Haveland at the other end—a double line of dons between them.

A modicum of confusion Mr. Deighton-Clerk had suffered in the name of the prescriptive, but when the table was once settled he resumed control. He whispered to Titlow; Titlow and he severally whispered to the servants; and cut glass and decanters, fruit and finger bowls, vanished untouched. It was a portentous symbolism—and it induced a portentous silence. The ritual of dessert had been metamorphosed into the ceremony of a meeting. The servants had withdrawn and the Dean spoke. He spoke, Appleby noticed, without the slightly strained formality which unfamiliar colloquy with a policeman had induced earlier in the evening.

"We have here tonight Mr. Appleby of the London police. Mr. Appleby has been sent on our direct application to the Home Office, and we will help him in every way. He is staying in college, in the rooms just opposite my own, until matters clear up. We realize, I think, that that may take a little time. It is useless to disguise from ourselves the fact that the circumstances in which the President has died, as well as being quite evidently sinister, are possibly complicated. Mr. Appleby will no doubt wish to see us all severally and discover what, if anything, we have to tell.

"Mr. Appleby, I will name my colleagues. On your left is Mr. Titlow. Dr. Gott, Professor Empson, Professor Curtis, Mr. Chalmers-Paton. . . ."

And so the Dean went right round the table. It was an uncomfortable proceeding, but sensible and efficient, and Deighton-Clerk went through it with level severity. It was not, Appleby decided, exactly a matter of introductions, and the process was completed without bow or word spoken. Most of those named looked direct at Appleby; a few kept their eyes on the bare table in front of them. Only Barocho's eyes went circling round with Appleby's, and he smiled amiably on each of his colleagues in turn, giving much the impression that he regarded the roll-call as preliminary to the starting of some pleasant paper game.

For a moment there was silence, and then Haveland suddenly spoke from the lower end of the table. He was a pale, almost featureless person, but there was a rigidity about such features as he had that suggested a quality of intensity or concentration. He was dressed, as the Dean had foretold, in morning clothes—clothes which conveyed, in their soft but clear colouring and negligent flow, something of consciously-worn æsthetic sensibility. But the hands were lifeless and the voice cold, thin, impassive as the features. He addressed the Dean.

"I take it that you are not suggesting that Mr. Appleby should begin by holding a conference. What information each of us may have, what impressions each of us no doubt has—all that Mr. Appleby had better get by going round privately."

Beneath the flat words, beneath the flat tone in which

they were uttered, there was discernible some latent cutting edge waiting to come into operation. "Information," "impressions," "going round"—there had been scepticism, irony, contempt delicately perceptible behind the successive words. Haveland continued.

"But there is something I take this chance of saying to everybody. It may deprive one or two of you of the pleasures of suddenly realizing that two and two are four, and give you an impression the less to convey to Mr. Appleby. Please forgive me.

"You all know that Umpleby's study has been found littered with bones. I wonder where they came from . . . Empson, can you think?"

There was some hidden art in this appeal: Empson seemed momentarily confused. But Haveland at once went on.

"I am sure you can. But I don't know if Mr. Appleby understands as yet the significance of bones amongst us? I am certain it is a point his rural colleague—with whom I am afraid I shall reveal myself as having been improperly reticent this morning—would scarcely appreciate. I suggest you say a word to Mr. Appleby on that, Deighton-Clerk."

Deighton-Clerk, thus appealed to, looked first puzzled and then startled. "Mr. Haveland no doubt means," he said, "that anthropology is a strong subject with us at St. Anthony's. Haveland is an anthropologist himself. Titlow's classical archæology has got mixed up—please excuse the expression, Titlow!—with anthropology of late. And Pownall's ancient history and Campbell's ethnology have linked up with the subject too. The linking-up was fostered by the late President. Dr. Umpleby himself came to anthropology through comparative philology, as did his pupil, Ransome, who is now abroad. In fact, St. Anthony's has been famous for team work on ancient cultures for years now. As a student of comparative religion I have been interested myself. I suppose that is what Haveland means by the significance of bones amongst us—though such an odd notion would never have occurred to me. . . . And now, Haveland, if you have something to say, pray say it."

Haveland had that look in his eye which a man might have who is putting a horse for a second time at a very stiff fence.

"Empson knew that I had a collection of bones in college. I wonder if anyone else knew?" His eye ran round the table, making a fleeting point before he continued. "The bones are my bones."

The common-room was hushed. None of Haveland's colleagues said a word, and Appleby said no word either.

"At least I presume they are my bones, for my bones have disappeared. And as mine happen to be of Australian aborigines they will be fairly easily identified. . . . I wonder if any of you has any thoughts as to how these exhibits of mine have come to be put to such picturesque use?"

There was absolute silence.

"Or perhaps I might ask not *how* they came where they did, but *why?* What do you think . . . Empson? Would you care to advance any theory?"

"I have nothing to advance. . . . Ask Titlow."

Why, thought Appleby, ask Titlow? And Titlow seemed to think the same. He was looking with much the same indignation at Empson as Empson was looking at Haveland. A little more of this and all the subterraneous currents of this little community would be rising to reveal themselves on the surface.

"I can imagine their being put there to incriminate you, Haveland," Titlow put in. "Pownall, does that not seem possible to you?"

Pownall, thus dragged in (why drag in Pownall?), responded: "I can imagine an explanation which is at once simpler and odder. Can you not, Haveland?"

It was as if Barocho had been right and some round game—a round game of which only a fragment of the rules was known to any one player—was in progress in the common-room. But now a venerable and bearded person sitting opposite the fireplace took up the conversation. "I wonder if any of you know the curious Bohemian legend of the Bones of Klattau . . . ?"

This was Professor Curtis, and to Appleby's ear and mind his perfectly irrelevant interjection had a curious effect. Its innocence—and, in the circumstances, absurdity—threw into sudden clear relief the animus with which the previous play of conversation had somehow been heavy. Pownall's *"Can you not, Haveland?"* had had it, and now Haveland, ignoring Curtis and the Bohemian legend, squared himself to reply.

"Certainly I can imagine another explanation. There is a concatenation of circumstances that comes to my mind at once. Empson, I think you should give some account of a conversation I had with Umpleby in your presence a month or two ago. You know what I mean. And I don't think anyone else knows of it."

"Pownall knows: I told him next day." Empson had replied impulsively, and seemed to regret it. "I don't see," he continued, "that I need give any account of anything here. If you want all that out, out with it yourself."

The Dean stirred in his seat—half uneasily, half authoritatively. "Haveland," he said, "is this expedient? If you insist on telling us something, tell us outright."

"I am going to tell you something outright." The retort was a neat and venomous imitation of the Dean's slightly magisterial accents. Haveland was certainly not playing for sympathy: the common-room could be felt to shudder at the impropriety of his tone. But he had controlled himself instantly and now continued unmoved. "I am going to tell you—as Empson seems reluctant to do it—of a certain occasion on which I quarrelled with Umpleby—badly."

From several quarters there rose protesting murmurs. The Dean, in evident perplexity, half-turned to Appleby. But Appleby seemed lost in absorbed contemplation of the table-edge in front of him. And Haveland continued unchecked.

"It was a matter, of course, of one of Umpleby's usual thefts."

If there was anything, Appleby decided, to be discerned in the expressions of the late President's colleagues at this opening, it was comprehension rather than perplexity. The Dean, however, was moved to some attempt at remonstrance. Haveland—and with a trace of unrestraint—thrust it aside.

"Deighton-Clerk, don't be a fool. Consider what we are up against. Umpleby, I say, had been stealing again. I needn't go into it all. Empson was there, and if he were not so uneasy about it could give you a cooler account than I. But I do remember one very definite expression I used."

Haveland's fence, Appleby sensed, was full in front of him now. And the whole room seemed to feel the strain that was in the air.

"When I taxed him with it he simply would not meet my point. He talked about his own work among the tombs down the Gulf. And I said I would like to see him immured for good in one of his own grisly sepulchres. . . . That is correct, Empson, is it not?"

Empson made no reply. There was absolute silence. Haveland was impassive still, but even down the candle-lit table Appleby thought he could discern the drops of sweat that stood upon his brow. At length a voice broke the spell.

"Haveland, what madman's trick are you suggesting?"

It was Pownall who spoke. And if there had been silence before, there was utter stillness now. Appleby had the feeling of a sudden horrid sense of understanding, a catastrophic dark enlightenment, running round the table. But Haveland had suddenly got to his feet. He looked directly across at Appleby, and seemed now to address him rather than the room.

"And there you have material for two theories. Titlow said something about 'incriminating': you can reflect on that. And Pownall said something about 'simpler and odder': you can reflect on that too. Good night."

And Haveland swung out of the room. For a moment the company sat staring rather blankly at an empty chair. But Deighton-Clerk had whispered to Titlow and Titlow had pressed a bell. Some soothing fragment of ritual was again being resorted to.

The door of the inner common-room was thrown open and the unemotional tones of a servant announced: "Coffee is served!"

III

The Dean motioned to Appleby and the two of them, together with Titlow, Barocho, and a silent person who had proved to be Dr. Gott, passed into the next room—Deighton-Clerk because he was Dean, Appleby because he was the Dean's guest, Titlow because he was Senior Fellow, Gott because he was at present a proctor and Barocho probably because he had simply forgotten to remain behind. Appleby was helped to coffee by the Dean, and the others helped themselves. Deighton-Clerk made no secret of his distress to Appleby.

"Mr. Appleby, it is a horrible business. Pray heaven you

clear it up quickly! I am coming to feel some wretched tone or atmosphere spreading itself around us."

Little more than an hour before Deighton-Clerk had been elaborately impressing upon Appleby, in direct contradiction to the strongest physical appearances, that Umpleby's death was the deed of some Unknown who had no part or lot in the life of St. Anthony's. Plainly, he was not a little shaken from that confidence—if genuine confidence it had been—now. He had drawn Appleby into a corner and was continuing with increased distress.

"It was a most improper observation of Pownall's. Even if Haveland was inviting accusation, it ought not to have been put to him by way of insinuation like that. We were all exceedingly shocked."

Appleby was in the dark as to the significance of this speech, but in a moment the Dean enlightened him. "I am afraid it is my duty to explain to you, Mr. Appleby, though it has much upset me. I had quite forgotten. . . . Did I remark earlier this evening when we were speaking of the bones that they were *mad* whereas we in this college were all demonstrably *sane*? At any rate, I think I implied it. And of course I had forgotten—though I was dimly aware of some sinister thing. I had forgotten the trouble poor Haveland had had. Some years ago, Mr. Appleby, he had . . . a severe nervous breakdown, and behaved for a time very oddly. Actually, he was found behaving very oddly among the sarcophagi in the Museum. . . . Where will this lead us?"

It might lead, Appleby thought, in more directions than one—but it did not look, at present, as if it would lead straight out of St. Anthony's.

"There was never any relapse," the Dean was continuing. "The whole thing has been long ago overlaid and forgotten—until Haveland and Pownall so deliberately dragged it up. You will realize that it has been so when I tell you that Haveland has been regarded as a not unlikely successor to Umpleby—despite the fact that he is, as you know, uncompromising in certain social matters. Haveland's attack was regarded at the time as the aftermath of war-time strain, and he is a thoroughly equable person."

There came back to Appleby upon this his first impression of Haveland, shortly before. Was it exactly of an equable person? He was *even,* yes. But was he even as a result of some constant control? Somewhere in the man there was high pressure—and where there is such pressure there may, conceivably, be chronic latent instability.

A few minutes only had passed since the break-up in the other common-room, and now, after the ritual interval, the other St. Anthony's Fellows (who, while divorced from their seniors, had tonight been without the compensating advantage of an extra moment with the port) came in to coffee. The company split into small groups and Appleby presently found himself taken possession of by Professor Curtis. It seemed likely that he alone was to be privileged to hear in full the curious legend of the Bones of Klattau. But it was something else that the *savant* had in his head.

"May I ask, my dear sir," he began mildly, "if you have ever condescended to interest yourself in the imaginative literature of your profession?"

Curtis, Appleby reflected, should be approaching Dodd. But he answered that he was not altogether ignorant of the field.

"Then," said Curtis, blinking amiably over the top of his steel-rimmed glasses, "you may be acquainted with Gott's diversions? I am not giving away any secret here, I think, when I tell you that Gott is Pentreith, you know. I suppose his stories are now fairly well known in the world?"

Appleby agreed that they were, and looked round with

interest for so distinguished a story-teller. But Gott, being a proctor, had departed on his nocturnal disciplinary perambulations of the city.

"It is a curious branch of literature," Curtis was continuing; "and I must confess, I am afraid, to being an indifferent scholar in it. Would you be inclined to maintain that Wilkie Collins has ever been bettered? Or Poe? Not that Poe is not, I always feel, inconsiderable—how curiously his reputation has been foisted on us from France! You younger men, I suppose, have passed beyond the Symbolists? But *The Purloined Letter* now; don't you think that is a little—*steep,* as they say?"

Appleby agreed that he thought it was. Curtis was delighted.

"I am glad to have my amateur's opinion—so to speak—professionally endorsed. Yes, I think I should have spotted the letter myself—almost at once. But I wonder if it was Poe's idea? I wouldn't be a bit surprised if the basis of it was as old as the hills, would you? There is an interesting story they relate in the Basque country. . . . But I will tell you that another time, if you will let me. What Poe put it in my mind to say was that these bones we hear of might *neither* be meant to incriminate somebody *nor* be evidence of any sort of mental unbalance. Not of mental unbalance in the strict sense, I mean. They might be—how shall I put it?—some perfectly sane man's idea of the humorously grotesque. . . . Do you know Goya's sketches? In the—dear me, what are they called? Barocho, those war-things of Goya's. . . ."

And Professor Curtis wandered away.

Looking round the room, Appleby now saw standing conveniently in one group three members of the commonroom of whom he as yet knew nothing: Lambrick, Campbell and Chalmers-Paton. He was particularly interested in

Lambrick, the married member of the college who retained a key to the fatal gates. And something about Campbell was familiar. Feeling that he might usefully pile up a little more in the way of impressions before retiring to sort them out, he approached this group and was presently sitting smoking and talking with them. Nothing could well have been more irregular. But St. Anthony's had enough of its own conventions to care very little, it seemed, for those of the world. The college was taking it for granted that it should treat a detective-officer come up to investigate a murder just as it would treat an architect come up to design it a new kitchen or an Academician making watercolours of its courts. It was an attitude that made a superior technique of investigation possible, and Appleby was not going to quarrel with it.

The conversation was running on the proctorial activities of Gott. The walk from hall to common-room had revealed a raw, unpleasant night, cold and with a lurking vapour that caught at the throat. And to Appleby's companions, comfortably smoking cigarettes in large leather chairs, with a leaping fire, more generous even than in the outer common-room, pleasantly warming their legs, the thought of their colleague pacing round the streets at the head of a little bevy of university police appeared to be particularly gratifying.

"Think of it," Lambrick, a large dreamy mathematician with a primitive sense of the humorous, was saying; "in he goes to the Case is Altered—two men drinking egg-hot—men duly proctorized and out goes Gott into the night, thinking of egg-hot. He goes across the way to the Mucky Duck (good pub that)—two men playing shove-halfpenny over a little rum shrub—proctorized—and out comes Gott thinking both of rum shrub and shove-halfpenny (capital hand he is, too). Over he goes to that flash place at the

Berklay—half a dozen smart men having a little quick champagne. Old Gott half hoping for a rough house. 'Your name and college, sir?'—all answer like lambs. Then out again to prowl around that college next my tailor's (never can remember its name) until the Hammer and Sickle Club is out and safely tucked away in bed. What a life!"

"Did you ever hear," asked Campbell, who was a dark and supple Scot, "did you ever hear how Curtis when he was Senior Proctor proctorized the Archbishop of York?"

It was an excellent anecdote, but over-elaborate for Lambrick, who vanished suddenly as he sat into some impalpable mathematical world. But Chalmers-Paton kept the theme going by remembering an exploit of Campbell's. "I say, Campbell, do you remember your climb up St. Baldred's Tower after that pot?" And despite something approaching positive displeasure on Campbell's part Chalmers-Paton told the story. It represented Campbell as a daring, even reckless man—and as a skilled climber. And then Appleby remembered.

"You went high, didn't you," he quietly asked the Scot, "in the Himalaya in 'twenty-six?"

Campbell flushed and seemed for a moment almost disconcerted. "I was there," he said at length. "Didn't you and I once do the Pillar Rock together when I hit your party in Wasdale?"

Appleby in his turn admitted to this—much as he might have admitted to Mr. Bradman that they had once played rounders together at a Sunday School picnic. But a subject had been started, and for a few minutes there was climbers' talk. Then Appleby dropped a casual question.

"Is there any roof-climbing in St. Anthony's in these days?"

"I believe not," replied Chalmers-Paton. "A few years ago there was a club, but undergraduates come and go, and

I believe it has lapsed."

His companions, Appleby noticed, were quite evidently aware that something had at length been said relevant to the President's death. Addressing Campbell, therefore, he came more directly to his point. "What is St. Anthony's like for climbing in, out, or about?" he asked.

Campbell laughed rather shortly. "I'm a mountaineer at times, as you know. But I assure you I'm not a housebreaker —or a steeple-jack, and I don't see that I'm qualified to give an opinion. Anyone could get on to the roofs through some trap-door or other and scamper round; but I should say, for what it is worth, that that would be about all. I should imagine that climbing up or down, in or out, is almost impossible."

"Even to a skilled climber?"

Campbell answered steadily.

"Even to a skilled climber."

CHAPTER V

I

APPLEBY sat in his bedroom and took stock—first, and by long habit, of his immediate surroundings; then of his mind. The room did not occupy him long. It was about eight feet square, eight feet high and for window it had a bewildering maze of traceried glass sweeping in a Gothic curve from the floor in one corner to the ceiling in another. St. Anthony's, willing to cram into its venerable fabric an extra dozen of undergraduates, had carried out some curious internal alterations in the venerable fabric's structure. The room bore traces of its regular occupant in the shape of an empty jar labelled *Rowing Ointment,* a religious text decorated with an exuberant floral border, a half-tone representation of Miss Mae West, and ten uniform photographs in uniform frames of exceedingly uniform young men—the other ten, doubtless, of some school eleven of the recent past. Why the owner of these *keimelia* was not in residence among them had not been explained: perhaps he had had some difference of opinion with authority; perhaps (Appleby speculated) he was having measles or mumps.

Appleby turned to his thoughts. He was feeling, on the whole, more confident than when he had parted from Dodd. Going over Dodd's facts had given him certain physical contours of the situation—contours that must be regarded as significant by reason of the definition with which they appeared to point, limit, exclude. But around them Appleby had felt a complete darkness; they were no more than a sort of braille recording of the facts. But later in the evening he had begun to see light, or the possibility of light —light flickering and uncertain, no doubt, as the dying fires in the common-room must be at this moment. From the stage and *décor*—that so elaborately constructed stage, that gruesome *décor*—Appleby had arrived at some view of the *dramatis personæ;* at some glimpse, perhaps, of the protagonists. . . .

A certain amount of Appleby's work lay among persons of considerable cunning. Occasionally he had the stimulus of crossing swords with a good or excellent natural intelligence. But for the most part he dealt with sub-average intelligence, or with normal intelligence circumscribed and handicapped by deficient training and knowledge. And here was what might be intellectually the case of his life. Here was a society of men much above the average in intelligence, the product of a variety of severe mental trainings, formidably armed with knowledge. The secret was hidden amongst them and intelligence and athletic thinking would be needed to reveal it.

Of one thing that evening he had begun to feel convinced. His earlier cautious refusal to take as conclusive those physical facts that cried *"Submarine!"* to Dodd might almost certainly be abandoned. The extraordinary fact of the freshly fitted locks and freshly issued keys had been almost conclusive of that in itself. Directly or indirectly, the murder had been brought about by one or more of the persons with keys. The only alternative—that a malefactor had climbed out of the locked orchard—was sufficiently unlikely to be put last in any line of investigation. The keys held the key. They gave a formula:

Deighton-Clerk, Empson, Gott, Haveland, Lambrick, Pownall, Titlow, the college porter, a hypothetical X (possessor of the missing tenth key); one, or some, or all of these murdered Umpleby—or so disposed of a key as to be able to throw light on the murder.

Appleby looked mentally at this and saw that he had missed something. He brought out pencil and paper and wrote an elaborated formula down:

Slotwiner; Deighton-Clerk, Empson, Gott, Haveland, Lambrick, Pownall, Titlow, the college porter, a hypothetical X (possessor of the tenth key); one, or some, or all of these murdered Umpleby, or one of the ninth last so disposed of a key as to be in a position to throw light on the murder. So far, none can be excluded, but if Slotwiner and Titlow are telling the truth they corroborate each other's alibis. . . . Dodd is having certain further alibi-statements checked.

So much he had learned that afternoon in the President's Lodging—and so much his subsequent impressions had come to confirm. But what else had he learned later? What had he learned from his interview with the Dean? First, certain facts about the Dean himself. He had been anxious to have it found that the murder was an *outside* murder— that was natural enough. And he had advanced an argument which was simply in effect, "Such things do not happen among us. And the quality of our knowledge that they do not so happen is really safer evidence than arbitrary physical indications to the contrary." Appleby had given the argument fair weight, but he was abandoning it now— and the Dean, he suspected, was doing the same. . . . What else had transpired? The Dean was apprehensive that routine investigation would bring to light matters of petty scandal within the college. And he had recently had some sort of quarrel with Umpleby himself. That was about all. As to more general impressions, they were difficult to form as yet. The man was upset—even thrown off his balance. He would not have given way slightly to a latent pomposity, would not have made pointless reference to the celebrations in which St. Anthony's was soon to indulge, had that not been so. But that he was insincere, that he was concealing any material information—of anything of this sort there was no evidence.

Appleby next passed to a review of the events in hall—or rather to the one significant event: the odd behaviour of Barocho. The Spaniard had possibly only the vaguest ideas on the circumstances of Umpleby's death, and was aiming something at random and for reasons of his own—at Titlow, had it been, or at Haveland? Or had there been no specific application; merely something tossed into the air for the purpose of watching the general reaction? Not much useful thinking, probably, could be done on the incident at present.

But on coming to the events in the common-room Appleby faced a complexity which made him feel suddenly cramped. He sprang up and passed into the absent undergraduate's sitting-room—a big, rather dingy apartment, its walls entirely panelled in wood that had been overlaid with chocolate-coloured paint. Turning on the reading-lamp, Appleby began to pace softly up and down.

The outstanding fact was Haveland's admission—that oddly public admission—of the proprietorship of the bones. He ought to have admitted this earlier to Dodd. That the bones would be traced to him he must have known as fairly certain: why then had he delayed owning to them? Obviously, in order to do so under the particular circumstances possible in the common-room, with all his colleagues around him. He had wanted to show himself publicly as aware of the existence of a case against himself. He had appealed to Empson to reveal a most damaging story that he believed only Empson knew—the story of a quarrel with Umpleby which had led to his expressing a malevolent wish now almost literally fulfilled: "I said I would like to see him immured in one of his own grisly sepulchres."

It was a terrific admission to have to make, and Haveland must have been aware that Appleby would soon be in possession of information which would make it doubly —and more than doubly—terrific. Haveland had once experienced a fit of serious unbalance—and the circumstances had apparently suggested some morbid attraction to symbols of physical dissolution.

What had happened, then, was this. Confronted by these disquieting facts, Haveland had come forward and said, "You are at liberty to believe that in a fit of aberration last night I killed the President and made good my wish as to his lying amid a litter of bones. Or you can suspect that somebody aware of all this has put a plant on me."

Somebody aware of all this. . . . "Empson knew I had a collection of bones in college: I wonder if anyone else knew . . . ?" "Empson, you know what I mean, and I don't think anyone else knows of it. . . ." "That is correct, Empson, is it not . . . ?" Haveland had, in fact, as good as pointed to Empson. And what had Empson done? Perhaps the most striking fact, Appleby reflected, was that Empson, aware enough of the insinuation, *had not pointed back*. Empson had, after a manner, pointed *sideways*. "Ask Titlow . . ." There was nothing in the words, but there had been no mistaking the existence of some significance behind them. There had indeed been an electrical atmosphere round that table, and now Appleby was feeling his way to recreating it—conjuring it up imaginatively in order to test and explore it anew.

The facts pointing at Haveland. Haveland pointing at Empson. Empson (like Barocho?) pointing at Titlow. And

Titlow himself? "I can imagine their being put there to incriminate you, Haveland. Pownall, does that not seem possible to you?" Had there been anything in that? Appleby thought there had—but amid all these charged utterances was he now reading a charge into something uncharged, casual merely? Anyway, Pownall in his turn had certainly pointed. It was he who had, at length, pointed back at Haveland: "I can imagine an explanation which is at once simpler and odder . . ." "Haveland, what madman's trick are you suggesting?" Appleby knew how, on the level of intellectual dispute, these men would toss a ball around in just that way, each trying to embarrass the other. It was the habit in any mentally athletic society, no doubt; and no doubt the same process would have its pleasures on the level of scandal and gossip. But when it was a case of murder that was in question . . . ?

Appleby felt that he had run over the salient facts. Now he turned to contemplate those less obtrusive. And the less obtrusive facts, he well knew, were often finally the vital facts: the neglect of some minute observation, the leaving of a single fugitive query unattended to, was often the ruining of an elaborate and laborious detective procedure.

The candle grease. Slotwiner and the candles. The *Deipnosophists* upside down. The safe. Barocho's gown. The Dean, hitherto so reticent about college scandal, describing Haveland's old attack. Curtis so casually, so vaguely making sure that Appleby should know that Gott was Pentreith. . . . And finally there was Campbell, the man who had gone high; more significantly, the man who had scaled St. Baldred's tower. He was married and lived out of college. He had no key. But he was an ethnologist and so connected with the Umpleby group. And although Appleby did not believe in the probability of Campbell scaling the heights of St. Anthony's as it were alpenstock in hand, probability was not enough. Troublesome red herring as he might be, he must be kept in mind.

Appleby's thoughts swam up from these speculations to a consciousness of his surroundings. He had been staring unseeingly at a rather scanty shelf of books: *Stubb's Select Charters, Poems of To-day, The Forsyte Saga, Trent's Last Case.* . . .

He turned round and swung impatiently across the room. A kettle, a commoner's gown, a football "cap"—its tinsel already tarnished by those vapours that were even now floating round the courts. Kneeling on a window-seat he threw open a window and looked out. It was black, damp, cold. But it was cold too inside, and Appleby was not at all sleepy. Obeying an impulse, he switched off the light, groped his way out to the landing and then softly made his way downstairs. There was a light under one door, and a murmur of voices. Excited undergraduates sitting up over the case, no doubt, and fortifying themselves lawfully within college with some of those pleasant potations denied to the unhappily prowling Gott. But by this time Gott would be comfortably in his bed in Surrey: as Appleby reached the open air there came to him, muffled and solemn, one deep note from a distant bell, followed by fainter chimes from other quarters. One o'clock.

The Dean's staircase, where Appleby had his rooms, was in the corner of Bishop's diagonal to the common-rooms. On the left, over the archway to Surrey, a lamp still burned. But it had been turned low and its light hardly reached across the gravel path to the edge of the lawn which Appleby knew stretched in front of him. The night was starless and obscure. Almost nothing could be seen except an uncertain line separating two contrasting textures of darkness—textures which would reveal themselves at dawn as stone and sky. And yet Appleby had never felt the place more keenly than under this spell of silence and night. He began to pace up and down the near side of the court, cleaving a path through the darkness, absorbed.

II

Two o'clock found Appleby still pacing. But the echo of the bells once more made him pause, and in the pause there came to him the second impulse of that night. Behind the screen of buildings in front of him lay Orchard Ground, and in his pocket reposed a key. It was now the only key, with the exception of the problematical tenth, not in the possession of his colleagues. The keys had been collected from their owners that morning (a bold exercise of authority by Dodd); a constable armed with one had stood guard all day; and a relief, similarly armed, was now sitting in the porter's lodge. Empson, Haveland, Pownall and Titlow, once they had been let into Orchard Ground for the night, were thus virtually prisoners of the police until the morning. As things stood at the moment—and they could hardly so stand for long—no one could get in or out of Orchard Ground without applying to the constable on duty—or to Appleby. The latter's impulse to use his key now was quite irrational, for in the almost impenetrable darkness nothing certainly could be done. But impulses of the sort he did not think it necessary invariably to resist, and he moved cautiously off to the nearer of the two gates—that between chapel and library. Then suddenly changing his mind, he struck across the lawn, skirting the library and chapel, to reach the western gate instead—that between hall and the President's Lodging. This was, of course, the gate he had seen when moving to the common-room after dinner, and the gate through which the constable would have admitted the four Orchard Ground men to their rooms.

He rounded the last of the great south buttresses of the hall and found himself upon gravel—upon the path, that was, that led through the gates and skirted the President's Lodging before striking into the orchard proper. He walked warily on; the hall on his right, what must still be the common-rooms on his left. He felt for the key in his pocket, keeping his eye meantime on the faint gleam of the path at his feet. In the darkness distance was hard to judge; he put his hand out before him to avoid running full into the gate, and paced steadily on. And then suddenly he was aware of something inexplicable to his right: the hall, close to which he had been walking, had vanished, to be replaced by empty space. At the same time he dimly discerned the path at his feet forking right and left. He was in Orchard Ground. *The gate lay behind him.*

A moment earlier Appleby, though walking cautiously through the night, had been almost a disembodied intellectual machine, the emphasis of his attention turned inwards. Now he was a tense mechanism of physical potentiality and sensory awareness. For perhaps thirty seconds he stood rigid, listening. He sank noiselessly down to the ground, crouching with his ear to the earth. There was no suspicion of a sound nearer than the subdued intermittent rumble of the night traffic on Schools Street.

Softly he straightened up again and retraced his steps. The north angle of the hall loomed up a few feet away and he progressed slowly, his left hand feeling constantly along the wall until presently he came to the gate. One wing only was open; he had walked unaware straight through the narrow aperture. And now he halted and debated his course of action. To leave the gate unguarded would be inexcusable: here was the chance of a discovery which must be waited for till morning if necessary. He could, of course, shout and rouse somebody. He could even, by advancing only a few paces, command the archway into Surrey, and through that archway the torch he carried might just convey a signal to the constable at the lodge, were he vigilant. But both these courses might warn somebody who, if unalarmed, would walk straight into a trap. Appleby drew up to the wall and waited. He was prepared to wait with unabated vigilance until sunrise.

His back was against the hall; his left hand was on the cold iron of the open wing of the gate: playing up and down, it touched the lock. His body stiffened. In the lock was the key—the tenth, problematical key!

He set about exploring the gate thoroughly—or as thoroughly as darkness allowed. The open wing was so hung that it swung to of its own weight, and would then lock automatically. But in the wall of the hall was a catch by which the gate might be held back in the day-time, and this catch had been applied. Out of Appleby's pocket came a fine tool. He disengaged the key from the lock without touching it with his fingers and stowed it in his pocket-book. Then he stepped through to the Bishop's side and let the gate swing to behind him. He noticed a faint creak as it closed. All the keys were now in police keeping.

And now Appleby ran. Silently across the grass, rapidly through the archway and to the lodge. It was the work of a moment to beckon to the constable doing porter's duty to follow him, and both men were back at the gates within a minute of Appleby's leaving them. Appleby unlocked the gate and murmured: "Somebody may come—from either side. Get him. And wait till I come back." Then he slipped once more into the darkness of Orchard Ground.

He made first for the eastern gate, that between library and chapel. A glide across the grass brought him to it: it was closed and securely locked. And now he set off along the faintly discernible path that led in the direction of Schools

Street and at the end of which he would find the wicket that connected St. Anthony's with the outer world. Presently he lost the path and was groping among the apple trees. But still he judged it better not to use his torch, and after a few minutes' wandering he touched what he knew was the wall bounding the eastern side of the orchard. The grass ran up to the wall, so that he made his way silently forward. Presently he reached the wicket. It too was locked.

He turned round now and made off down the orchard, trying to recall to his memory the lie of the paths as he had seen them on Dodd's sketch-map. But he failed and had to proceed by judgment. Two paths in succession ran off to the right; he bore left till he came to a little cross-roads. He guessed where he was now: to the right was Little Fellows'; to the left the west gate where he had left the constable; straight on were the French windows of the President's study. Appleby went straight on. And presently he knew that something was wrong.

The French windows, he knew, had been bolted from the inside at top and bottom and locked in the middle. But now the window, like the west gate, swung open. Within was blackness. Appleby listened once more and then slipped inside. The curtains were only partly drawn back; as silently as possible he drew them to behind him and switched on his torch.

The body had been removed that evening. But the bones had been left—and the bones were still there, as were the crudely chalked death's-heads on the wall. He stepped over to the door; it was locked, and he did not doubt that on the other side the seal applied by Dodd on leaving would be still intact. The French windows had simply been forced and the room rifled. Appleby turned on the light now and walked to the far end with a premonition of what he would find. In the bay by the *Deipnosophists* the dummy shelf swung loose. The concealed safe was open. Some documents lay scattered in it. Something, doubtless, was gone.

An observer would have found Appleby pale at this moment. He had lost a trick—perhaps a decisive trick. He ought to have insisted to Dodd on more surveillance than was represented by the constable at the porter's lodge. He ought to have had a team of locksmiths up from London, working at that safe all night. . . .

He set himself to an inspection. Nothing, as far as he could see, had been disturbed. The desk was untampered with. And the safe had not been forced. Whoever had been in the room had known what he wanted, where it lay concealed and how to gain access to it. The safe, the very existence of which appeared to be unknown to the rest of the college, had held, even in the combination that opened it, no secret for this intruder. Who had the intruder been? Appleby turned to the probabilities. One of the four men sleeping in Little Fellows' next door could have broken in easily enough. He slipped once more through the curtains and examined the window. What had happened was clear. The burglar had made three circles with a diamond and to each of these he had applied a piece of sacking treated with some sticky substance; through this deadening medium he had then smashed the holes which enabled him to get at bolts and key. It was a trick out of fiction rather than out of current burglarious practice, and it was surprising that it had worked as well as it had done. A resounding splintering of the whole great pane ought to have been the result; as it was, the fractures had almost confined themselves to their diamond-scrawled boundaries and the noise would have been insufficient to penetrate either to the quarters of the dead President's domestic staff or round the corner to Little Fellows'.

It might have been one of the Little Fellows' men—but

what then was the meaning of the open west gate? The key had been on the orchard side. If the burglary and the open gate were connected, and if one of these four—Empson, Haveland, Pownall, Titlow—was responsible, he had gone on through the gate to one of the other courts—*and was there still*. Or somebody from outside St. Anthony's had entered with this tenth key through the wicket, committed the burglary, and similarly gone on to the other part of the college.

But the indications might be deliberately misleading. Why had the key been left in the lock? As a deliberate false trail? Supposing the burglary had been committed not from the orchard side but from the Bishop's side? The perpetrator might then have left the key on the orchard side to suggest the contrary. But what would that suggestion, logically followed up, imply? It would imply that somebody had passed from Orchard Ground (or perhaps from Schools Street) into the main courts of the college and had then (as a fictitious person could obviously not be discovered there) passed back, leaving the gate open and abandoning the key. The pretence was too thin to have been worth putting up. Almost certainly somebody had passed from Orchard Ground to Bishop's; and almost certainly that person was there still. For if (as the creak suggested) the gate had been left open to cut down noise pending a return and one final shutting of it, then the key might have been forgotten in the moment that such a procedure was decided upon. But if the person concerned had passed back to Orchard Ground his whole instinct would be to cover his traces: he would almost certainly take the very slight risk of shutting the gate, and would almost certainly repossess himself of the key.

If this was indeed the situation, if the burglar was now somewhere in the main buildings and had his escape to make through the gates he was virtually in Appleby's hands. Leaving the gate open, with police possibly prowling round, had been a gross error of judgment; abandoning the key in the lock had been more careless still: both acts implied a sort of mind that Appleby had not hitherto associated with Umpleby's murderer. If this was the murderer who was operating now the St. Anthony's mystery might be past history within half an hour. It was somehow a disconcerting thought.

And now Appleby glided into the darkness again and made his way back to the west gate—to find himself looking into the dimly gleaming barrel of a revolver. It was not a weapon with which the sturdy constable holding it was likely to be over-familiar, and Appleby was relieved when his identity was established. At least, this was a vigilant man; he might safely be left on guard alone a little longer. In a whisper Appleby gave directions. He himself was going back to explore Little Fellows'. The constable was to continue to keep watch and to make sure of anybody who came along. By lying low there was a chance of capturing the burglar neatly with his spoils upon him. A general alarm and search might discover somebody who would have difficulty in explaining his presence, but that somebody would be unlikely to have anything incriminating still upon his person. Meantime, a search of Little Fellows' might discover one of its four occupants missing; and this would be evidence in itself supposing anything were to go amiss with the hoped-for capture by the west gate.

Appleby was on the point of turning back into the orchard when he became aware that during this prolonged night prowl he had grown exceedingly cold. And in front of him, after he had searched Little Fellows', lay what might be a long vigil beside his colleague. Just across the lawn, at the foot of the Dean's staircase, was hanging his overcoat, and as his course to it would be untouched by the dim light over the Surrey archway he decided he could cross once more without any appreciable risk of giving alarm.

With a word of his intentions to the constable he set off and in a moment was round the corner of the hall and making for his staircase with fair certainty. He came upon the gravel path again just by his doorway and slipped inside. He groped his way forward to where he knew the coat hung. His hand had gone out to it when he sensed a movement in the darkness behind him. And before he could turn there came a smashing concussion. He crumpled up on the floor.

CHAPTER VI

I

IN something under half an hour Appleby regained consciousness. His head was throbbing and he felt sick. Nevertheless he had barely become aware of these circumstances before he was aware too that his brain was beginning to work clearly. Almost his first reflection was that he had by no means been made the victim of a murderous attack: he had merely been neatly and not unmercifully stunned. It required little thinking to tell why. His pockets, he discovered on passing a hand over himself, had been rifled and his key to Orchard Ground was gone. But not the key which he had found: that was safely in his pocket-book still —with whatever tell-tale finger-prints it might conceivably bear. The assailant had been content with securing *a key:* beyond that he had not stopped to think. And this was Appleby's second indication that night that something less than a perfectly efficient mind was at work.

The unknown had been content to secure a key; there was little doubt to what purpose. The west gate was guarded but the east gate was not; as long as all the keys had been in police custody there had been no need for that, for whoever was lurking in these courts could get out only by the open west gate where the constable stood. But now Appleby's assailant was as good as a free man. All he had to do was to hurry down the east side of Bishop's, down the passage between library and chapel—all this being remote from the hearing or observation of the constable across the court—and let himself into Orchard Ground by the alternative route. Then if he were Empson, Pownall, Haveland or Titlow he could go straight to bed; if he were an outsider he could let himself through the wicket and vanish.

Appleby got painfully to his feet. The movement started a trickle of blood from the wound on his scalp; as he bent forward it ran down his forehead and dropped suddenly and sickeningly into his eyes. Impatiently he made a rough bandage with his handkerchief, and wrapped his now shivery body in the coat which had been the cause of his downfall. For it was a downfall. Twice he had been outwitted that night: first in suffering the burglary of the President's study to happen, and now again in this closer and somehow more personal duel. For the second time he had the mortification of vain regrets. If only he had gone to Little Fellows' before consulting his comfort in the matter of the overcoat, what might he not now know! Something that he would not be given the chance, perhaps, to learn again.

At least he could go to Little Fellows' now. Bracing himself to hold at bay the giddiness and nausea that were upon him he stepped out into the court. It had been cold in the little stone lobby but it was colder in the open. The extra chill, numbing as it was, steadied him and he crossed the lawn confidently enough.

The constable had done the right thing: as long as Appleby was absent he had stuck to his post. But as time passed he had been in considerable perplexity and now he was anxious to know that he had committed no error of judgment. Appleby reassured him and dismissed him to an easier vigil in the President's study. To guard the gate any longer would serve no useful purpose: the bird had flown. . . . Appleby made his way once more into Orchard Ground. He looked at the luminous dial of his watch as he did so: it was a quarter to four—and impenetrably dark.

That anything would come of this final reconnoitre he had little hope. But it was preferable to going back to his room to think when his brain was too tired to think at its best. And if he went back he would, he knew, attempt to think: sleep immediately after defeat was impossible to him. So he rounded the corner of the President's Lodging and presently became aware of the bulk of Little Fellows' a few paces ahead. He would do a little burglarizing on his own. If one of the four occupants had been his assailant there was just a chance that some tiny indication of the fact might be discoverable. And if he were detected rummaging about the rooms of one of his St. Anthony's hosts at four o'clock in the morning it might not be altogether unfortunate. A bare feeling that the police were uncompromisingly at work on a trail is a thing often surprisingly productive in criminal investigation.

No glimmer of light came from Little Fellows' as Appleby stepped into the stone-flagged lobby. Little Fellows' was a modern building, but it had been constructed on the old orthodox plan. Right and left of Appleby as he entered were the heavy outer doors of a set of rooms: Pownall's, as he knew, upon the left; Haveland's upon the right. Both doors were ajar and Appleby's torch ran cautiously round the little inner lobby revealed beyond each. Within the lobbies was one single door only; this would lead to the owner's sitting-room, from which an inner door, in turn, would serve as the only entrance to the bedroom beyond. In front of Appleby, and against the right-hand wall, the staircase ran up into the darkness to a similar lobby on the upper floor—the floor on which were the rooms of Titlow and Empson. Again in front of Appleby, and along the left-hand wall, a short passage led to a flight of stairs running downward—no doubt to some small service basement. There was little to explore here, but Appleby made a minute examination first of the paved floor of the outer lobby and then of the wooden floors beyond. Outside, it was slightly damp underfoot and there was the chance that a fresh footprint might give some clue to who had been stirring in the small hours.

But a careful search revealed nothing, and Appleby started on the staircase. Softly he mounted the bare wooden treads, scrutinizing them one by one. Half-way up was a small landing with a coal-locker, and then a full turn brought him to the upper lobby—and still nothing. He began to think that this in itself might be evidence, for in the lobby down below, and on the first few treads of the staircase, his own feet had left distinct traces. If anybody had passed indoors within the last two hours it seemed likely that traces would remain. But it was a doubtful point. Appleby himself had been walking a good deal on the grass; if his assailant had kept to the gravel paths his shoes might have remained comparatively dry. Or it was not unlikely that a careful man would have removed his shoes on the threshold.

And now Appleby decided to make sure that the occupants of Little Fellows' were indeed all in the building. He quietly opened the door of Empson's sitting-room and slipped inside. His flitting torch revealed a large book-lined room, handsome rugs on a polished floor, deep leather chairs, and, by the door where Appleby stood, a bronze bust on a pedestal. By an impulse of artistic curiosity that was natural to him he turned his torch for a moment full on this. The head, obviously, of a *savant*—and then he noticed a plaque on the pedestal: *Charcot*. Empson's master, perhaps—and Freud's.

Next—and again characteristically—the torch ran over the books. It was a severe library, almost without digressions, hobbies or loose ends of any sort. . . . Ancient philosophy, massed together. Modern philosophy, similarly massed. *The International Library of Psychology, Philosophy, and Scientific Method*—uniform, complete, overwhelming. Academic psychology—what looked like a first-class collection. Medical psychology—a great deal of this, too. General medicine—something like the nucleus of a consultant's library. Criminal psychology. Straight criminology. . . . And that was all. Now for the bedroom.

Stepping deliberately from rug to rug, like a child on the pavement baffling the bears, he reached the inner door and heard, his own breath suspended, low regular breathing from within. He turned the handle and opened the door a couple of feet until the bed was visible. Then he shone his torch upon the ceiling of the sitting-room behind him: the light was just sufficient to reveal Empson clearly. He was sleeping soundly, and in his sleep he looked worn and delicate. The lines of his mouth suggested pain; the skin stretched tight in a clear pallor over the cheek-bones and the jaw. Appleby recalled a slight hesitation—barely a stutter—in Empson's speech; recalled too that he was lame, walking with the assistance of a stick that even now stood beside his bed. The two disabilities were perhaps symptomatic of some congenital delicacy, and the dry, slightly acrid spirit of the man was the protective shell over a suffering and perhaps morbid sensibility. Appleby's mind went back to the books in the room behind him. The mainspring of such a personality as Empson's would be described there as the restless urge to power of one who feels in certain physical particulars subnormal. He softly closed the door on the worn, almost bitter figure. He felt an unprofessional impulse of shame at his spying: a man appears so helpless in sleep—so helpless and so revealed. . . . Appleby passed out to the landing once more and entered Titlow's rooms.

He made no pause this time to scrutinize the sitting-room, for he wanted to be downstairs again without delay. Tiptoeing over to the bedroom door, he bent down to listen. There was no sound from within. And Appleby's ear was almost abnormally acute. Either Titlow was an exceedingly light sleeper or . . . Appleby boldly opened the door. The room was empty. The bed-clothes were disarranged and Titlow's evening clothes lay on a chair—but Titlow himself was missing.

There was as yet no faint glimmer of light in the eastward-fronting windows of the rooms, and Appleby kept his torch burning as he made his way thoughtfully downstairs. He would wait for Titlow, and while waiting he would have a look at the two men below. He had recovered from his compunctions; if sleep was revealing he wanted more of it. Turning right as he got to the foot of the stair, he had his hand on Pownall's door, when he checked himself. Beneath the door was a thin luminous line. Within, someone had turned on the electric light.

Appleby's first thought was that it might be Titlow: while he himself was in Empson's rooms Titlow might have slipped down to Pownall's for purposes of his own. There was no murmur of voices from within: only the sound of slight physical movements. Was Pownall still in bed and asleep, unconscious that he had a visitor—even as Empson had been a few minutes before? Appleby tried the keyhole —unenthusiastically. No aperture is more exasperating to the would-be spy than is a keyhole. It gives him a strip of floor, a strip of wall—even a strip of ceiling; but its lateral range is wretched. The thicker the door, moreover, the narrower the view—and college doors are commonly good stout barriers. Through Pownall's keyhole Appleby could just discern movement, and no more. It seemed to be a case of either walking in or going away uninstructed. And then it occurred to him that the windows might be more hopeful. He slipped out into the orchard and was rewarded. The curtains of Pownall's room were drawn, but from one cranny there came a streak of light and by standing on tiptoe in a flower-bed he could just peer in.

Something large and black was moving about the floor, and it took a moment to sort out this appearance from its surroundings and impose an intelligible form upon it. Analyzed, it proved to be a pair of human buttocks, the curve of a human back and the soles of two human feet. A dinner-jacketed form, in fact, was kneeling on the floor and crawling slowly over the carpet. It could not be Titlow—unless he had unaccountably changed out of one dinner-jacket into another. But at this moment the form circled round and rose to its feet. It was Pownall himself.

Inadequate as was his means of vision, Appleby was struck by the concentration on the man's face. Pownall was a clumsy man, and possessed at once of the bluest and the slowest eyes that the detective remembered. These eyes were cold now—were felt as cold even through the little chink of window-curtain—and the brow above them was heavy with effort. There seemed no fear that he would spot the dim face at the window. His gaze was intently fixed upon the floor; without shifting it he sidled out of range for a moment, and returned holding some small object with which he sank down upon the floor once more. Inch by inch he was going over his own carpet.

Appleby was as absorbed as Pownall—so absorbed as to start almost violently at the sudden murmur of a pleasant voice behind him. "Ah, my dear Mr. Inspector, you begin early—or continue late!"

Switching on his torch, Appleby swung round. It was Titlow—Titlow in pyjamas and a frayed but gorgeous silk dressing-gown, regarding him over that weak nose, through these luminous but fathomless eyes. There had been amused irony in the voice, in the "Mr. Inspector." But suddenly there was concern as the Senior Fellow added, "But bless me, man, are you not hurt—injured in some way?"

Appleby, pale, exhausted, with a bloody bandage round his head and clotted blood down his face, was discernible in the ray of light from the window as a sorry sight. He admitted dryly that an unexpected misadventure had befallen him. Titlow continued concerned. "If you have concluded your momentary observations, will you not come upstairs to my rooms? I have just been fetching myself a tin of coffee from the basement pantry here—I have wakeful fits sometimes. But you, if I may say so, need something stronger. And after that, I doubt if you could do better than go to bed. . . . Now, come away."

Beside all this easy benevolence, Appleby discerned, was the same nervous excitement, the same irritability and impulsiveness that had struck him in Titlow already. And Titlow, if no more intense than say Empson or Haveland, was deeper than the others: there was layer upon layer to him—the several layers none too firmly bound together perhaps into any coherent personality. But he was smiling urbanely now, simply amused, it seemed, at having detected a detective in an absurd situation. And Appleby did feel a little uncomfortable. He experienced an idiotic satisfaction that Titlow had not come upon him while he was at the keyhole: there were several shades of ignominy, somehow, between keyholes and windows. He pulled himself together. "I shall be delighted," he said, "if you will excuse me one moment." And turning into the lobby of Little Fellows' once more, he went straight into Haveland's room, straight into his bedroom, discerned him indubitably asleep, and came straight out again. And this gesture accomplished, he followed the now frankly smiling Titlow upstairs.

II

Titlow's whisky was very good—or so it seemed to Appleby, who would have consumed the rankest poteen with relish at this melancholy hour of four-thirty on a November morning. Stretched in front of a large electric radiator, he sipped, munched biscuits from a large tin delusively labelled "Msc. clay-tablets: Lagash and Uruk," and looked round him with interest. He had already—although Titlow did not know it—had a glimpse of this room; now he scrutinized it in detail. A living-room is always revealing, and particularly so when clothed with books. Titlow's books, like Deighton-Clerk's, and unlike Umpleby's and Empson's, came up only waist-high round the room, but they were two deep everywhere on the broad shelves—an arrangement the inevitable inconvenience of which seemed enhanced by the completely haphazard arrangement of the volumes. Carelessly disposed along the tops of the low bookcases was a mass of ancient pottery—shapes subtle, free and flowing; shapes angular, abstract and austere; brilliant glazes, delicate crackles; textures that flattered the sense of touch through the sense of sight. Above the pottery on one wall was an enormous ground-plan of some large-scale excavation, a yearly progress marked on it in coloured chalks. Next to this, and set up for study it would seem rather than for ornament, was a series of large and technically magnificent aerial photographs of the same site, with sundry lines and crosses delicately traced on them in chinese white. And next came a perfect miniature picture gallery, photographs and colour-prints covering a vast field of art—or covering rather all that field of prehistoric, barbaric and pre-Hellenic culture which is still "archæology" to most although it has become "art" to some. All the forms of natural life, the human figure chief among them, stylized and distorted to convey implications of permanence, rigidity, abstraction: the art of peoples who feared life. And hard upon these, in subtle juxtaposition, an art despising it: the art of the Middle Ages—an erudite collection, dominated by a big German *Dance Macabre*. And, single against this, in violent disharmony upon the opposite wall, all the physical glow and warmth of the Renaissance pulsating from a colour-print of Giorgione's Sleeping Venus.

Titlow in fact—it came to Appleby—was dramatizing an inner incoherence in this room. And in addition to the deliberate sounding of major disharmony there had been a scattering of little grace-notes of pure oddity. There was a stuffed dog, oddly reminiscent of Queen Victoria (who would scarcely have felt at home here); there was a small cannon; one of the chairs was simply hollowed out of some porous stone. But Appleby looked chiefly at the *Dance Macabre* and then at the Sleeping Venus. And he sipped his whisky and finally murmured to Titlow, with something of the whimsicality that Titlow had been adopting a little before, *"What truth is it that these mountains bound, and is a lie in the world beyond?"*

There was silence while Titlow's eye dwelt meditatively on a policeman conversant with Montaigne. Then he smiled, and his smile had great charm. "I wear my heart on my wall?" he asked. "To project one's own conflicts, to hang them up in simple pictorial terms—it is to be able to step back and contemplate oneself. You understand?"

"The artist's impulse," said Appleby.

Titlow shook his head. "I am not an artist—it seems. I am an archæologist, and perhaps that is not a very healthy thing to be—for me. It is unhealthy to be something that one can be only with a part of onself. And it is with a very small part of myself, I sometimes think, that I have become what I am. By nature I am an imaginative and perhaps creative man. But it is difficult to become an artist today. One stops off and turns to something else. And if it is something intellectual merely, so that other impulses lack expression, then perhaps one becomes—freakish. Irrational impulses lurk in one, waiting their chance . . . do you not think, Mr. Appleby?"

Odd the abruptly pitched question. And odd the whole man, talking thus under some queer compulsion to a stranger—and a policeman. Appleby's answer was almost at random: "You think the thwarted artist . . . unstable?" But it set Titlow off again.

"Artists or scholars, Mr. Appleby—we are all unstable here today. It is the spirit of the age, the flux growing, the chaos growing, the end of our time growing nearer hourly! Perhaps one has not to live in imagination much amid the long stabilities of Egypt and Babylon to know that? But it is to the scholars, the men of thought, of contemplation, that the first breath of the whirlwind comes. . . ."

And pacing nervously, convulsively up and down Titlow talked . . . of the rhythm of history . . . the rise and fall of cultures . . . *das Untergang des Abendlands,* Decline of the West. He talked well, with a free, unashamed rhetoric, at once logical and full of bold ellipses. And Appleby listened quietly to the end. Titlow was talking as he was because Umpleby had died as he did.

"You know where we come from here—whence we derive, I mean. We are clerks, mediæval clerks leading this mental life that is natural and healthy only to men serving a transcendental idea. But have we that now? And what then does all this thinking, poring, analyzing, arguing become—what but so much agony of pent-up and thwarted action? The ceaseless driving of natural physiological energy into narrow channels of mentation and intellection—don't you think that's dangerous? Don't you think we could be a dangerous, unbalanced caste once the purposes have gone and the standards are vanishing? Don't you think it?"

Titlow had paused; he was perched outlandishly on his outlandish little cannon. What was the compulsion behind this queer talk—talk that was indeed but contemporary commonplace in substance but, in some personal relationship in which the man now stood to it, so decidedly queer? Appleby remembered Deighton-Clerk talking—talking, it had seemed, to convince himself. And somehow—surely—Titlow was doing the same? Again he had concluded on a question, an appeal for corroboration. Again Appleby had to evolve a reply.

"No doubt it is, as you say, the scholars and men of thought who feel the whirlwind coming. But do they really—give way? Is it not they who survive—survive because they are removed from the world? Do they not—well—guard, hand down?"

What, Appleby was wondering as he spoke, would Dodd think of all this as a technique of investigation? But his eyes were as searchingly on Titlow as if his question had related directly to the President's death. And there was strain, something even of anxiety or alarm lurking in Titlow's eyes as he replied.

"It should be as you say, Mr. Appleby. Indeed, it *is* so—essentially."

There was a silence of calculation. It was as if Titlow were feeling his way, testing the ground he would be on were he to abandon some position to which he had trusted—and all this with no reference to how he stood with Appleby. "It is so—really," he reiterated.

"But you think that a society such as this, in what you see as a disintegrating age, is unstable, erratic?"

Titlow made a gesture almost as of pain. And when he replied it was with an impersonality that plainly revealed the intellectual man's habit of striving for objectivity, for dispassionate truth. The personal pressure he had contrived for the moment to sink.

"Erratic, yes. But I have been overstating—or oversuggesting—greatly. Any fundamental unbalance there is not. What there is, is—nerves. And personal eccentricity, perhaps some degree of irresponsibility—our modern scholarship, I know, is essentially irresponsible. But basic instability—no. Except perhaps"—softly, firmly Titlow added —"in such a one as myself. . . ." Again he made his little gesture of pain.

"You would not say—regarding the matter untemperamentally—that the spirit of the age, and the rest of it, is likely to incline any of your colleagues to homicide?"

If there was a hint of irony in Appleby's question it was lost. Standing now before the fire, Titlow weighed it. And replied: "No."

"You would not think of any of your colleagues, while in his right mind, as remotely likely to murder?"

"Certainly I would not think anything of the sort—spontaneously."

"Only on proof?" Sitting nibbling Titlow's biscuits and drinking Titlow's whisky, Appleby felt he could get no nearer direct inquisition than this.

And Titlow's response was enigmatic. "What is proof?"

III

Appleby rose. Of all this there must be more on the morrow, or rather later this same day. Meantime it would be discreet to withdraw from a slightly uncomfortable position. But Titlow had something further to say. His restlessness, the characteristic nervous agitation which had expressed itself in his earlier talk, and which he had by some great effort controlled later, was back again now in full possession of the man. He had paced across the room; now he turned round with a new and tempestuous gesture, as if to say some conclusive, some final thing. But for a moment he seemed to seek delay on a minor theme.

"Who could have told, Mr. Appleby, that *you* would come amongst us? Not one of us would have believed there was such a person—outside Gott's nonsense. . . . Tell me, when were you here before?"

Appleby answered the unexpected question with some reluctance, but truthfully. "Eight years ago."

"Exactly—obviously! A good head that has had the right training—of course one knows it anywhere. But talk of erratic conduct . . . ! What of erratic walks of life? From our angle, you know, you yourself are the oddest thing in the case."

"You mean," said Appleby, remembering a facetious remark of Dodd's, "that you expected Gott's other stock figure, the village policeman?"

"I say we should not have been inclined to count——" And suddenly Titlow was off on another tack. "Did you ever read De Quincey's *Murder considered as one of the Fine Arts?*"

This was not the aimless belletristic habit which had prompted the venerable Professor Curtis to discourse on *The Purloined Letter*. Titlow meant something—was indeed poised again to take his plunge. But for a moment he wavered anew from the issue. "Rather in your line. But poor stuff really—much slack erudition on a thread of feeble humour. . . ." And then he said what he had to say. "It records an anecdote about Kant. You would find that interesting, if only because it deals with an academic attitude to murder. And if you turned it upside down it might even be illuminating."

Appleby smiled. "Thank you. I will look it up with all speed." He moved to the door. And when Titlow spoke again it was easily, benignantly, as when he had first invited Appleby to his rooms.

"Well, you ought certainly to be in bed. You can get three or four good hours—and so perhaps can I. Put a notice on your door and the servant won't disturb you."

Easy, benignant again—but with a difference. Titlow *was* easy now. It was as if, in giving some hint or pointer through De Quincey's essays, he had reached a position, or come to a decision on which he could rest. He moved to the door with his guest.

"Later—we shall see," said Titlow. He gave his agitated little gesture—by way of farewell this time—and turned back into his rooms. Appleby went slowly downstairs. Through the orchard was seeping the first glimmer of dawn.

CHAPTER VII

I

INSPECTOR DODD walked down Schools Street in stolid satisfaction. The business of the burglaries was going well. In his pocket nestled a sheaf of notes for his London colleague that witnessed to the efficiency of his department. The morning was cold but pleasant, with gleams of sunshine filtering down the street, gilding St. Baldred's tower, playing hide and seek in the odd little temples in front of Cudworth, exploring the dusty intricacies of the ornate and incongruous portals of the Museum, straying across the way to Ridley in an effort to brighten up the heavy-featured effigies of Jacobean divines. A group of undergraduates passed in riding-kit: a solitary and exquisite youth, in the most beautiful scarlet slippers, was crossing the street with the evident purpose of breakfasting with a friend in Joseph's; occasionally a female student, capped and gowned, bicycled hurriedly past in that zealous pursuit of early morning instruction proper to her kind. A small boy was sitting innocently on the doorstep of the Warden of Dorset, selling an occasional newspaper to unenthusiastic purchasers. No one could have guessed that the same boy had been dashing wildly up and down Schools Street the evening before, waving the *Evening Standard* and bawling of the death of Dr. Umpleby. . . . The Master of St. Timothy's, venerable, bearded and magnificent, swept down the street on his morning perambulation as he had done every morning these forty years—plainly untroubled either by the decease of his colleague or by the reflection that St. Timothy's rather than St. Anthony's might have been the seat of the crime. It suddenly occurred to Dodd to rejoice that he was not a policeman in Chicago or Sydney or Cardiff. Praising heaven for his lot, he turned down St. Ernulphus Lane.

Mr. Appleby was to be found in Six-four. Meditating on this unorthodox way of conducting police investigation, Dodd found Six—which was a staircase—passed Six-two with its unacceptable announcement, "The Rev. the Hon. Tracy Deighton-Clerk: Dean," found Appleby's temporary quarters and knocked loudly. There was no reply, so Dodd walked in. A big fire was burning ruddily. Appleby's table was laid for breakfast; Appleby's coffee was keeping warm on the one side of the fire; a covered dish that was certainly Appleby's bacon and eggs was keeping warm on the other. But of Appleby himself there was no sign—until Dodd's eye lighted on a sheet of paper pinned to the inner door. Its message was short and to the point: "Breakfast at nine —J. A." Dodd looked at his watch. It was just nine-ten. "Well I'm damned!" said Dodd, and was just about to penetrate into the bedroom when Appleby emerged.

"Morning, Dodd," he said. "Have some coffee? I expect there's plenty, and fairly warm still." And then, noticing his colleague's doubtful glance at his still-bandaged head, he chuckled. "Yes, I've been in a rough house all right. Nocturnal rioting in St. Anthony's. The police attacked with sandbags, lead pipes and the butt-ends of heavy revolvers. . . . But I think this picturesque touch might come off now." And Appleby disposed of the bandage before proceeding to fall upon his coffee and bacon and eggs.

Dodd looked at him wonderingly. "You've really been knocked out?"

Appleby nodded. "Knocked out, gently but firmly—and on the very verge of solving the St. Anthony's mystery. I'm in disgrace." He took a large gulp of coffee and nodded again in solemn assurance. "One of your henchmen will be going home this morning with a sadly diminished respect for the conception of the metropolitan sleuth."

"Who was it attacked you?"

"I don't know. But he—or perhaps she?—was the possessor of the tenth key. At least he was, and then I was, and then we did a bit of an exchange. I've got his tenth and he's got my ninth, so to speak. He took it from me after hitting me on the head."

"Took it from you! And where did you take the tenth from?"

"The lock, Dodd; I found it in the lock. Natural place for a key, no doubt."

Dodd groaned.

"And, by the way, Dodd, Umpleby's safe has been burgled—very successfully. Not a thing in it now—to interest us."

Dodd fairly started to his feet. "Burgled? Who in heaven's name can have done that? Someone in college?"

"I don't know."

The local inspector looked at his colleague for a moment with what might have been positive mistrust. "Have you had *any* light on it—on the whole affair, I mean?"

"Indeed I have. Lots. Light comes flooding in from every angle—far too much light, from far too many angles. And I'm quite sure you've brought another surplus of it yourself. . . ."

"I've got something," responded Dodd. "But in a general way I'd like to be hearing what has happened. If you've got time, that is." And he glanced with a sort of humorous severity at his watch and at the notice on the bedroom door. His admiration for Appleby was increasing rapidly. If he himself had lost that key he could never have contrived this air about it all. And Appleby, he felt, was doing something more than simply carrying the matter off: he was showing a quite natural and unforced faith in himself. He could be hit on the head and still remain in control of the situation—or so it seemed. If Dodd were hit on the head he would be hot and angry for days afterwards.

"Very well," Appleby was saying. "Here is an abstract of what has turned up.

"First, your friend the Honourable and Reverend Tracy is in a stew. But whether he's simply worried about the reputation of the college, or whether he's worried somehow on his own account, I don't know. St. Anthony's is due to come into the limelight in the near future, and he seems to have got his worries mixed up with that.

"Secondly, I know where the bones come from——"

Dodd sat up straight. "Where?"

"Australia, my dear Dodd. Earth's last-found jewel. *Terris magna Australis incognita.*"

Dodd looked bewildered. "You're sure they don't come from Athens or Sparta?" he asked sarcastically, "same as the *Deipno*-what-was-its in Umpleby's library?"

"The bones were abstracted from Australia—by no irrational ferrety, as Sir Thomas says. They were snatched from the pious care of an aboriginal posterity to gratify the scientific proclivities of one Johnnie Haveland."

"Haveland! They're his?"

"They're his. And he was suitably apologetic about refraining from explanations when you were making inquiries yesterday. Apparently Johnnie kept the skulls and what-not in his own little toy-cupboard—and now they're in Umpleby's study. He invites us to consider two possibilities about the murder. One, that he did it himself and left the bones as a sort of signature; two, that somebody has tried to frame him. And he as good as invited his learned friends to explain to me that there had been a time some years ago when he wasn't quite sound in the head. He seemed to think that would fit in with either possibility. . . . Oh! and he wasn't very nice about Empson.

"Thirdly, in the matter of keys, submarines and scaling ladders. St. Anthony's turns out to harbour a man who is likely to make the summit of Mount Everest one day—and who has already made the summit of St. Baldred's tower in this city. That's Campbell—and I hope you have a little information about him in your pocket at this moment.

"Fourthly, President Umpleby was not beloved. Johnnie Haveland alleges that Umpleby stole from him in a learned way. And that, when you consider it, is more excessively unlikely than any number of murders—nevertheless, it undoubtedly struck some chord in the assembled confraternity.

"Fifthly, Umpleby's safe, as I've told you, has been opened by one X—who incidentally knew the combination. X had the tenth key. He came either from Little Fellows' or through the wicket from outside. X is erratic but brilliant. He left the west gate open behind him, apparently because it squeaked—an error of judgment. He left the key in the lock—a piece of colossal carelessness."

"But," Dodd interrupted, "why should he come through the gate into the main body of the college at all?"

Appleby shook his head. "After his successful burglary perhaps he wanted a little chat with somebody in the other courts. As I say, he is erratic—and brilliant. He found himself trapped when he came to get back—and he got out of the trap ruthlessly, effectively and without losing his head and hitting too hard." And Appleby stroked his own skull tenderly.

"Sixthly, under the prosaically named Giles Gott, at this time Junior Proctor in the university, is shadowed no less a person than Gilbert Pentreith."

Dodd fairly leaped. "And I never knew that!"

"Yes. He sits over there in Surrey giving his spare time to imagining just such pretty affairs as this. I told you there was a great deal of light flooding in.

"Seventh, Mr. Raymond Pownall, an eminent ancient historian, spends his nights crawling about the floor of his room in a panic.

"Eighth—and, for the moment, lastly—Samuel Still Titlow lures honest policemen into his apartments, bemuses them with large and convincing talk of the end of the world, and just thinks better of concluding that the times are so out of joint that St. Anthony's may well be a hot-bed of murder. And he counsels a little reading in the minor English classics. And he drops dark hints about being in at the death."

"Would you say," put in Dodd with his sudden shrewdness, "that Titlow, like X, is erratic but brilliant?"

Appleby nodded thoughtfully. "Yes," he responded, "he is. But it's just one of his points, I imagine, that that is a habit here. And I rather agree. I hope my next case is in Hull."

Dodd smiled a slow smile. "You just love this," he said. And then a sudden thought struck him. "What about traces of the burglar in that study? What about his slipping back 'o obliterate any later?"

Appleby shook his head. "Your man's been sitting there all night since I recovered from my knock—I expect he'll have rung through for a relief by now. There was an interval, of course, after X got back from Orchard Ground, in which he could have gone to the study and cleared up. But I expect he'd pretty well obliterated himself already—even if he is erratic. I had a shot at the cigarette-ends and whatnot earlier—and nothing doing. And I don't much look to find the damning thumb-print on the tenth key either."

The two men were silent for a moment and then Dodd took his papers from his pocket. It was characteristic of Dodd that he always had something on paper ready to produce; he moved in an atmosphere of neat dockets and conscientious documentations. Appleby at the same time produced the notes and statements that had been made over to him the day before. As yet, his study of them had been superficial; direct contact with the personalities they dealt with had been taking up his time.

"Constable Sheepwash," Dodd began in the peculiarly wooden manner he adopted when cautiously savouring the absurdities and ironies of his profession—"Constable Sheepwash had a bite of supper last night with the Lambricks' cook. Earlier in the evening the lighting installation failed at the Chalmers-Patons'. Sergeant Potter represented the Electricity Department and after prolonged operations, mostly in the servants' quarters, the lights went on again. Constable Babbitt, as a Press reporter, failed to make an impression on the Campbell establishment yesterday, but he has done better as a milkman this morning. Station-Sergeant Kellett undertook to trace the movements of the Junior Proctor, Mr. Gott, round the places of refreshment and amusement in the city for the material times. Kellett was unable to avoid the purchase of considerable quantities of liquor, but his report is nevertheless substantially coherent." And Dodd, having had his little joke, became business-like. "How would it be," he asked, "if you read out the statements as made yesterday and I followed each with my check-up here? That would begin to get us clear, I think, on these four people who were out of college on the night of the murder."

Appleby nodded his agreement. "We'll begin with Campbell," he said. "I see these are not *verbatim* statements in evidence?"

"No, they're simply abstracts of preliminary statements got out of these folk in a hurry. I don't think they could be evidence. I think you will have to take formal statements today. Anyway, we must have some before the coroner fixes the inquest."

Appleby nodded and began to read:

"Campbell, Ian Auldearn (29). Became a Fellow of the college six years ago; has been married for four years; lives in a flat at 99 Schools Street; has never possessed a key to the St. Anthony's gates. Declares that he has no knowledge whatever likely to elucidate mystery of Umpleby's death. Was associated with Umpleby in scientific investigation but was never in any sense a personal friend of the President's.

"9.30. Left college and went home to flat. About half an hour later went out again to the Chillingworth Club in Stonegate.

"11.50 (approx.). Left club for home, but remembered that he had certain business matters to discuss with Sir Theodore Peek, who lives at a house called Berwick Lodge up the Luton Road. Knowing that Sir Theodore keeps late hours he walked out there and arrived just at midnight. He had a brief conversation with Sir Theodore and then walked back to Schools Street, arriving home a few minutes before half-past twelve."

Appleby had no sooner finished reading than Dodd took up Constable Babbitt's report as a sort of antiphonal chant:

"Acting on instructions received entered into conversation with Mary Surname Unknown at 99 Schools Street 7.25 a.m. Subsequent to general remarks not necessary to record Informant declared (1) her employers kept fine hours, (2) Mr. Campbell came home night before last shortly after 9.30 but went out again about three-quarters of an hour later, (3) she believes she heard him returning long after midnight, (4) he remarked to Mrs. Campbell at breakfast next morning that he had looked in on that old gargoyle Peek at midnight and found him in a sleepy, growly state (? a sick dog). No further information elicited."

Appleby nodded and made a note. "Questions at the club," he said, "and questions at Sir Theodore's—the sick dog! The material time was at the club, and it seems to hang together." And without more ado he turned to his next note.

"Chalmers-Paton, Denis (40). Lecturer at St. Anthony's —also at two other colleges. Married and lives at 12 Angas Avenue. Can make no suggestion on President's death.
"9.30. Left college and went home. Read *The Decline and Fall of the Roman Empire* aloud to Mrs. Chalmers-Paton. Mrs. C.-P. then went to bed. C.-P. retired to his study and continued to read *D. & F. of R. E.* until shortly before midnight. He then went to bed too."

Again Dodd followed with his subordinate's report. Chalmers-Paton had indeed come home, had read to his wife and had then retired to his study "a little before eleven." But after that the servants knew nothing, and Sergeant Potter had not been authorized to approach Mrs. Chalmers-Paton in any way. He had, however, timed the walk from Angas Avenue to St. Anthony's and made it just twenty minutes. Chalmers-Paton had no car.

"Almost satisfactory," said Appleby, "and yet not quite. The man disappears into his study just too soon. If he was home at ten to ten and reading by ten, then 'a little before eleven' *might* be twenty to eleven. And with the possibility of some emergency sort of conveyance that is just not good enough. And we don't *know* that he hadn't got the tenth key."

"Just not a good enough alibi. And Campbell's at that club looks an uncommonly good one. Always sound to suspect the good alibi."

Appleby smiled. This was the story-book Dodd speaking. But he did not altogether disagree. He turned to his next note.

"Lambrick, Arthur Basset (54). Fellow of the college for twenty-four years. Married and lives next door to Chalmers-Paton. Has had a key to the gates for a long time. Said to Inspector D.: 'I cannot persuade myself that it was I who murdered our poor President.'"

"9.30. Went home and stayed at home, 'not knowing there was anything on.'"

"Our humorous friend," murmured Appleby. And he listened to Dodd's reading of Constable Sheepwash's researches. There seemed no doubt here. Lambrick had got home shortly before ten, played shove-halfpenny with his eldest son till eleven and danced to the wireless with his eldest daughter for half an hour after that. A housemaid who had still been up thought both proceedings immoral and consequently had them firmly fixed in her head.

"Not much good suspecting *that* good alibi," admitted Dodd. "But he might always have lent his key, you know."

"And danced, so to speak, while Umpleby was cooling? It is possible. He might have lent his key, for instance, to Chalmers-Paton next door." Appleby's tone was absent and it was a moment before he came back to his sheaf of papers.

"Gott, Giles (32). Came to St. Anthony's six years ago. Has had key to gates since becoming Junior Proctor this year. Can give no information about Umpleby's death.

"9.15. Left St. Anthony's by the wicket gate and proceeded to the Proctors' office. Transacted university business there until 11.15. During this time he was quite alone.

"11.15. The Senior Proctor returned from his rounds, accompanied by the four university officers on duty. Gott then took over, proctorizing various parts of the city in turn. He was later than usual, only dismissing the officers outside St. Anthony's at about twenty past twelve."

Appleby finished this recital with a shake of his head. "No alibi there," he said, "nor the shadow of one. He was alone in his office until fifteen minutes after the shot and the discovery of Umpleby's body. And by way of the wicket that office is not more than seven or eight minutes from Orchard Ground." Appleby's topography was remarkably sure. "I don't see that your sleuth can have done anything useful about Gott?"

"Kellett has simply been round the town inquiring about the movements of the Proctors the night before last. It all squares so far. Between nine-thirty and eleven the Senior Proctor was patrolling about here and there. And after that Gott did apparently take on, going to various places until well past midnight. He wasn't seen before about eleven-thirty, but he might have slipped down from the office to St. Anthony's and back easily enough without being recognized. It was a pretty dark night. Kellett, incidentally, hasn't made any inquiries direct at the Proctors' office, or seen the four officers. That would have to be done formally and openly, I think. As you say, there's no alibi— or rather any alibi there is is for the wrong time: it begins too late. Kellett has followed it all up, but it seems irrelevant."

"Kellett has followed Gott up after eleven-fifteen? Better let us have it." There were times when Appleby was a stickler for routine.

"Well, Gott must have gone straight to the railway station first. He and his men were there meeting the eleven thirty-two from town. Then he went straight back to Town

Cross and was seen by one of our men on duty there just after eleven-forty. He turned up Stonegate and must have gone straight ahead, because just on midnight he was at the Green Horse."

"What's that?"

"It's a dubious pub out the Luton Road and a likely place to proctorize after hours. But Gott didn't spend long there, for he was back at Town Cross by twelve-fifteen and went down Schools Street, presumably to St. Anthony's as he said."

"About this Green Horse business. Did Kellett get his information from the people of the pub?"

"No, he got it from a farm-hand who had left a bicycle in the yard and was collecting it at midnight when Gott more or less ran into him. Kellett was uncommonly smart to tap him. The fellow knew what was up, of course: everybody in these parts knows the Proctor in his gown. And when he got out of the yard there were the four 'cops' as he called them waiting."

Appleby had got up and was striding restlessly about the room, seemingly in more perplexity than the St. Anthony's mystery had yet driven him to. Suddenly he halted.

"Dodd, you haven't by any chance got a street map on you?"

Without a word Dodd produced a map. Appleby opened it and pored over it for a minute. "Odd," he murmured, "distinctly odd. And the first oddity that hasn't pretty well been thrust at us. And at the same time, as you say, irrelevant. I tell you, Dodd, there is too much light in this case—too many promising threads." And he fell to striding up and down the room once more.

"Well," asked Dodd, slightly aggressively after an interval of silence, "what are you going to do now?"

"I think I'm going to go for a walk. But there is one other

matter first. Can you spare a little more time this morning . . . ? Well, I want you to send for Pownall to Umpleby's dining-room and take his formal statement. And I want the proceedings to last something over half an hour."

II

Mr. Raymond Pownall's was a colourless room. The books looked drab and were interspersed with unbound journals that looked drabber. The few pictures were of classical statuary—the kind of photographic reproduction in which the marble is thrown against an intensely sooty background. The carpet was a discouraged blue and a still aggressive black.

It was the carpet that interested Appleby. Secure in the knowledge that its owner was closeted with Dodd, he crawled over it with every bit as much concentration as he had witnessed in the small hours of the morning. First, he studied the design,—a largish floral one. Then, guided by the pattern, he made sure that his eye travelled over every inch of the surface. At the end of twenty minutes he had covered the whole area—and found nothing.

He straightened up, sat down, and thought. And then suddenly he shivered; his adventure of the night before had left him susceptible to cold. . . . *Cold.* He looked round the room. On this bleakly sunny and decidedly chilly morning every window of Pownall's room was open to its fullest extent. He began again, crouched over the carpet, not looking this time but smelling. . . . After a few minutes he sprang to his feet and, stepping into the orchard, sent a lurking subordinate with a message to Dodd. He must have another hour. And he fell to the carpet again.

Pale blue had been turned to black. In eight symmetrical places the pattern had been minutely altered—and in eight places the faint smell of ink remained. A brisk rub with a handkerchief produced from eight places a faint but amply confirmatory smear: Indian ink.

"Of all the tricks . . . !" murmured Appleby—and proceeded to rummage a packet of envelopes from Pownall's desk. Presently he was on his knees once more, industriously plying a pocket scissors.

III

In Two-six in Surrey the immemorial System was in operation. Mr. David Pennyfeather Edwards, the Senior Scholar of St. Anthony's and owner of the rooms, was squatting in front of the fire—appropriately, he had just pointed out—upon a large copy of the *Posterior Analytics*, superintending the preparation of a simple matutinal beverage mainly compounded of milk and madeira. Mr. Michel de Guermantes-Crespigny, the cherubic bible-clerk of the evening before, was lying on a window-seat with Sweet's *Anglo-Saxon Reader* upside down upon his stomach. Mr. Horace Kitchener Bucket, an exhibitioner of the college, was playing a rather absent-minded game of patience—involving four packs of cards and every inch of space—round the chairs and tables on the floor. And all three were improving themselves by conversation.

"The elimination of the Praeposital Pest," said Mr. Edwards, "suggests a number of nice speculations. For instance, what would you do, Inspector, if you knew who had performed this useful and sanitary act?"

Mr. Bucket, referred to as Inspector in allusion to the immortal masterpiece of Charles Dickens, wriggled a few inches across the floor to impound a ten of hearts, and shook his head.

"Dunno, David. Wait and see if there was a reward, I suppose."

"I really believe," murmured Mr. Crespigny from the window-seat, "that such is our Inspector's petty-bourgeois passion for the till that he would accept blood-money without a qualm. You shock me, Horace. . . . How's the drink?"

Horace, peering round the sofa in hope of a clinching ace, answered without heat. "Aristotle—or perhaps it was Plato—was a shopkeeper—or perhaps the son of one: I forget. And your own namesake, dear Mike, the sage of Perigord, was a fishmonger. And you are a nasty, unwholesome, misshapen, degenerate and altogether lousy scion of outworn privilege. And the increasing unpleasantness of your personal habits, your thick and incoherent utterance, your shambling gait, and above all your embarrassing and indeed painful inability to talk sense have long since convinced David and myself—though we have striven to conceal it—that you are already undermined beyond human aid by the effects of retributive disease. And your tailor—whose taste perpetually astonishes me, let me add—would be grateful for any blood-money *you* might raise on Umpleby: it would help feed the eight children your bad debts are depriving of sustenance."

Long before Horace had finished these remarks he appeared to have lost interest in them. The words came automatically from his lips as his hands deftly manipulated the cards round the coal-scuttle. But presently he added, "Who *did* kill Umpleby?"

"Umpleby," Mike ventured, "was stabbed by a dishonest serving-man, a rival of his in his lewd loves, and died swearing. Don't you think, David, that it must have been that Crypto-Semite Slotwiner? Passion had run high between them over Mrs. Tunk the laundress. And all to no purpose, for Mrs. Tunk is firmly pledged to our own omnivorous and promiscuous Horace."

"But what *would* one do," asked David, suddenly jumping up to distribute the adulterate madeira; "what *would* one do if one did really know?" Whereupon Mike swung himself erect on his window-seat, closing Sweet with a snap; Horace scrambled up from the floor, scattering his cards as he rose; and all three eyed each other attentively over their mugs. A moment before the rules of the game had required the slackest sort of interest, the laziest, sleepiest sort of wit. Now interest was allowed. It was rather like a flock of birds rising abruptly from the ground at the instance of a sudden and mysteriously communicated excitement.

"Would it depend," asked Horace, "on how bad we knew Umpleby to be?"

"Or on how good we knew the murderer to be?" asked Mike.

"What d'you mean—how good?" demanded David. "If he was a good man and in murdering Umpleby did a bad act, his goodness couldn't be a relevant point to our decision, could it? He would have to be good in his character as a murderer, not simply in his character as a man, before we should have to begin reckoning with his goodness. I mean that if he murdered from some sort of ethically pure motive—then we should have to consider."

Horace protested. "Can one murder from a pure motive?"

"Well, suppose Umpleby were a very bad man in ways the law couldn't touch. Suppose he did things, and was bound to go on doing things, that would inevitably result in other people committing suicide and smothering their babies and being ruined by fraudulent speculation and all that. Would eliminating him be ethically pure?"

"Would the motive but not the deed be ethically pure?" asked Mike, who was untrained in these disputes but always put in a word.

"But suppose Umpleby were a good man," suggested Horace, "*chiefly* a good man, but with . . . but with a kink or something. Suppose him a *split personality*—yes, now, suppose him just that—one of those people Morton Prince studied: one person one day and another person the next——"

"Jekyll and Hyde," said Mike, very pertinently—and was ignored.

"Suppose he had two personalities, *a* and *b*. And *a* was, say, a blackmailer. And *a* knew about the existence of *b* but *b* didn't know about *a*. And now suppose his murderer happened to be a split personality too—with three personalities: *x* knowing about *y* but not *z*, *y* knowing——"

"Steady," said Mike. "Stick to the corpse—and to who stuck Umpleby. When we find out that it will be time enough to debate whether we can morally seep in and collect the cash. And why *shouldn't* we find out—if Gott doesn't?"

"What d'you mean, if Gott doesn't?" asked both his companions.

"Gott could find out if he wanted to," maintained Mike, who had boundless faith in his tutor; "only quite likely he doesn't want to."

"Quite likely it *was* Gott," declared David. "The man must have a morbid mind, turning out such tripe. A man who could write *Murder among the Stalactites*, with all that stuff about how long a well-nourished, middle-aged man would take to petrify, must be capable of anything. Did I tell you I tried pumping old Curtis yesterday evening, and he said the President had been murdered with 'grotesque concomitant circumstances'? What do you think that meant? I wonder if Gott *disembowelled* him?"

Mike, ignoring this offensive suggestion, pressed his own point. "I don't see why we shouldn't amuse ourselves by finding out. We haven't got the facts, but I expect a lot can be done just by intelligent thinking. And you and I are intelligent, David—and even Horace has his moments."

Horace, secure in the classical man's consciousness of a superior training, was undisturbed. "No doubt we're brighter than the police," he said, "although this Scotland Yard man is probably smart in a ferrety way. But we're no brighter than Deighton-Clerk or Titlow, and they know more of the facts." Horace, in his turn, would maintain the almost ideal intelligence of his preceptors. "They're more likely to guess than we are."

There was a brief pause. Then David said, "I have a fact." There was another pause and he added, "But what's more interesting: I have a notion too."

In all tiny coteries there is always a leader, and David was the leader here. Attention was immediate. "It's what no one will have thought of—and it opens a line. I'll tell you."

And he did.

CHAPTER VIII

I

POWNALL, irritated and pale after his long interview with Inspector Dodd, halted, suddenly paler still, on the threshold of his room. For from beside the fire there rose to greet him Inspector Dodd's colleague, Mr. Appleby of Scotland Yard.

Appleby was, as the occasion demanded, politely and conventionally apologetic. "I hope you will forgive my waiting for you in your room. I thought I would wait a few minutes on the chance of your coming back. And I was tempted to sit down by your fire. It is a chilly morning." And Appleby's eye, moving as lightly as his apology, swept the uncompromisingly open windows of the room.

Rather slowly, as if gaining time to collect himself by the act, Pownall shut the door. And having closed it he seemed to realize, with a fresh failure of composure, that he had thereby closeted himself with the detective. But he kept his eye steadily on his visitor as he crossed the room and sat down. He was a grey, dim creature, Appleby thought; his beardless, fresh complexion the sort that makes a close guess at age impossible; his greying hair cropped Germanically short. His head went a little to one side and his hands had a trick of falling lightly into each other in front of his chest —a gentle, almost feminine attitude that was strangely at variance with the hard chill of the slow blue eyes. The eyes, so cold in the small hours, were indeed cold again now—and they were unwavering as the man sat down opposite Appleby. He sat absolutely still. He was clumsy—and it was as if he feared that a single clumsy movement of body would bring some fatally clumsy revelation in its train.

"I have just signed a statement for your colleague, and been questioned at great length. And now, can I help you?"

Pownall spoke quietly and colourlessly—severity only hinted at in his choice of words. But as he spoke he let his glance glide over his room, a resolutely casual, yet cold and searching glance. And all the time his head kept its fixed, slightly sideways-inclined posture—oddly like the sooty photograph of Alexander the Great on the wall behind him.

"You have been unable to add anything to your informal statement yesterday?" Appleby too spoke colourlessly, but the question took an emphasis not of his giving from the pause of silence that followed it. At length Pownall replied.

"I have added nothing." And again there was a pause.

"You are aware of no circumstances connected with the President's death that would be useful to us?"

"No."

"In effect, you have just sworn to that position?"

Again there was a pause. And then Pownall suddenly sprang up and crossed the room. His objective turned out to be a little glass box containing cigarettes, which he apparently intended to offer to Appleby. But the oddly-timed gesture of hospitality never accomplished itself: the box suddenly slipped from Pownall's fingers and its contents were scattered on the floor. The touch of clumsiness about the man made the accident seem natural enough. But to Appleby there was no accident—only a fresh illustration of the general proposition that in St. Anthony's minds worked well.

Pownall had stooped down instantly. His fingers, gathering the cigarettes, ran here and there over the carpet. And when he straightened himself again his face, which might have been flushed with the exertion, was even paler than before. For a moment the two men looked into each other's eyes. And then—obliquely—Pownall answered the question which had been directed to him a minute before.

"I can throw no light, by way of evidence, on the death of the President. But there have been certain matters, connected with his death but not elucidating it, that I have considered it my duty to myself not to advance up to the present."

"What you have signed before Inspector Dodd can be used in court, Mr. Pownall. You must know that. And the fact of your having omitted material facts from your statement can be used too."

"It is not perjury, Mr. Appleby, to make one's own decisions as to what is relevant in a statement offered to a police-officer."

Appleby bowed his acceptance of this proposition. But an edge had come into his voice when he spoke. "A course far short of perjury may, under certain circumstances, be very injudicious. It is injudicious, for instance, to spend the night following a murder in doctoring the floor of your room. As you have guessed, from every spot where you put ink I have taken a specimen; and what is under one or more of those spots analysis will reveal."

Appleby had a good deal more faith in extracting a revelation from Pownall himself than from any chemical analysis. Pownall would realize that the doctored carpet was a most uncomfortable fact in itself, irrespective of what the doctoring might be proved to conceal. And he did realize. Coldly, abruptly came the confession. "The ink covers blood."

There was a pause, and then Pownall made his first movement since he had sat down again—something like a gesture of resignation over what he had just said. And then he went on.

"You will wonder how an intelligent man could act in so foolish a way as I have been acting. Well, the answer is —*blood*. They say that to shed blood is an intoxicant—that one feels like an angel. I have been drunk too, and drunk from—blood. But not blood that I had shed. And I have not felt like an angel. . . . No."

There was another of the pauses which seemed characteristic of any conversation with this dim, still, clumsy creature. But this seemed—despite the incoherence of what had just been said—a pause of intense calculation, as if the man had made a first move at some intricate game of skill and was striving with complete concentration to assess the result.

"It was blood on the carpet. Just here"—and Pownall, rising, strode almost to the middle of the room and pointed with his foot. "Not much, a little pool—two inches perhaps . . . and half clotted. I took blotting-paper. I remember wondering if it would work; if blotting-paper would absorb blood—clotting blood. It did, and there was left just half an inch of stain. On the black, it didn't show—only on the pale blue there. So I took the ink, a dead black Indian ink I have, and enlarged the pattern. It was a panic action —the fear of what had been planted on me drove me. And the panic kept coming back. Every time I looked at the carpet yesterday the irregularity—the minute half-inch irregularity—seemed to leap at me. But the ink on the blue seemed a perfect dye, giving exactly the normal black of the carpet. And it worked on me till I went over the whole carpet in the night, making it regular. It was only when I had made all those half-inch blots that I found it would smell. But with the windows open . . ."

Pownall stopped. He seemed simply lost in thought.

And this time Appleby had to speak.

"Will you please give me a more coherent—a less dramatic—account?" Expressed in Appleby's tone was the conviction that the pressure under which Pownall appeared to speak was a fabricated pressure, that the man was playing a part. And yet he was not sure; the strange blend of agitation and impassivity with which he was confronted was almost baffling. And now Pownall took up the request simply.

"Yes," he said, "I will." And after that pause which had established itself as an essential rhythm of the proceedings he added, "It began, really, with a dream."

Inspector Dodd, had he been treated to these confidences an hour before, would undoubtedly have betrayed some impatience at this point. Appleby did not. But he took a notebook and pencil from his pocket and began to make a shorthand entry. The action seemed to stimulate Pownall, who plunged into something like connected narrative.

"I keep early hours, usually breaking the back of my day's private work before breakfast. It is a habit I got in hot countries: I have done a good deal of archæological research in Egypt as well as Greece. I am up normally before five and therefore I go to bed fairly early. The evening before last I got back from the common-room perhaps a few minutes before half-past nine. I sat here reading for about twenty minutes. Then I got some hot water from the servants-pantry out on the landing there, washed, and went to bed. I must have been asleep before ten-fifteen: I like to be asleep a quarter of an hour earlier than that if I can.

"Well, it began, as I said, with a dream. I was a rowing man as an undergraduate and this dream was about the river. We were practising just as they are practising now—in tub fours. Our coach was shouting to us and I remember being worried by some quality of his voice—perhaps he was using a megaphone—I know I was unreasonably worried by something about the shouting. . . . We were practising starts and the same shout ran through the dream again and again: *'Come forward—Are you ready?—Paddle!'* The last word was a tremendous shout, like the crack of a whip, and then we were straining up the river. There were other things that I forget, or perhaps the dream lapsed. But anyway, the same situation came back again, a sort of recurrent nightmare. And presently some stiffness seemed to come over me and interfere with my stroke. The coach was calling to me over and over again, *'Drop them, Bow! Drop them, Bow!'*—meaning my wrists. But I couldn't get them away and finally I caught a crab.

"And that woke me up with a start. I was in a cold sweat of terror. But not terrified enough not to be puzzled by my terror. For though I sometimes have nightmarish dreams they don't leave me really scared. And then I knew somebody had been in the room. I don't know how I knew, but I suppose that my sleeping consciousness somehow told me. And a moment later I received confirmation. I heard a distinct, heavy sound from this sitting-room. If I had been in an accessible part of the college I might have suspected an undergraduate joke, although such things are rare. But only one of my colleagues, or the porter, could normally be in Orchard Ground at that hour. And although a colleague might quite naturally and properly enter my sitting-room, he would hardly be likely to come secretly into my bedroom while I was asleep. And I concluded therefore that a burglar had broken into Little Fellows'.

"I am not a particularly courageous man. It took me perhaps two minutes to compel myself out of bed and into the sitting-room. As I entered I was aware of a streak of light from the lobby beyond—and then the streak disappeared. Somebody had just closed the door. Oddly enough, I think (for I am, as I say, a coward), I went straight after him. And I got out just in time to see someone disappear into the darkness——"

"Which way?"

The sudden question came from Appleby like a pistol-shot. But he could not feel with any certainty that it had caught Pownall out. The man hesitated, but only for a moment. "There is only one path," he answered, "and he was lost to sight long before it branches. I shouted, and I know he heard me, for he instantly broke into a run."

Appleby's question was soft this time. "Who was it, Mr. Pownall?"

And this time Pownall did really hesitate—the old trick of marked pause again. Once more he seemed to be calculating effects and chances before he finally replied, "I don't know."

"You have no idea? It was just a back? What about the build, the clothes?"

Pownall shook his head—and returned abruptly to his narrative.

"I went back to my room, meaning to telephone to the porter at once. But as I glanced round to see if anything had been rifled or upset I saw——"

"You saw the blood, Mr. Pownall—two inches of half-clotted blood. And you mopped it up with blotting-paper and got out your bottle of ink. . . . What else?" Appleby was really formidable now. The cold, measured disbelief in his voice might have unnerved a hardened criminal. But Pownall was entirely master of himself.

"That is so," he said. "I discovered the blood—and something else. Two charred pieces of paper in an ash-tray caught my eye—an ash-tray which I knew had been empty when I went to bed. And when I examined them I found that they were two pages torn from a diary—nearly all burnt, but not quite. There was a corner preserved with a fragment of the President's writing."

Appleby, in whose pocket the dismembered diary of the dead man reposed at this moment, knew that here at least was something not sheer fiction. But he showed no sign of being impressed. "This might have come out of the brain of Mr. Gott," he said—and half started at the unintentional two-edged nature of the remark. "And you immediately concluded from these indications . . . *what?*"

Pownall rose to his fence as Haveland had done the evening before. "I concluded," he said, "that someone had murdered the President and was trying to blame me."

"It is in Chicago surely, and not here, that that sort of conclusion is lying ready to come into people's heads? You seriously put it to me that you thought of that?"

Pownall looked coldly at his guest. "I thought just that."

"These rather odd facts—a spot of blood, a couple of scraps of paper, a night-prowler of some sort—actually suggested murder and conspiracy?" Appleby's tone was openly incredulous.

Pownall did not hesitate this time. "It was the blood," he said. "It threw me off my balance—made me, in a way, drunk, as I told you. My actions became abnormal. The attempt at concealment was abnormal. But my inference was perfectly sound and reasonable. From these facts—the clandestine visit to my rooms, the blood, the half-destroyed fragments of Umpleby's writing—induction could take me to only one conclusion: Umpleby, incredible though it was, had been attacked or murdered—and the blame was in course of being put upon me. Probably the blood, the diary pages, were only first steps. Probably I had interrupted the plot. I ought to have been still asleep, allowing further stages of the plan—but now the plotter knew I was awake. Probably he had relied on the fact that I am a notoriously heavy sleeper to enable him to leave yet further traces in my bedroom. It is worth while remarking, by the way, that when we had an alarm of fire some years ago I slept so soundly through the hubbub as to become a college jest.

"I guessed, then, that the plotter intended to leave the body near at hand and then give the alarm and somehow direct the search to my rooms. And these things would be found, like fatal traces I had overlooked before going callously to bed. If I had not awakened when I did, the first thing I should have been aware of would have been being hauled out of bed to face a murder charge."

Pownall spoke confidently and—beneath the resolute chill—even passionately. *Almost*, thought Appleby, like a man speaking the truth. And yet Pownall, in rising so resolutely to that fence, had made a mistake. And Appleby, with that effect of intuitive awareness that experience and training bring, knew that Pownall knew that he had made a mistake. (He thought, said Appleby to himself, that a knowledge of Umpleby's murder was necessary to explain his getting into a panic and monkeying with the carpet. So he has invented this story of guessing at it. And in doing so he has landed himself in simply psychological impossibility. He ought simply to have put up the story that he was scared by what had happened and acted out of mere indefinite, massive sense of danger. He has made a mistake which no talk about inference and induction can cover—and he knows it.)

Aloud, Appleby said: *"And you gave no alarm?"*

The mention of Chicago had been one absolute point. This was another. And Pownall took a moment to square himself to it.

"My hands were tied. Once I had—unnerved by the

blood and with, I admit, the gravest folly—used that ink, I dared not risk another move. Hiding the bloodstain had been the result of some morbid streak of fear rising up in me: it rose again the next night when I continued to tamper with the carpet. And I felt at the time, I think, that I would rather be hanged than admit to it."

The man could make a good come-back—knew what and when to concede. They were all able . . . what a case it was . . . ! And suddenly Appleby found himself shocked at the quality of pure intellectual pleasure that he himself could get from this wretched business—this wretched murder where murder had no reason to be. He remembered thoughts which had come to him pacing up and down Bishop's in the darkness that morning. The darkness, the silence, pregnant somehow with the spirit of the place, had brought him momentarily a strange bitterness—bitterness that he had come to these courts he knew as an instrument of retributive justice. And that mood had been succeeded by anger. He remembered touching the cold carved stone of an archway and feeling a permanence: something here before our time began; here while our time, as Titlow was to paint it, moved fearfully and gigantically to its close; to be here in other times than ours. He remembered a significance that the light over Surrey archway, shining steadily amid the darkness and vapour, had taken on. And he remembered how he had sworn to drive out the intrusive alien thing. . . . And now here he was with the problem coldly before him again—a frankly enjoyable intellectual game. . . .

And yet it was impossible altogether to suppress the element of emotion—of piety. Why was this scholar sitting here coldly telling fibs—in a matter of life and death? Had he taken a revolver and shot Umpleby in the head? After all, why should he do such an idiotic thing? A little wave of exasperation came over Appleby and he let himself go farther than he had yet done.

"Well, Mr. Pownall, did your observation extend to the hour at which these interesting events took place?"

But Pownall was not to be rattled by a tone of contempt any more than he was to be shaken by disbelief. "I looked at my watch as I got out of bed. It was ten forty-two."

"Ten forty-*two*." Irony emphasized the precision. "But was not ten forty-two, sir, eighteen minutes before we knew that the President was shot? Just how was the living Dr. Umpleby, do you think, persuaded to part with—well, even two inches of blood? There seems to be some difficulty."

"I suppose it needn't have been Umpleby's blood. I suppose the plotter—whoever he was—was laying as many false clues beforehand as possible. Then he would simply have to kill Umpleby somewhere close at hand, run, and then cause the alarm to be given."

"But we know that the President was shot in his study, where the shot would almost certainly be heard and mark the time. And then the President's body was found there, surrounded by Mr. Haveland's bones. Does that square?"

"Yes, it does. Remember, the plotter knew that I had found out what was afoot. He had heard me call after him. And so he might abandon the plan of putting the crime on me and attempt to put it on Haveland instead."

There was a long pause. Resolutely Appleby said nothing. And eventually Pownall added something more. "Or the murderer might abandon his plan of fathering the murder on someone else. If he were an unbalanced person, for instance, and his elaborate plan miscarried, then——"

"He might turn round on himself and leave his own signature, as it were, openly on the deed? I see."

Appleby got up. And then a thought seemed to strike him. "By the way, if your first suggestion holds—if the murderer, knowing he had failed to frame you, decided to frame Mr. Haveland, he must have counted on your unlikely folly in concealing what you ought immediately to have revealed."

"I do not suppose my first suggestion to hold," said Pownall.

II

It was a thoughtful and perplexed Appleby who walked slowly back through Orchard Ground to the President's Lodging. He felt a disposition to react against these odd little interviews by which the case seemed to be conducting itself. He had an uneasy feeling that his own favourite technique, which was that of sitting back and watching and listening, was somehow inadequate—dangerous, indeed—in this case: something more aggressive was required. In discussion, all these people would be endlessly plausible—and they would hardly ever make a mistake.

What had he really learnt? Or what, rather, had he really learnt that he was not *meant* to learn? His one success, so far, had been in this last encounter with Pownall: he had at least forced Pownall from one position to another—convicted him of very injudicious conduct. But that success had been the result of orthodox police methods: a little successful prying through a window, a little successful bullying. Had he made a mistake in trying to follow these people over their own discursive ground? And these palavers took time; the morning had slipped away without appreciable gain. He would not have another of these face-to-face interviews until he had done a little preliminary backstairs work. And the need for one piece of concrete investigation was pressing upon him vividly—had been pressing upon him when he told Dodd that he was presently going to take a walk. He had to solve a puzzle that seemed at once irrelevant to the case and at the same time too *near* the case to be really irrelevant. . . . And meantime he turned into the President's Lodging to persuade Dodd, if Dodd himself was impatient to be gone, to provide another officer sufficiently senior to go on with the business of taking formal statements. He was not yet prepared to give time to that himself.

He was still somewhat gloomy as he crossed the President's hall. Quick results were not to be looked for, to be sure, in a case so complicated as the present. Nevertheless, certain things should now have emerged or be beginning to emerge that had not in fact done so. Certain threads of motive there should be by now—and, actually, what was there? Umpleby had been disliked by Haveland and others, and there was a dubious story of his having made free with other people's intellectual property. Very insufficient, so far. What else might have emerged? The weapon . . . ?

Appleby turned into the dining-room. At one end of the table the sad sergeant was gathering together a bundle of papers. At the other end sat Dodd, apparently in meditation. And on the polished mahogany between them lay a tiny gleaming revolver—a delicate thing with a slender barrel of chilly blue steel, a slender curved ivory butt. Barely a serious weapon—but at three or four yards just serious enough.

Appleby was analysing his surprise at this appearance when Dodd awoke from his meditations and beamed. "The coppers," he said, "have managed a little more of the rough work for you"—he waved his hand at the pistol—"and will now withdraw." And he began gathering his own papers together.

"Without divulging the hiding-place of this interesting object?"

"To be sure—I was forgetting. We found it among the Wenuses and other fabulous animals." Inspector Dodd had his own power of literary allusion.

"Quite so," said Appleby; "among the Wenuses. What could be more obvious?" And even the sad sergeant joined discreetly in the mirth. Then Dodd explained.

"Babbitt found it in the store-room of Little Fellows'. You know how a passage runs back on the ground floor to the little staircase that goes down to the servants' basement pantry and so on? Back there on the ground floor itself, just over the pantry, there is a little store-room or big cupboard full of all manner of junk. Babbitt"—Dodd continued with a momentary return to the meditative manner—"was routing about there before you were facing that breakfast of yours. . . . Well, there is all manner of stuff, apparently, including a good many of Titlow's cast-off oddities. Quite a museum of a place: there's statues and mummy-cases and bits of an old bathroom floor—or so Babbitt says, but your learning will doubtless recognize a Roman pavement or such-like. And the door is more or less blocked by an old bath-chair that Empson used to use (it seems) when he was lamer than he is. And behind that are these heathen females, and the revolver had been chucked behind them again. Not a bad hiding-place, really."

"It no doubt had its points," Appleby agreed rather dryly. He was staring thoughtfully at the little weapon. And for some moments he continued to stare.

"You seem to be waiting for it to jump up and out with the whole story," said Dodd.

"I have a feeling that it has already told me something just as it lies. But I can't fix it. *Abondance de richesse* again. A few minutes ago I was feeling that perhaps I had learnt nothing after all. And now in a minute I learn far too much."

"The approved cryptic manner," said Dodd with a chuckle.

Appleby almost blushed—and certainly became brisk. "Got a railway time-table, Dodd? Good. Sergeant, have you had a jaunt to town recently? Go over, will you, and get my suit-case from Six-two."

"The Yard in action," continued Dodd in the same humorous vein. "And now, in my own humble way, I'm off after my burglars. Kellett will be here presently to continue taking statements and so forth as you want them. I think you said you were going to take a nice walk. Don't let them bludgeon you again in our rural solitudes. And if your learned friends aren't claiming you, will you meet Mrs. D. over supper?"

Appleby accepted cordially: it would be a failure in propriety, he felt, to appear at the St. Anthony's board again. The arrangement was just completed when the sergeant returned with the suit-case, and Appleby fell rapidly to work before a lingering and attentive Dodd.

"You don't think he'll have left finger-prints, do you?" the latter asked incredulously.

"You never can tell." Appleby's fingers were busy twisting up a stout length of wire.

"I never heard of dusting for finger-prints with a sort of rabbit-trap before." Dodd was amused and impressed and happy in the contemplation of these mysterious proceedings.

"Good Lord, Dodd; how out of date your shockers must be! You don't think I'm going to tackle what may be a hundred-to-one chance myself, do you? It's a job for the best chemists and photographers we have. And they will want the bullet too, by the way, when it's available." The little wire cage was finished as he spoke; the revolver, delicately lifted, fitted miraculously into it; the whole, together with the notorious tenth key, fitted into a small steel box. The box was locked and handed to the sergeant; its key pocketed.

"There you are, Sergeant, and there's the time-table. The first train to town and then a taxi to the Yard. Mr. Mansell in the east block. Time is an element in these diversions—so off with you. And you'd better stay the night: you might be useful to bring back reports. So have a good time."

The sad sergeant went off transformed. And Dodd went off too. He carried away with him for meditation a new image of Appleby—an image, momentarily caught, of a startled and startling eye.

CHAPTER IX

I

UNDERGRADUATES were strolling through Bishop's—more of them than usual, perhaps, and more slowly than the bite in the air might seem to warrant. Some lingered to converse with friends at windows—and the windows of the court were remarkably peopled too. But Appleby, pacing in the filtered winter sunshine where he had before paced in darkness, was oblivious of his character as a spectacle. The excitement detected by Dodd was on him still.

To Dodd he had complained earlier of too much light—but it had been light, or a multiplicity of lights, playing brokenly and confusedly on a blank wall. Now the light had suddenly concentrated itself and revealed an opening, an uncertain avenue down which it might be possible to press. He was beginning that exploration now. And as he went cautiously forward the avenue narrowed and defined itself; the light grew. . . .

He knew now something that he ought to have known the moment he first entered the President's study. The shot heard by Titlow and Slotwiner could not have been the shot that killed Umpleby. Barocho's gown was next to absolute proof of this. Appleby had found it—carefully replaced as it had first been discovered—swathed round the dead man's head. And for this the murderer had surely had no time. Between the report from the study and the entry of Titlow and Slotwiner scarcely a quarter of a minute could have elapsed. To scatter the bones, to scrawl however hastily on the wall and then to escape into the orchard would take every available second. The murderer would have had no time to wrap a gown round his victim's head—and he would have had no motive to do so either.

And all this, which should have come home to Appleby at once—which must, indeed, have been lurking deep in his mind from the first—it had needed a chance piece of information from Dodd to bring to consciousness. And it had come to consciousness in the form of a vivid picture. For as he had stood in Umpleby's dining-room his inner vision had recreated for itself all the impenetrable darkness of a moonless November night—darkness such as he had himself experienced a dozen hours before. And through the darkness had lumbered a dubious shape, creaking and jolting—a shape indefinable until, stopping by the dim light from a pair of French windows, it revealed itself as a bath-chair in which was huddled a human body, its head swathed in black. . . .

And as the picture came now once more with renewed conviction to Appleby's mind he turned round and hurried into Orchard Ground. A minute later he had found the store-room of which Dodd had spoken. The bath-chair was there. Would it be possible to say that it had recently been used—that it had recently been outside? He fell to an absorbed examination. It was, even as it had presented itself to his imagination, an old and creaking wickerwork thing—a hair-raising vehicle for the purpose to which he suspected it of having been put. But it was in sound enough order. He studied the hubs. There was no trace of oil—slight evidence, perhaps, that if the chair had been used it had been used in an emergency, without previous plan. And nowhere was there any blood. That, of course, would give the motive for the swathed head: nowhere must there be blood except in the President's study. . . . And next, Appleby turned his attention to the tires. They were old and worn, the rubber hard and perished, with a surface to which little would adhere. But here and there were minute cracks and fissures which offered hope. In these, in one or two places, were traces of gravel—but all bone dry. Supposing this gravel to have been picked up a couple of nights before could it be as dry as this? Appleby thought it could—and searched on for better evidence. And when he had almost finished minutely scanning the perimeter of the second wheel he found it. Between tire and rim, caught up as the chair had scraped against the border of some lawn, was a single blade of grass. And that clear green, which clings even in mid-winter to an immemorial turf, was on it still. Recently—very recently—the bath-chair had been used.

Appleby turned to the back. The chair was propelled by a single horizontal handle of the kind that can be removed by unscrewing a knob at each end. Mechanically, following the routine search for finger-prints, Appleby unscrewed. And then he glanced round the little room. It was, as Dodd had reported, full of lumber—and obviously of Titlow's lumber chiefly. There was a harquebus. There was a meek-looking shark in a glass case. And there were one or two plaster casts, including one of a recumbent Venus—the goddess, no doubt, behind whom the revolver had been found. Appleby, not venturing to sit down on the chair, sat down on this lady's stomach instead—and thought hard.

Umpleby alive in his study at half-past ten. Umpleby shot, elsewhere, between that hour and eleven. . . . And suddenly there came back to Appleby another impression of the night before. The quiet of Bishop's, protected by the great barrier of chapel, library and hall. The intermittent rumble and clatter of night traffic heard in Orchard Ground, increasing to uproar as one came nearer and nearer Schools Street. Every five minutes there must come, even in the night, a moment in which it would be safe to fire a revolver without fear of detection.

Umpleby killed here in Orchard Ground and his body trundled back to his study. Umpleby killed at one time and place and given the appearance of being killed at another time and place. At another time and place and *therefore by someone else*. Alibi . . . no, that wasn't it: there had been the second shot. Stay to fire a second shot and you can't be establishing an alibi. *Destroying someone else's alibi* . . . that was better. . . . And then to Appleby's picture of that grim conveyance emerging from the darkness there was added a new detail. At the feet of the dead man was a box—perhaps a sack—filled with bones.

He heaved himself up from the chilly and unyielding abdomen of Aphrodite and went slowly out of the storeroom. In the lobby he paused. On his left, Haveland's rooms: the bones had lived there. On his right, Pownall's —and on the carpet, blood. He turned into Orchard Ground once more and fell to pacing among the trees—this time a spectacle to none. His mind was absorbed in testing a formula—a formula which ran:

He couldn't prove he didn't do it there and in twenty minutes' time—were some indication left that he was guilty. But he could prove he didn't do it here and now.

And he added a rider: *An efficient man; he reloaded and let the revolver be found showing one shot.* And then he added a query: *Second bullet?* And finally, and inconsequently, he appended a reflection: *Nevertheless I must take that walk still—best do it now.*

II

Appleby had not set foot outside St. Anthony's since the big yellow Bentley had deposited him at its gates the afternoon before. And he was beginning to feel the need of a change of air. He had planned a little itinerary for himself which was to subserve both business and pleasure; the carrying out of it had been interrupted by the discovery of the revolver; he was resolved not to delay it longer now. A sandwich and a pint of beer at the Berklay bar and he would be off. He was just slipping through the archway to Surrey when he became aware of the approach of Mr. Deighton-Clerk. And on Mr. Deighton-Clerk's countenance there showed, in addition to its customary benevolent severity, the clear light of St. Anthony's hospitality. Appleby's heart sank—justifiably, as it quickly appeared.

"Ah, Mr. Appleby, I have just been seeking you out. Pray come and take luncheon with me if you can spare the time. I should much like to have another talk with you. Something simple will be waiting in my rooms now."

Appleby scarcely *had* the time—and certainly not the inclination. But he lacked the courage to say so. Perhaps long-buried habit was at work: the habit of intelligent youth to jump to the invitation of its intelligent seniors. Or perhaps the detective instinct subterraneously counselled a change of plan. Be this as it may, Appleby murmured appropriate words and followed Mr. Deighton-Clerk meekly enough. He took some pleasure in the mysterious handle of the bath-chair which he carried delicately with him. It would puzzle the Dean.

The luncheon was doubled fillet of sole, *bécasse Carême* and *poires flambées*—and there was a remarkable St. Anthony's hock. College cooks can produce such luncheons and undergraduates—and even dons—give them. But it was an odd gesture, Appleby thought, with which to entertain a bobby off his beat—or on it. About Deighton-Clerk there was some concealed uncertainty. His beautiful but rather precious room, his excellent but untimely woodcock, were the gestures of an uncertain man. And, once again, his conversation began uncertainly. With his colleagues, even in a difficult and untoward situation, the Dean was efficient, easy and correct. But add to the untoward situation a stranger whom he had difficulty in "placing" and he was frequently a shade out. During the meal his talk held frequent echoes of the formality and pomposity which had appeared in his first exchanges with Appleby. But now, as then, he managed finally to achieve forthrightness. He talked at length, but without more than an occasional suggestion of speech-making.

"You may remember my saying yesterday evening how particularly unfortunate the President's death was at this particular time—just before our celebrations. It was an odd and irrelevant thing to feel—or to imagine I felt—and I have been thinking it over. And it seems to me that I was really trying to invent worries that didn't exist in order to cloak from myself the worries that did—and do—exist. I was determined to repulse the idea that our President could have been murdered by any member of his own Society; I was anxious—at the expense of logic as you no doubt felt—to see the murder traced out and away from St. Anthony's.

"I am impressed now by the extent to which—quite involuntarily—I ignored or even distorted evidence. I was inclined to see those bones, for instance, as evidence of some irrational outbreak *from without* upon the order and sanity of our college. I contrived to ignore the reflection that the interests of a number of my colleagues made it possible that they should have bones in their possession. And—what is more remarkable—I succeeded in repressing my memory of poor Haveland's aberration."

There was a pause while the Dean's servant brought in coffee. Appleby remembered the periodical pauses in

Pownall's room that morning. But while Pownall's pauses were involuntary, Deighton-Clerk seemed to contrive his for the purpose of underlining a point. If not an outside madman, then at least an inside *madman*. That, in effect, was what the Dean was saying—and his motive, as before, was thought for the minimum of scandal. . . . But now he was continuing.

"But what I want to say is this: that last night I failed in my duty. The urgency of my feeling that this or that event or situation in St. Anthony's *could not* bear any correspondence to murder made me, I am afraid, insufficiently communicative. I tried to impress upon you the fact that such disharmonies as have existed here are on another plane from murder. I would have been better leaving that —which I still of course believe—to your own common sense when you had heard a dispassionate account of what those disharmonies have been. That account I want to give you now."

Most long-winded of the sons of St. Anthony—Appleby was murmuring to himself—get on with it! Aloud he said, "It is difficult to tell what may be helpful—directly or indirectly."

"Quite so," responded Deighton-Clerk—much as he would reward a discreet observation by an undergraduate—"quite so. And I must tell you first—what indeed I hinted at before—that for some years now we have not been an altogether happy society. You heard the shocking remark that Haveland tells us he made to Umpleby, and you will have noticed other signs of friction. I mentioned to you a dispute I myself recently had with the President—of that I must tell you presently. But the first thing I must say is that for the disputes we have had amongst us I am unable to apportion blame. Irritations arising one cannot tell how have hardened into quarrels, enmities, accusations. There have been accusations—a thing shocking in itself—and accusations of mild criminality. But it is significant of the scale of the whole miserable business that a dispassionate mind would find it difficult, I believe, to say where the blame really lies.

"I should tell you something of Umpleby himself. He was a very able man—and in that, perhaps, lies the essence of the situation. We have no other intellect in St. Anthony's which could touch his—unless, it may be, Titlow's. But Titlow's is an intellect of fits and starts compared with Umpleby's. Umpleby had all but Titlow's ability, and far more intellectual tenacity. The great strength of Umpleby lay in his being able to cover a number of fields—of related fields, I mean, and organize useful affiliations between workers in one and another. And here in St. Anthony's he had gathered together a team. Only the team fell out.

"As I told you last night in the common-room, Haveland, Titlow, Pownall, Campbell and Ransome were all pretty closely associated—and the association was really thought out and organized by Umpleby. I was interested in the work myself, in an inactive way—or at least in those aspects of the work that touched the Mediterranean syncretisms. So I had an eye on the relations between Umpleby and the others from early on and was aware of the trouble pretty well from the beginning."

Appleby had brought out his notebook—not without a certain diffidence over the remains of the Dean's elegant and unpolicemanly luncheon. Deighton-Clerk, seeming to recognize the diffidence, made a permissive gesture—not unepiscopal in its rotundity—and proceeded.

"I would put the beginnings of a certain awkwardness about five years ago, after Campbell got his Fellowship. He was a very young man then—I suppose about twenty-three. And that would make him only two or three years younger than our other young man, Rowland Ransome, the research Fellow. Ransome had been working for some time, practically under Umpleby's direction, when Campbell came to St. Anthony's and the two young men became close friends. Ransome is a clever creature but—well— intermittent: one thing he will do well and indeed brilliantly, and the next carelessly and ill. He is a careless, happy-go-lucky and often obstinate person, with very little thought for his own reputation or success. And presently Campbell got it into his head, rightly or wrongly, that Umpleby was exploiting Ransome. Ransome, he thought, was content to work under Umpleby's direction to an extent not proper to his status, and Umpleby was profiting by Ransome's results as a man should not profit from the results of his pupil. And he convinced Ransome himself that this was so.

"As I said, it is a matter very difficult to judge. Umpleby was printing steadily—and printing without more than occasional reference to Ransome. But you have to remember that Umpleby was organizing and co-ordinating the work of a number of people with those people's consent—and a good deal to their advantage. I record here the opinion, Mr. Appleby, that Umpleby never appropriated other people's intellectual property for any good it would do himself in the learned world."

This was a dark saying and Appleby, remembering his own incredulity over Haveland's insinuation of plagiarism, challenged it at once.

"'For any good it would do himself'—will you explain that qualification, please?"

"You will find, Mr. Appleby, that it explains itself presently. To put it briefly, Umpleby came to relish annoying people. And if he himself worked out, say, *Solution x*, he was capable of working still harder to persuade, say, Colleague A that *Solution x* was Colleague A's achievement—simply for the amusement of annoying Colleague A by appearing to steal *Solution x* from him later on."

"I see," said Appleby. (And what, he was wondering, would Dodd make of *this*?)

"I can now take up my thread again," continued the Dean, "without further emphasis on the fact that Umpleby was not an easy or amiable man. When he heard that Ransome, who had been his pupil since he came up, and whom he regarded as his pupil still, was complaining (behind his back, as he said) in the way I have mentioned he was furious. The situation was exceedingly awkward until Ransome went abroad four years ago. He was away for two years and when he came back the trouble flared up again. There were scenes—incidents, perhaps, is a better word—and finally Umpleby acted in what was generally thought a very high-handed manner. He had in his possession certain valuable documents which had always been understood to be preponderantly Ransome's. When I say valuable documents you will understand, of course, that I mean valuable in a learned sense: they constituted, in fact, an almost completely worked out key to certain inscriptions which promised to be of the greatest importance —I need not particularize. Umpleby simply hung on to them. When Ransome, he said, was out of the country again he might have them: Ransome's presence here was offensive to him and that was his only means of getting him away. Well, Ransome went, and has been away ever since. And over this arose my own quarrel with Umpleby—the quarrel to which I referred yesterday evening."

Deighton-Clerk was absorbed in his narrative now: the self-consciousness, the orotundity were gone in the intellectual effort to attain the completest clarity. Appleby was listening intently.

"A few months ago I had a letter from Ransome saying that the documents had not come back to him. And he added some hint that set me making certain inquiries. And presently I found to my great uneasiness that Umpleby was proposing to print matter bearing on the decipherment of the inscriptions in question in a learned journal. I was told this in the greatest confidence by the editor, Sir Theodore Peek, and I at once approached Umpleby privately. I could get no satisfaction from him. And then I considered it my duty to bring the matter up formally at a college meeting. It was not strictly in order to do so, but I did it. And it caused high words. Superficially, it was not a very serious affair—merely an unfortunate dispute between colleagues over a learned matter. But underneath there lay this ugly hint of plagiarism—or theft. Remember, please, that it is not a simple business. I have not the least doubt that Umpleby was capable of work on those inscriptions of a superior order to Ransome's, and beyond the fact that Umpleby was acting high-handedly and unjustly in retaining another man's property—or part property—the whole matter is perplexed."

"But other people besides Umpleby, Ransome and Campbell were involved?"

"Yes, indeed; that is what I have to come to. From the first the wretched business seemed to have an unhappy effect on the President. I think he was a wayward man. And when he came to feel that the weight of college opinion was against him in this matter he behaved wilfully. Or so it seems to me—though I would again say that such things are very difficult to disentangle. Umpleby quarrelled with Haveland. It was initially a sort of *teasing* of Haveland, I believe—a sort of mocking, 'I'm going to steal *your* work next.' Certainly it made Haveland both nervous and furious, and Umpleby came to like that. And finally he evolved for himself what was really a sort of curious intellectual game. He liked, in some queer ironic way, to keep the college guessing about his intellectual honesty. And he started new quarrels. And he made alliances. In particular he allied himself with Pownall against Haveland, and then to make the fight less uneven he jockeyed Titlow into Haveland's support. And then recently he decided it would be better fun (it is really dreadful to put it so) to fight them single-handed—with the result that he precipitated a violent dispute with Pownall.

"It was a game with Umpleby and he never actually overstepped certain limits, never, you may say, broke the rules he had invented for himself. He was always formally courteous, and I think that fundamentally he was quite dispassionate—quite detached. He was simply running an intellectual man's somewhat morbid recreation. But it set a bad tone in the college. And the minor actors were less dispassionate, less detached. Pownall and Titlow in particular I suspect of being somewhat carried away against each other: there is very real dispathy between them, I am afraid. And others have been implicated in one degree or another: Empson, Chalmers-Paton, even Curtis—dear old man! What a setting, Mr. Appleby, for this final horrible thing!"

Deighton-Clerk had come to the end of his narration. And as if in sign of this he threw himself back in his chair and fell for a moment into a gloomy and abstracted inspection of the dusky blue and silver of his ceiling. Appleby made a final note and fell to a no less abstracted study of the Aubusson carpet. And presently the Dean spoke again. "And now if you have any questions to ask arising out of what I have said—or on anything else—ask them."

But it was not Appleby's policy at the moment to worry his host with cross-questioning. He confined himself to a matter which had not been touched on. "This affair of the changing of the keys to Orchard Ground—I wonder if you can throw any light upon that? It was Dr. Umpleby's idea?"

"Yes. He told us at the last college meeting that he thought it was desirable, and that he would make what arrangements were necessary. Our Bursar died recently and the President took upon himself a good deal of the practical business of the college."

"Do you think there was anything behind the resolution to have the keys changed—that Umpleby had the idea of protecting himself in any way, for instance?"

Deighton-Clerk looked startled. "I hardly think so," he replied. "Umpleby had the idea that there were unauthorized copies of the old keys in existence. That was the motive for the change, and it certainly never occurred to me that he was in any personal trepidation in the matter."

"But it was from the Orchard Ground angle, so to speak, that he was vulnerable? His study, for instance, is barred on the Lane side, and the doors to Bishop's and the common-room and the Lane were locked every evening. But from Orchard Ground entry would be easy enough."

For a moment Deighton-Clerk's face brightened. "That would imply," he said, "that Umpleby was apprehensive of attack by somebody other than an authorized possessor of a key—by some outside person who had got a copy of the old key?"

Appleby nodded. Deighton-Clerk considered for a moment. And then he shook his head. "No," he said regretfully, "I don't think there can be anything in that. I am sure—I am *almost* sure—that Umpleby's concern was simply as he declared it to be. He *was* concerned, and I must admit to an odd degree. But it was genuinely over the reputation of the college. There had been rather an ugly business arising out of an undergraduate escapade, and he was determined to stop illicit egress from St. Anthony's. Umpleby, by the way, had been a poor boy and he had certain rather morbid social anxieties. He liked a particular sort of undergraduate to come to St. Anthony's—and nothing frightens good families away from a college like a vulgar scandal. I think the whole of his perturbation over the affair lay in that. I don't think he can have been alarmed for his own safety at the hands of an illicit holder of a key."

But for a moment Appleby stuck to his point. And he inserted a pause of his own this time before dropping his next question.

"By the way, did Ransome have a key?"

Deighton-Clerk started in his chair. "Yes," he said, "he did."

"But he would not have one of the new keys?"

"No; I suppose not."

"Just how did the President distribute the new keys, can you tell me?"

"As far as I know he simply walked round the college, handing them over personally."

"In what order?"

Deighton-Clerk looked puzzled. "You mean to whom he went first, second and so on? I have very little idea. Except that he came to me last but one, saying he had only Gott's to hand over after that."

"And this was about noon the day before yesterday?"

"Yes."

Once more Appleby was silent. His luncheon had not been unenlightening. Only the light was breaking up again, playing brokenly here and there. That evening he would have to report to Dodd yet again, it might be, that there was too much light. . . .

The Dean was looking at his watch. "I have a meeting

presently, Mr. Appleby, and shall have to hurry away. But I wonder if there is any other matter you wish to raise?"

"There is one thing," Appleby replied—and he picked up his enigmatical bath-chair handle as he spoke. "I am afraid I must have the finger-prints of the Fellows of the college." The policemanly demand at last: the bouquet of the Dean's hock and the savour of his excellent rendering of Carême's masterpiece haunted Appleby's palate as he spoke.

Certainly, Deighton-Clerk was slightly taken aback. "Finger-prints!" he exclaimed, "to be sure. But I thought that nowadays malefactors always wore gloves?"

"So they do often—and then, as far as that goes, we are baffled. Though in Germany they are claiming to have evolved a technique for getting prints through any ordinary glove.... Anyway, taking prints—of course with the permission of the persons concerned—is routine work we are required to put through. If there is any objection——"

"There will certainly not be any objection," the Dean interrupted firmly. "I agree that it is a most necessary procedure. My—ah—fingers and thumbs are at your disposal to begin with. And with the rest of us it will be the same."

Nevertheless, there was a shade of reluctance or misgiving in the Dean's voice, and Appleby proceeded cautiously. "In that case, Mr. Deighton-Clerk, if I may send a sergeant round——"

The Dean's face brightened instantly. It had been a point of propriety that was worrying him. That Mr. Appleby, who had dined at the St. Anthony's high-table, should go round with a little pad of ink, jabbing scholarly fingers and thumbs upon police record-cards, was disagreeable. A subordinate was necessary.

"Certainly, Mr. Appleby, certainly—a most proper suggestion. It will be—ah—quite a novelty. You have had no prints taken so far?"

"Only from the corpse," said Appleby, a little disconcertingly. And, looking at his own watch, he got up and took his leave. The Dean concluded the interview on a note of polite inquiry as to Appleby's comfort in St. Anthony's. But his eyes were meditatively on the wooden bar that Appleby bore delicately away with him. It was curiously like a symbolical truncheon.

CHAPTER X

I

It is in our universities that the conservative spirit finds its most perfect expression. Long after the reform of our ecclesiastical institutions, mediæval habits and conventions survive within these venerable establishments. "The Monks" (as the learned denizens were indignantly described by the sciolistic historian of the Roman Empire) are seldom up-to-date. They loll deep in what economists call a "time-lag." They teach out-moded subjects by exploded methods. They remain obstinately unconvinced of the necessity of the modern amenities either for themselves, their wives or their children. Only recently, indeed, did they *discover* wives and children. Only yesterday did they discover baths. Only today, despite much undergraduate example, are they beginning to discover the motor-car. It is notorious that the late Master of Dorchester, who died only a few months before Dr. Umpleby, maintained to the last that the convenience of a private locomotive was far outweighed by the dangers arising from the proximity of the boiler: himself, he would always travel by rail, and in a carriage towards the rear of the train.

But the motor-car does gain ground. For one thing, unlike the train (another institution that won but tardy acceptance and distant sufferance), it can change its mind. And there is something in the mental constitution of the retiring scholar to which this is a grateful circumstance. How delightful to set off of a morning in pursuit of the high dry air of the British Museum—to end the day instead in Beaconsfield churchyard, meditatively scanning the epitaph of the poet Waller, *inter poetas sui temporis facile princeps!* And earlier on this same road—many miles indeed before one reaches Aylesbury—there is a spot especially associated with such changes of plan. A by-road branches off—perhaps in the direction of Bicester, perhaps in the direction of Tring—and brings the initiated truant after a few miles to a most excellent—indeed a most Chestertonian—inn. Here one may lunch, here one may dine *well:* there is *bortsch* not inferior to that once known at the —, and a simple *schnitzel* that would have won the commendations of the eminent Sacher himself. There is a good straight claret; there is a genuine Tokay; there is a curious Dalmatian liqueur. The garden is erudite, remarkable in summer and winter alike. If you are lucky, you will find no similarly knowing colleague there; only an alien and abstracted *savant* from the academic deserts of Birmingham or Hull, come to meditate in solitude the remoter implications of the quartic curve, or a London novelist of the quieter and more prosperous sort, giving a lazy week to the ruinous correction of page-proofs. Only one disturbing presence there may be: that of undergraduates—for undergraduates too, with a sad inevitability, have discovered this earthly paradise. But even undergraduates become more urbane, less restless, in the *milieu* of the Three Doves.

It was an undergraduate party that was in possession of the Three Doves now. Mr. Edwards, Mr. de Guermantes-Crespigny and Mr. Bucket were sitting over the remains of luncheon, engaging in quiet and ingenious obscenities at the expense of the only other occupant of the coffee-room, a fluffily-bearded old party who was consuming soup noisily in a corner while sitting huddled over an obviously learned volume. Not the novelist from London; quite possibly the Birmingham mathematician in retreat; almost certainly not the master of esoteric misbehaviours elaborated by the gentlemen from St. Anthony's. But presently a look somewhat askance from the fluffy party, suggesting an awareness of comment which St. Anthony's good manners did not intend, coupled with the necessity of lighting pipes (a thing forbidden by custom in the coffee-room of the Three Doves), took the trio to another room. And presently they had settled down to discuss the formal business of the day.

"I had a shot at Gott this morning," Mike announced, "but he was pretty close. I asked him who he thought had done it. Or rather I asked him who *had* done it. He said the murderer was almost certainly the Chief Constable—or just possibly the President's demented grandmother, who was kept in an attic and made scratching noises in the night. So then I tried the 'But-seriously-now' note and he said he stuck to fiction. And he asked my advice about his new book."

"Asked *your* advice!" exclaimed Horace incredulously. "You mean tried bits out on you as a pretty average specimen of the *dumm* public?"

"No. Asked my advice. About an epigraph."

"A what?"

"Epigraph. As in *The Waste Land*, you know. *Nam Sibyllam quidem Cumis ego*——"

"Silly ass! He didn't ask *you* for a Latin tag for his pre-adult fictions?"

"Not Latin. And not a tag exactly. You see he makes up excerpts from imaginary learned text-books and sticks them at the beginnings of his chapters. Scientific touch. This one was all about taking slices of criminals' brains and looking at them with gamma-rays or something."

"What foul fatuity. And where did you come in?"

"I provided a title. '*Statistical Researches into Twelve*

Types of Homicidal Algolagnia—by Professor Umplestein of the University of Göteborg'—that's in Sweden, you know. Gott accepted the title, but vetoed Umplestein. Quite right, no doubt. It was, as they say, not in Good Taste."

"And *therefore* not suitable for one of Gott's lucubrations," said Horace with heavy irony. "What, I ask, is the university coming to? We shall be hearing of Deighton-Clerk doing advertisement copy-writing on the quiet next."

"Did you say *lucubrations?*" asked David, bethinking himself of a belated pedantry. "Wrong word. Means something done in the night."

"Like Umpleby," said Horace. "He was done-in-nin the night all right. *And* I'm not convinced *he* wasn't really one of Gott's lucubrations."

But David, ignoring this witticism, had produced a map. "Gentlemen," he said, "let us confer." They all stared rather vaguely at the map.

"It is a matter," said Horace, "of penetrating to the mind of the quarry. Did you ever read *The Thirty-Nine Steps*, Mike? An altogether healthier type of fiction than the morbid perpetrations of Uncle Gott. Well, there was a man there who wanted to pass as a Scottish road-mender. And he did it by thinking himself into the part. He gave his whole mind to *being* a road-mender. And as a result he survived the keenest scrutiny of the emissaries of the Black Stone—and all that. Now, all we have to do is to identify ourselves with the criminal; we can then put our finger down quite confidently on David's map and say: *There he is!*"

"It depends on the size of the map," said Mike. "I think he's in London."

"Too far."

"No, not really. And a capital place to hide—to lie concealed, as they say. At his club, quite likely. Terribly close London clubs are about their members if you go to inquire. Very nice point Gott makes of that in *Poison at the Zoo*——"

David and Horace gave a concerted groan.

"Anyway," said David, "do dons *have* clubs? I don't believe they do—except the very old ones who belong to a special place down by the Duke of York's Steps. . . . But town's no good: we bank on a radius of about twenty miles. Let's see what that takes in."

He busied himself with a pencil and presently announced: "Just misses St. Neots, takes in Biggleswade, goes through Hatfield, misses Amersham, goes through Princes Risborough, misses Kingswood by a few miles and Bicester by a good deal more, just misses Towcester, takes in Olney and a bit beyond——"

"Got it!" cried Mike suddenly, "and we're all wrong!"

"Olney and a bit beyond," David reiterated severely, "misses Rushden—and so round to just short of St. Neots again. And *now* what is it, Mike?"

"It is," replied Mike in bubbling excitement, "that we're miles out. Olney, you see, made me think of Kelmscott at once——"

"And why should Olney make you think of Kelmscott, you moron?"

"Because of the English poets, you ignoramus. And now listen. When I was, as the uninstructed say, a fresher, I made a pilgrimage one vacation to this Kelmscott—a *literary* pilgrimage. And making my way from Kelmscott to Burford I came to a hamlet of which the name escapes me. And outside the hamlet was a manor house or some such—much retired in its own grounds. And just as I was passing, out he came."

"Out *who* came?"

"Our quarry—as Horace so picturesquely puts it. And even in those days, when I come to think of it, he nursed a criminal conscience. Because he started perceptibly on seeing me, as they say, and appeared, again as they say, to wish to avoid observation. In fact, he seeped out and was gone before I could really distinguish his features. But I recognized him absolutely and instantly by a trick he has—walking with his fists to his shoulders like physical jerks."

"Is this thing *true?*" demanded Horace.

"Split true. Old David's prosing away brought it back to me. Of course it's *miles* away. But if my frail old car can get us there—let's go quick."

David nodded his agreement. Horace, who had been lying in his favourite position on the Three Doves carpet, puffing smoke at a sleeping cat, scrambled up, and all three bundled out into the yard. Mike's frail old car—a thoroughly robust and recent De Dion which had cost a doting aunt a small fortune—was purring in a moment. And presently they were careering exhilaratingly through the tingling winter air in the direction of Farringdon. That there was any sense whatever in their operations none of them believed: they were simply diverting themselves after the complicatedly ironic fashion of their order—the order of more mental undergraduates. To lunch at the Three Doves, to spin through the country drinking the wind of their own speed like Shelley's spirits, to sing and chant and chatter, and in the intervals play this elaborate make-believe; these were excellent things. And so they ran through Wantage.

Suddenly Mike threw out his clutch and jammed on his brakes with a reckless abruptness that made Horace shut his eyes in the expectation of catastrophe. But the De Dion merely glided smoothly and instantly to a standstill. Over the way was an unbeautiful brick building announcing itself as a Steam Laundry.

"Here," Mike explained, "we make a purchase." And he climbed out. "You may come too, if you like," he added politely.

And so the three crossed the road and entered a damp and forbidding office, presided over by a severe—and already surprised and misdoubting—lady of uncertain years. Mike had already removed his hat. Now he bowed—the same bow he was accustomed to give nightly in his character as bible-clerk to the St. Anthony's high table.

"I wonder, madam, if your establishment uses—I believe they are called skips?"

"Skips? Yes, of course."

"Of course you use them?"

"Of course they are called skips. *And* of course we use them."

"Will you sell one?"

"Sell one, sir! This is a laundry, not a basket-maker's. We haven't any spare skips."

"My dear madam, are you sure? It is really quite urgent. May I explain? My grand-aunt—you may know her: Mrs. Umpleby of St. Anthony's Lodge—is sailing for India tomorrow, and she has always been accustomed to pack blankets and eiderdowns and things of that sort in a skip. And she has just discovered that her own skip has been damaged by mice, so she asked me——"

"Mice!" interjected the misdoubting lady incredulously.

"Asked me to see what I could do. I understand the usual price is about five pounds——"

Mike produced his pocket-book, and the misdoubting lady, now no longer misdoubting, produced the skip. It was an enormous wicker-work thing, secured by a formidable iron bar, two staples and a padlock. Mike gravely superintended the hoisting of it into the back of the car, paid the surprised lady, assured her of his grand-aunt's gratitude, distributed substantial tips and waved his friends aboard. The De Dion purred on.

Mike, Horace thought, was probably Aristotle's Magnificent Man. His fun was on a lordly scale. . . . But the expenditure on the skip had rather shocked him. "What's it for?" he asked.

"One cage for Bajazeth," Mike replied—and continued cryptically: "one city of Rome, one cloth of the sun and moon, one dragon for *Faustus*. . . ." The day before he had been deep in the study of Elizabethan stage properties. And presently he was declaiming:

*And there, in mire and puddle, have I stood
This ten days' space; and, lest that I should sleep,
One plays continually upon a drum;
They give me bread and water, being a king . . .
Tell Isabel the queen, I look'd not thus,
When for her sake I ran at tilt in France. . . .*

And Horace, behind, was thumping the skip and answering:

*I am Ulysses Laertiades,
The fear of all the world for policies,
For which my facts as high as heaven resound.
I dwell in Ithaca, earth's most renown'd
All over-shadow'd with the shake-leaf hill,
Tree-famed Neritus. . . .*

And then David started on Pindar, and remembering a lot grew more and more excited in the effort to remember more. And the De Dion sang through the air like a thing of victory, and the other two listened much as when the world was young. And so they came to Lechlade and stopped in the square to consider. Presently they were nosing up narrow lanes and for a long time were completely and oddly silent.

"There has come upon us," said David, "a nasty sense of the possible reality of our quiet fun."

And it was true. After all, it was *true* that Mike had once seen him near here. . . .

"This," announced Mike presently, "is my hamlet—and there is the house."

The hamlet was small and unremarkable. The house was large, gloomy and repellent—a raw red brick affair not unreminiscent of the steam-laundry, and an offence in this country of mellow stone. But it was decently hidden away behind a large well-timbered garden and high brick walls. There was a lodge with high iron gates and a postman's bicycle leaning against an open wing.

"I think," said David, "we will put a question or two in the village."

Mike backed the car out of sight of the lodge and they all got out. It seemed an ill-populated hamlet. No one was visible except two very aged men, sitting against the side of a house and sunning themselves in the bleak and diminishing November sun. These worthies David approached.

"Good afternoon," he said. "We are rather lost: can you tell us the name of this village?"

One of the very aged men nodded vigorously.

"Oi, oi," he muttered, "powerful great pigs. True it is, there was never such come I was a lad. True it is."

Conjecturing that this was part of an interrupted conversation rather than directed to his own question, David tried again—loudly.

"What place is this, please?"

Both aged men looked at him kindly and comprehendingly. The second appeared to be on the verge of revelation. But when he spoke it was himself to take up some anterior theme.

"And do 'ee tell oi so!" said the second aged man. "And do 'ee tell oi so!"

Horace was giggling. Mike was making unintelligible signs. And then the first old man suddenly made contact with the new factor in his environment.

"This be Lunnontawn," he said.

"London town!" repeated David and Mike blankly together.

"Noa! Not Lunnontawn; *Lunnontawn*."

"And what," asked Mike, taking up the running and slightly changing the subject, "and what is that house there?" And he pointed to the aggressively red, steam-laundry-like building amid the trees.

"That be White House," said the second old man, darkly and unexpectedly—and spat.

"White House: who lives there?"

The two aged men looked at each other apprehensively. And then, mysteriously moved by a common impulse, they both struggled to their feet. They were old, old men—gone at the knees and with hands like claws. And they tottered away. The first disappeared at once into the house against which they had been sitting. The second made for a decrepit cottage next door. But on the threshold he paused and shuffled himself painfully round.

"A terrible haunt of wickedness that do be," he said. He spat, and disappeared.

Mike was shaking his head sadly at Horace. "I heard the old, old men say, All that's beautiful drifts away like the waters. . . . Chaps, let us drift away." And the three moved back, rather uncertainly, towards the big house.

"We will go straight in," said Horace, "and inquire."

"Horace," said Mike, "scents *une maison mal famée*."

"Come on," said David, "he was lurking here once and may be lurking here again." The gate was still open and the postman's bicycle still leaning against it. No one noticed them as they went in, but they caught a glimpse, over a low hedge, of the postman gossiping with someone at the back door of the lodge. "Straight on," said David. The drive wound among shrubberies. Presently they rounded a bend and saw the White House—saw, that is to say, in addition to the large and garish red structure which was alone visible from the road a long, low and rather dubiously white residence on to which it had been built. It was a depressing place; house and grounds alike seemed decently but lovelessly and unenthusiastically kept. From somewhere behind the shrubbery came a murmur of voices. The three stopped to listen.

And then an odd thing happened. Round the final curve of the drive in front of them there swung the figure of a man, coming from the house. But no sooner had he seen the three intruders bearing down on him than he plunged into the bushes—from the crashing noise that resulted, apparently the thick of the bushes—and disappeared.

"Was it him?" cried David. It had all been tremendously sudden.

"Of course it was him," shouted Mike, and started blindly forward. He didn't really know, but he did want excitement. All three went galloping up the drive, Horace making blood-curdling noises by way of ironic reference to the sport of fox-hunting. The fugitive, by plunging through a few yards of laurel, had gained a narrow winding path and disappeared. But he could be heard still retreating rapidly, in a direction roughly parallel to the drive, and towards the house. The pursuers followed in single file.

But presently the little path branched—and just ahead both branches could be seen branching again. And the hedges were high and thick. Horace, who was ahead, stopped, and pulled up the others. "Bless me," he exclaimed, "if it isn't a regular maze!"

It was. And the fugitive could now be heard more faintly, as if he had put several thicknesses of hedge between himself and his pursuers.

"Split up!" cried Mike, jumping with excitement.

"No," said David, "keep together. We'll know then that any noise is *him*."

David had the master mind: his would be the best First in Schools at the end of the year. Obediently bundled together, they explored ahead, stopping constantly in an endeavour to locate such noise as the fugitive made. Sometimes it was ahead and sometimes to the side; now it was fainter and now louder. But presently it became clear to the pursuers, as they swung round the abrupt angles of the maze, that they were astray. It could hardly be otherwise if the man ahead had his bearings. And at length the sounds died away just as the trio, turning a final corner, found themselves in a little clearing. It was the centre of the maze.

"What a mess!" gasped Horace. "He's clean away—which will take *us* some time."

But David pointed and ran forward. In the centre of the little clearing was a raised wooden platform reached by a ladder—a sort of gazebo from which wanderers in the maze might, if necessary, be directed. David was up in a flash.

"I can just see him," he called down presently. "He's nearly out too. Listen, Mike. Have you got any paper? We're for a paper chase now. Out you both go and I'll direct you. And leave a trail so that I can follow."

It was the most efficient plan, but a tedious business nevertheless. The afternoon was already fading into twilight and David from his perch was only just able to trace out the path that led from the maze. It took him some twenty minutes to get his companions out and five minutes to follow by the aid of the paper trail himself. Finally they found themselves reunited on the main drive, a little farther from the house than where they had broken off.

"Poor show," said Horace.

"Distinctly where we step off," said Mike.

"Down to the lodge," said David: "he's likely to have made a complete break-away. Come on."

And down they went. And just as they came within sight of the gates they heard a loud and angry voice exercising itself in picturesque imprecation in front of them. It was the postman. And he was lamenting the disappearance of his bicycle. "Come *on!*" cried David—and all three dashed into the road, with no more than a fleeting glimpse of the gesticulating official, a scared and surprised woman by the lodge, a gardener or groom hurrying up from a side path. On the open road no bicyclist was in sight—and indeed the fugitive might have pedalled off a good twenty minutes ago. The postman seemed just to have become aware of his loss: he had followed up his gossip, perhaps, by going within for a little refreshment.

"Which way—that's the question! Which way?" Mike, as he made for his car with his companions at his heels, threw the question desperately to the wind. But it was answered in an unexpected fashion—by nothing less, in fact, than the appearance of the two very aged men, gesticulating excitedly. They were old, old men; their hands were like claws and their knees were gone. But they shuffled rapidly up the road, waving their sticks that were as crooked as themselves and screaming together in a weird, unpremeditated unison.

"There 'ee do be gone, there 'ee do be gone, zurs! There 'ee do be gone in his wickedness away!" And they pointed ahead down the narrow country lane.

In a moment the De Dion was purring. Another moment and it was roaring up the lane. "I rather think," Mike shouted, "that this runs without a break to the Lechlade-Burford road. That's in about two miles. We ought to get him." He was right in his bearings. The lane ran winding between low hedges for something under a couple of miles, with no more break than here and there a gate giving upon bare fields. It seemed likely enough that the fugitive had ridden straight on. David was studying his map and by the time the car had slowed down to swing into the main road he had located their position.

"Left for Lechlade," he said, "with a cross-road about a mile along from Bampton to Eastleach. Right for Burford, and no cross-road until the Witney-Northleach road just short of the village. I vote for Burford."

"Wait a minute," exclaimed Horace. "Here's a bobby who can probably tell us for certain." A very fat policeman was cycling slowly towards them from the Burford direction. David called out to him.

"I say, constable, have you met anyone on a bicycle along this road?"

The fat policeman got off his machine with slow dignity. "Yes," he said, "I 'as." And his attention being directed to the matter, a new aspect of it seemed to strike him. "Come to think on it," he added, " 'twas Will Parrott's bicycle." He paused, broodingly.

"Will Parrott the postman?" David asked.

The policeman nodded. "But 'twern't Will on un." He brooded again over this reflection, and as he did so vague possibilities, undefined implications seemed to be hovering on the borders of his consciousness. "Come to think on it," he added slowly, "fellow on un were going fast and wild. Happen——"

He was interrupted by the sudden roar of an engine. The De Dion had dispatched itself like a bullet from a gun in the direction of Burford. The fat constable allowed himself a few moments to incorporate this fact in his reflections. And then light seemed to break on him. "It be them dratted Lunnon gangsters come about these parts at last!" He turned his bicycle round and set off in heavy pursuit.

The short November twilight was closing into dusk. It was just on lighting-up time. Peering ahead, Mike and David could discover nothing. But Horace in the back with the skip suddenly called out. "Chaps! There's another pack on the trail—a whacking great Rolls. Open out."

It was evidently true. Mike was already driving fast, but only a moment after Horace had spoken a large grey Rolls-Royce loomed up in the dusk almost abreast. Its horn sounded urgently and at the same instant its head-lamps flashed into brilliant illumination. Mike swerved to allow free passage—and thrust at his accelerator at the same moment. The Rolls was in a hurry, but not suicidally so. It drew in behind and the cars tore down the road in single file.

Visibility was poor; it was the uncertain hour at which headlights just fail to help. And suddenly, just ahead, Burford cross-roads came into view. And somewhere the telephone must have been at work, for standing across the road were three policemen. And between cars and police was the fugitive, bending low over the handlebars of the purloined bicycle and pedalling furiously. The next minute was one of confusion. The cyclist was up with the policemen, two of the policemen had made a lunge, there were shouts, a stumble—and the fugitive, by swerving wildly, had got safely through the cordon and was shooting over the cross-roads to Burford Hill. Another second, and the police were jumping to the side of the road to let the pursuing cars sweep past. But Mike, who was perfectly level-headed when driving a car, had checked for the main road, and by the time the cars were across the bicycle was some way ahead again and just dipping down the steep slope.

"We'll get him!" cried Horace.

"If there's anything left to get," said David grimly. "He's going down a good deal faster than he meant to."

It was true. Mike was plunging down the long steep street that is Burford as fast as was safe in a large, perfectly controlled car. But he was scarcely gaining on the cyclist, who had let himself plunge ahead as madly as if death itself were on his tracks. His continued equilibrium seemed a matter of miracle. But in a moment it was all over. The Lamb flashed by on the left, the church on the right; the road levelled and curved to the bridge; the fugitive, by some freak of control, was safely over; the De Dion was up with him and had edged him into the ditch. The quarry was run to earth. . . .

"It's not him!" exclaimed Mike, gazing at the dazed, red-headed creature in the ditch. And he was conscious of the quite slender reason there had been to suppose that it was.

"It's a looney," said David gently, looking at the red-headed creature's vacant eye.

"It was a looney-bin," said Horace, looking with his inner vision at the dismal red structure known as White House. . . .

The grey Rolls-Royce drew up with a swish of brakes. An excited but competent little person of medico-military appearance jumped out. "Is he hurt?" he cried. "Is his lordship hurt—damn him?" And he jumped straight into the ditch and began an examination.

"His lordship," murmured Horace sadly. "This *is* where we step off."

The little doctor was out of the ditch again. "Nothing broken. Bit of a bruise—bit of a daze—that's all. Yates!

Davies! Help his lordship into the car. Leave that damn fool postman's bicycle where it is. Damn these policemen—couldn't stop a child on a tricycle. Nearly had a neck broken. Rogers! Turn her round. And now, gentlemen."

The gentlemen eyed his lordship's warden warily. They were decidedly uncertain as to where they stood. But it did not occur to the little doctor, seeing three prosperous youths and a more than prosperous car, to see himself confronted by the villains of the piece. "Much obliged to you, gentlemen, for your—ha—intervention and assistance. I think the circumstances will be clear to you. Lord Pucklefield is one of my patients—Dr. Goffin of the White House. Nervous fellow—if anything occurs to startle him off he goes. Can't think what can have done it this time. Gates open too—gossiping postman—won't happen again—damme. Yates! Davies! Get in!"

And Dr. Goffin took off his hat very punctiliously (Mike just got in his high-table bow) and jumped into the Rolls. A moment later Lord Pucklefield and his friends had purred smoothly away into the gathering darkness.

Horace thrummed meditatively on the skip. David took out his pipe. Mike took out his watch. "Quarter to six and ever so far from home. We *could* just make hall—hurrying." The suggestion was unenthusiastically made and unenthusiastically received. "And I drop ten bob if we don't," the errant bible-clerk added.

"You've dropped five pounds already," said Horace brutally, and giving the skip another slap. "Another ten bob won't do *you* any harm. I think we'd better go and have a decent meal."

David's pipe was alight. "There's the Three Doves," he said.

With one accord the party moved to the car; in a minute they were running down to the Fulbrook cross-roads to turn. And as they swept back to take the long hill down which they had recently come their lamps caught for a moment a ponderous figure who had dismounted from a bicycle and was contemplating the bicycle in the ditch. It was the fat constable. He must have missed his colleagues at the top of the hill. He was brooding over an impenetrable mystery.

II

The great De Dion, foiled but not ashamed, glided beneath the discreetly flood-lit sign of the Three Doves. In the lounge there was comfort in the great fires, rest in the mellow candle-light, refreshment in the preliminary sherry. The fantasy of the day was over—fantasy fortunately untouched by the fatality that had at one moment threatened. David had gone back to Pindar, Horace was lost in reverie, Mike was thinking of the dinner. They were early and the pleasures of anticipation might be enjoyed.

At the Three Doves things always fall out well. The sherry had been drained, the ode finished, the reverie dispersed, the wine planned; the moment at which anticipation turns to impatience was hovering on the clock—when the waiter hovered at the door and murmured the awaited words. They rose luxuriously, and in a formal sentence Mike dismissed the cares of the day. "You know, chaps, I should have hated really to catch him."

They were the first in the long, dim, gleaming coffee-room and the smoked salmon was consumed before the next diner arrived. It was the fluffy old party of their luncheon speculations. He was without his book this time, and he ambled over to his table with his fists pressed oddly to his shoulders. . . .

"*Tally-ho-ho!*"

Mike's cry was unearthly—and it sent the fluffy old party out of the room.

"*Gone a-way-ay!*"

The ensuing scene was unique in the history of a well ordered hostelry.

CHAPTER XI

I

THE ability to smell a rat is an important part of the detective's equipment. Appleby had smelt a rat—in the wrong place. But he was too wary to take it that a rat in the wrong place is necessarily a red herring: it may be a rat with a deceptive fish-like smell—and still a rat.

To be exact, this rat had been not so much in the wrong place as at the wrong time. Just an hour after the discovery of Umpleby's dead body two Fellows of St. Anthony's, Gott and Campbell, had converged on one spot up the Luton road. It might have been fortuitous; it might have been by design—but if by design the purpose behind the manœuvre was obscure. At any rate, there was a field for investigation and Appleby had felt drawn to it when he first announced to Dodd that he wanted to take a walk. He was walking rapidly down Schools Street now and as he walked he concentrated on the first point he had to consider.

On the night of the crime Campbell had gone to the Chillingworth Club in Stonegate. He claimed to have arrived there before the hour at which Umpleby was last seen alive and to have remained until within ten minutes of midnight. That, as far as the murder was concerned, was Campbell's alibi and it would have to be checked anyway. He would begin with it now.

The entrance to the Chillingworth Club from Stonegate is down a few yards of covered alleyway. This gives upon a meagre little court with a meagre little fountain and fish-pond—the whole about fifteen feet square and known to members as the "garden." . . . A subterraneous approach to the Chillingworth, Appleby decided as he traversed this retreat, was impracticable: there was nothing for it but a frontal attack upon the secretary. With this plan in view he rang the bell.

The secretary was an elderly youth of great discretion. Appleby's credentials produced his assurance that the club would render all proper assistance with all possible expedition. Nevertheless, in a matter involving an inquisition into the movements of a member while on the premises, he was afraid he could not act without the sanction of the chairman. Could the chairman be consulted forthwith? Unfortunately not. Lord Pucklefield was in delicate health, and for some time his physicians had forbidden business matters being referred to him. An acting chairman? Well, yes; no doubt Dr. Crummles's authority might suffice. Ring up Dr. Crummles? The Inspector would realize that it was scarcely a matter to confide to a telephone conversation. . . .

Appleby was accustomed to getting over difficulties of this kind and in something over an hour he had obtained from a succession of club servants almost all the information he required. And his requirements, as far as Campbell's movements were concerned, were minute. Campbell had arrived at ten-fifteen. Just before half-past ten he had been served with a drink in the smoke-room. A few minutes later he had entered the card-room, with this drink still in his hand, and had cut in upon a four at bridge. The game lasted till half-past eleven, and for ten minutes after that Campbell had remained talking to another of the players. But at exactly a quarter to twelve he had collected his hat and coat and gone out. Of the precise time of his leaving the servant concerned was convinced: just before getting up Campbell had looked at his watch, and this had had the effect of making the man glance at the clock. Moreover, something else had occurred to fix the matter in his mind. Campbell had gone out by way of the little court. But he had evidently forgotten something in the club, for a minute later he was seen in the building again. And then almost immediately he had finally left—this time by the side entrance that gave directly on Stonegate somewhat farther north.

This seemed detailed enough and Appleby did not feel disappointed when, on certain minute points on which he inquired, he did not succeed in getting a clearer picture. It was remarkable that of the casual movements of a member some nights before so much had been noted and remembered. Appleby was now almost certain that he was on the trail of something. Thoughtfully he emerged on Stonegate—as Campbell had done—and turned left for the Luton road. His next call was to be on Sir Theodore Peek—and on Sir Theodore's neighbour, the Green Horse. For in this topographical fact lay the germ of Appleby's present proceedings. Dodd's street map had shown him that the Green Horse must be almost in the stables, so to speak, of the eminent scholar. And the exact topography, he hoped, would be finally illuminating.

It was. The entrance to the Green Horse Inn was from the inn yard. And the yard, which opened on one side to the high road, opened on the other to a secluded suburban avenue. And the nearest house was Berwick Lodge, Sir Theodore's home. Appleby spent a moment conjuring up the whole venue in the dark. Then he ran up the steps of Berwick Lodge and knocked at the door.

II

The city abounds in venerable men. Particularly are its suburbs thronged with scholars of enormous age. The fact is not immediately observable—because once having abandoned their colleges they never go out. But hidden there in that humdrum Ruskinian villa is a greybeard who remembers the publication of Lachmann's *Lucretius;* over the way, behind that imitation Tudor timbering, is the historian who quarrelled with Grote; down the road is an ancient whose infant head was patted by the great Niebuhr himself. . . . Moreover there is something special about the generation of these primigenius *savants*. They are themselves the sons and grandsons of scholars who, having given a long working life to the furtherance of humane knowledge, and feeling, round about ninety or so, the first mists of senescence begin to gather about their minds, have retired from their intellectual pursuits to the solaces of matrimony and procreation. It thus comes about that the man who remembers Lachmann remembers too his father's anecdotes of Porson, and that he who received the blessing of Niebuhr preserves the liveliest family anecdotes of Bentley and Heinsius and Voss—the sense of personal contact scarcely growing dim until it disappears with Politian and Erasmus into the twilight of the fifteenth century. This is the tradition of the true University Worthies—and of all living University Worthies Sir Theodore Peek was the oldest and the dimmest, the most sunk in the long and foggy history of scholarship—and the most truly bathed, perhaps, in the remote and golden sunlight of Greece and Rome.

Appleby found him in a small and gloomy room, piled round with an indescribable confusion of books and manuscripts—and asleep. Or sometimes asleep and sometimes awake—for every now and then the eyes of this well-nigh ante-mundane man would open—and every now and then they would close. But when they opened, they opened to decipher a fragment of papyrus on his desk—and then, the deciphering done, a frail hand would make a note before the eyes closed once more. It was like being in the presence of some animated symbol of learning.

Sir Theodore was finally aware of Appleby, but scarcely aware of him in his character as a policeman. Rather he seemed to think of him as a young scholar who, having just taken a creditable First in Schools, had come to consult authority on matters of post-graduate study. It was only with difficulty that he was headed off from a discussion of the Aristarchic recension of Homer to a consideration of the reiterated name "Campbell."

"Campbell," said Appleby firmly. "Campbell of St. Anthony's!"

Sir Theodore nodded, and then shook his head. "Able," he murmured, "able, no doubt—but we are scarcely interested—are we?—in his field. Umpleby is the only man at St. Anthony's. I advise you to see Umpleby. What a pity that he too has taken to these anthropological fantasies! You know him on Harpocration?"

"*Did . . . Campbell . . . visit . . . you . . . on . . . Tuesday . . . night . . . ?*" asked Appleby.

"Indeed, *you* might consider Harpocration," Sir Theodore went on. "He preserves, as you know, a number of passages from the Atthidographers Hellanicus, Androtion, Phanodemus, Philochorus and Istrus—to say nothing of such historians as Hecatæus, Ephorus and Theopompus, Anaximenes, Marsyas, Craterus——"

Appleby tried again.

"Yes," he said emphatically, "yes; Harpocration. *Was . . . it . . . about . . . Harpocration . . . that . . . Campbell . . . was . . . talking . . . here . . . on . . . Tuesday . . . night?*"

Dimly, remotely, Sir Theodore looked surprised. "Dear me, no," he said. "Campbell knows nothing about it, I am afraid. He simply brought a manuscript for the Journal—

we don't object to giving a little space to that sort of thing. He was here only a few moments. And now, if you should want introductions when you go abroad . . ."

Sir Theodore Peek was venerable, but exhausting. Respectfully, Appleby withdrew—and betook himself, for more purposes than one, to the Green Horse.

III

Appleby got back to his rooms in St. Anthony's at half-past eight. The visit to the Green Horse had not finished the day's ferreting. There had been interviews with surprised and uncertain clerks; telephone messages to the Senior Proctor, to the Vice-Chancellor; minute interrogation of pugilistic-looking persons clutching bowler hats. . . . But the evening had ended pleasantly in supper with Inspector Dodd, and in restfully irrelevant talk which would have been prolonged had not that excellent officer had to take himself hurriedly off. The very crisis of his operations against the burglars was approaching. Now Appleby, refreshed, was seeking the solitude of his room for a spell of hard thinking on the material available after the day's investigations. But he stopped as he opened the door. Sitting waiting by the fire, much as he had waited by Pownall's fire that morning, was Mr. Giles Gott.

Mike's enthusiasm for his tutor was understandable. Gott began well by being, in repose, quite beautiful. When he moved, he was graceful, when he spoke, he was charming; when he spoke for long, he was interesting. Above all, he was disarming. "Plainly"—he seemed to say—"I am a creature whose life is more fortunate, more elevated, more effortlessly athletic and accomplished than yours, but—observe!—you are not in the least irritated as a result; in fact, you are quite delighted."

Mr. Gott rose gracefully now—and said nothing at all. But he looked at Appleby with a whimsical, tentative familiarity such as few men, being total strangers, could have achieved without some hint of impertinence. In this creature, it was most engaging.

Appleby saw no present need to decline the atmosphere suggested. Quite silently he sat down at the other side of the fire and filled his pipe. And when he spoke his opening remark seemed obligingly calculated to the slight oddity of the encounter.

"And so," he said, "you are a bibliographer?"

Gott was filling his own pipe, and he merely chuckled.

"You are," Appleby pursued didactically, "professionally a bibliographer—which is as good as being a detective. You make a science of the physical constituents of books and you are able, by means of the most complex correlations of the minutest fragments of evidence, to detect forgery, theft, plagiarism, the hand of this man or of that man in a text, an interpolation here, a corruption there—perhaps hundreds of years ago. By pure detective work, for instance, you have found out things about Shakspere's plays that Shakspere never stopped to learn. . . ."

Appleby paused to puff at his pipe and stir the fire.

"And this technique—or at least the type of trained mind behind this technique—you have actually turned (I am told) upon crime. Pentreith's books are the best in their kind; pleasantly fantastic, but pleasantly closely-reasoned. I fancy you must take quite a professional interest in the pleasantly fantastic, pleasantly closely-reasoned death of Dr. Umpleby?"

Gott shook his head. "Mr. Appleby, you don't believe it. Amid all the sad puzzles in which this case is involving you, you have one or two certainties. And you know that although—to my embarrassment—I write thrillers, I did *not* plan this real murder."

"I know that you planned—something."

"To be sure. But remember *Don Juan*. 'The fact is that I have nothing planned except perhaps to be a moment merry.' . . . What do you think?"

"I think that it is dangerous to make merry in the vicinity of murder. And I think it is wrong to make murder a matter of disinterested observation. It would be wrong to go into a thieves' kitchen and be simply *interested* in murder. And—sentimentally, perhaps—it is wronger here."

Gott had listened seriously. "Yes," he said soberly after a silence, "that's true. But my affairs, you know, have nothing to do with the case."

Abruptly, Appleby was emphatic. "Mr. Gott, I have spent all this afternoon over your affairs, and a good deal of preliminary thinking too. And it happens that, in a case like this, my time has a certain scarcity value."

But this only brought Gott out of his sobriety. "What's the Green Horse bitter like, Mr. Appleby? And how did you find Sir Theodore? And I suppose you have worked it all out . . . ?" His laugh was mocking and friendly, his speech at once confession and challenge.

"Yes," answered Appleby, "I have worked it out. It wasn't *very* difficult."

"Ah!" said Gott. . . . "Can I have your story?" It was cheeky but charmingly topsy-turvy—and there was no denying that Appleby liked the man.

"You can have my story from first suspicion to proof. And the first suspicion was pure chance. I was not very interested in anybody's doings round about midnight on Tuesday. I should not have been interested in yours. But a conscientious colleague, commissioned to check up on you earlier on, actually followed your movements—or what he thought were your movements—just as far as he could.

"The Junior Proctor was at Town Cross at eleven-forty. Just after that he was going up Stonegate. At midnight he was at the Green Horse. Oddly enough, another Fellow of St. Anthony's, Mr. Campbell, declared himself to have been going in just the same direction at just the same late hour. There was just enough coincidence (to use, I am afraid, a very unscientific term) to arrest my attention and make me call for a map. And the map was suggestive enough to make me take a walk. And the walk showed me why Campbell was visiting Sir Theodore Peek at approximately the same time as the Junior Proctor was visiting the Green Horse."

Appleby paused. His visitor was contemplating him mildly through a haze of tobacco-smoke.

"Mr. Gott, you and Campbell were faking an alibi for yourselves on the night of Umpleby's murder, but as far as that murder went you were faking it for the wrong hour. Your alibi was an hour too late."

"Odd," said Gott. "But won't you tell me a little more of how you thought of all this? I like it."

"When I remembered," Appleby responded quietly, "how a proctorizing procession moves, it became quite simple. The proctor doesn't go along with his marshals in a bunch; they follow him a good twenty yards behind. And when he enters a building they don't follow unless they are signed to: they remain outside."

"You seem," interjected Gott dryly, "familiar with the process. Please go on."

"You and Campbell had eleven forty-five as a sort of zero hour. From eleven-fifteen to eleven forty-five both your alibis were genuine. I mean that you were each where you appeared to be: Campbell in his club, you proctorizing about the town. But at eleven forty-five you came up Stonegate and at the same moment Campbell emerged from the alleyway to the Chillingworth. The marshals saw him—actually recognized him, as it happened—but there was no harm in that. You greeted each other and Campbell made as if to draw you back into the alley and into the club. Nothing odd in that, during such a visit the marshals would simply wait outside. But once in the alley you slipped off your proctor's gown and handed it over to Campbell. You then simply lay low while Campbell, with the gown bundled up, passed through the club and, slipping the gown on himself, passed out into Stonegate again by the entrance further north. And so there was the Junior Proctor striding ahead of his marshals once more. If anybody recognized him in the street it would never occur to them that Campbell was not acting as a pro-proctor in a perfectly regular way."

"It would read well," Gott murmured.

"And so to the Green Horse—and Sir Theodore's. The marshals as usual wait outside. Campbell goes into the inn-yard and noses about for a minute in his gown. And anybody that's about knows that the proctor has been at the Green Horse. Not that that is important, because the marshals know—or think they know. Then Campbell offs with the gown again, passes out of the other end of the yard, and within a couple of minutes it is established that Campbell—the real Campbell—paid a fleeting visit to Sir Theodore at midnight. Two good alibis: one faked, and one, so to speak, faked-genuine."

"And the get-away?" asked Gott softly.

"Campbell as proctor again just shows himself under the arch of the yard, signals to the marshals, turns round and is off the back way—past Sir Theodore's, in fact. And so the marshals follow right to St. Anthony's. And here's the last point. You usually return to college on these occasions, you know, by way of the wicket on Schools Street. But on this occasion you returned to St. Anthony's by the main gate on St. Ernulphus Lane, knocking for the porter quite in a regular way to let you in. . . . Oh, yes, it *was* you. Campbell made the turn off Schools Street to the Lane, and there you were in a doorway. A quick change of the gown again and Campbell is sauntering home to his flat. And you, I say, walk down to the main gate, wait for the marshals, turn round and cap them gravely. Off come their little bowlers. Good night, Mr. Gott. And you knock for the porter. Again, Good night, Mr. Gott. . . . *Actually, you had had from about eleven-fifty to twelve-twenty to do what you liked, and a nice alibi manufacturing for you all the time.* It was rather a shame to squander (fruitlessly, as you see) on crude actuality what would have done so nicely for a book!" And Appleby looked with a rather dangerous mockery at the celebrated novelist.

Gott puffed thoughtfully. "It is very ingenious," he said, "but surely a little wanton? *You* might have made it all up surely, rather than Campbell and I? Until you collect a little evidence—someone who saw me where I oughtn't to have been, or who saw that it was Campbell in the proctor's gown—it hangs a trifle in the air, does it not? And have you thought of a motive for all these surprising proceedings? Were we going to murder Umpleby at midnight, and were we forestalled?"

"Perhaps," replied Appleby, "it all had nothing to do with St. Anthony's. My colleague Dodd here is grappling with the problem of a series of burglaries in the suburbs. Perhaps, Mr. Gott, you are the master mind behind the gang?"

Gott laughed—a little shortly. "You think it's a burglar I am?"

"Yes, I do."

"In the suburbs?"

"No." There was a moment's silence and then Appleby added, "And now, am I to have *your* story?"

"If there were a story, you know, it mightn't be mine to spin."

There was another silence while Appleby debated how to take this charming, cool and unhelpful person. To Pownall he had been almost rude—a horrid technique. And he doubted if much could be extracted from Gott by bullying. . . . His thoughts had only arrived at this stage when there came an interruption. From outside the door of the sitting-room there suddenly arose a succession of bumping and creaking noises, followed by a loud thud and the sound of a number of rapidly retreating feet. Appleby sprang over to the door and threw it open. In a little lobby stood a large-sized wicker laundry-basket.

Gott too had risen and come over to the door and for a moment the two men regarded the problematical object in silence. And in the silence they became aware of equally problematical sounds. "I think," said Appleby, "we may open up." And he proceeded to remove the sizeable iron bar which kept the hamper fast shut.

There is something eminently absurd in the spectacle of a human being confounded with a laundry-basket—a fact known to Shakspere when he fudged up *The Merry Wives of Windsor*. And it was a somewhat Falstaffian apparition that emerged now—a Falstaff in distinctly damaged theatrical disguise. For some species of paint was dripping down the apparition's face, and from one pink and angry ear hung the remains of a false, fluffy-white beard.

Appleby was quick on his bearings. His extended arm was helpful; his voice was bland.

"Mr. Ransome, I presume?"

CHAPTER XII

MR. RANSOME had gone off for a bath and a raid on the buttery. As he darkly remarked, he had *not* dined. . . . And Mr. Gott was left to explain.

"Our whole story," said Gott, "may now, I suppose, emerge. You have no doubt heard of the business of Ransome's papers—those Umpleby was holding on to? Well, Ransome came back to England a month ago, furious that Umpleby hadn't sent the stuff on to him. And instead of coming openly up to college he stayed in town and sent for Campbell. He and Campbell were always pretty thick, and Campbell was all for taking drastic measures against Umpleby. Presently they decided to take the law into their own hands. And when they had decided on that, they decided, too, to call me in as—an authority."

Gott's pipe was going again. He was telling his story with disarming simple pleasure.

"I came in on it—very foolishly, you will say—and I half turned it, I suppose, into a species of game. We could simply have raided Umpleby and forced the stuff out of him—he wouldn't have cared for public scandal. But we decided instead to plan a sort of perfect burglary and I worked it out. There were the three of us—Campbell, Ransome and I—and it was the alibi idea that interested me. I had to be in at the actual burglary, and so had Ransome——"

"Why the two of you?" Appleby interrupted crisply.

For a moment Gott seemed to see the question as almost awkward. Then he grinned amiably. "I had to be there," he responded, "because the circumstances of the burglary required—well, rather a special sort of brain—you'll understand presently. And Ransome had to be there simply because I wasn't going to carry out this rather risky and indubitably foolish proceeding for him while he lay safe in bed.... It was the alibi notion that interested me. First, I reckoned that Ransome himself was all right; for all that anybody but our three selves knew he was thousands of miles away. But there must be an alibi for me and, if Campbell were implicated, for Campbell. As I say, it was little more than a game. I didn't expect Umpleby to call in the police over the burglary and—forgive me—I didn't expect the police to dream of testing our alibis even if he did. Nevertheless, I tried to work it out thoroughly."

"The experimental approach to popular fiction," murmured Appleby.

"Perhaps so; perhaps I had it in my head in terms of a book. Anyway, you know how I worked the idea out. At eleven forty-five Campbell, as you guessed, was to slip into my shoes. I was then to go straight to St. Anthony's and join Ransome, who would already have reconnoitred the ground. We reckoned to be through with the burglary by twelve-ten. I was then going to slip out and round to St. Ernulphus Lane, where Campbell was due to arrive at exactly twelve-twenty, and at the same time Ransome was to make his own get-away. But we were going to make sufficient row on leaving the President's Lodging to rouse the household; in that way the burglary would be discovered at once and *timed*—timed at a moment when the supposed I, followed by the marshals, was yet some way off St. Anthony's, and when equally, of course, Campbell could not have made the college on foot from Sir Theodore's. Campbell and I were to change places again while hidden from the marshals by the corner of the Lane; he would be back in his flat in two or three minutes and I would simply walk down to the main gate of the college (I could hardly seem to turn back out of the Lane again, you see, for the wicket) and be let in by the porter, a comfortable ten minutes after the burglary was discovered."

Appleby had been following closely. And now he asked a question. "You say that Ransome was to have reconnoitred the ground before you joined him. Do you mean he was to have reconnoitred inside the college?"

Gott nodded. "You are thinking of the business of the new keys? Of course they nearly caused some alteration of the scheme. They would have done so, but for luck. Ransome has always had a key to the gates and although we knew that fresh keys were making we didn't think they would be forthcoming so soon. It wouldn't have mattered very much, of course; one key was enough. But one for Ransome and one for me was better and it was a nuisance when, on Tuesday morning, Umpleby suddenly appeared in my rooms to say the locks were changed and to hand me my new key. Even if he had had one made for Ransome he would of course hold on to it."

"Do you think," Appleby interrupted, "that the business of having new keys made had anything to do with keeping Ransome out of one—that Umpleby felt apprehensive in any way?"

Gott looked startled. "I never thought of such a thing. I think the keys were changed for the reason given; I don't think Umpleby had Ransome on his mind in that way at all."

Appleby nodded. "You can imagine a prosecuting counsel, Mr. Gott, making a good deal of the point." The words were spoken dryly.

"I see the prospects of awkwardness well enough," Gott responded, "otherwise I should not (as my fictitious crooks are fond of saying) be coming clean. There is obviously awkwardness in the fact that I got hold of the tenth new key—Ransome's key."

"*You* got it, did you," said Appleby tartly—and his hand passed reflectively over the still-tender crown of his head.

"Ah, I don't mean that time; I mean in the first place. I got it through luck and a simple trick. Umpleby came to me last, with two keys left in his hand. I took mine, and put down my old one on the table. Then I handed Umpleby a good fat folio I had been working on and asked his opinion on some point or other. He grabbed it nicely with both fists: he had a brain that could get the hang of anyone's trade in three minutes, had Umpleby—and he liked showing it. And, quite automatically, down went that last key on the table. I got him into a good hot dispute—to break any thread of connexion in his mind—meanwhile palming the tenth key. Then presently I poked the old key with my finger: 'Whose is this?' I asked casually, and he growled 'Ransome's, if he comes back'—and off he went. Result: Ransome got his key."

"Result," Appleby amplified tersely, "one step nearer a crime. . . . And now, what actually happened on this unfortunate night?"

"Nothing. Ransome slipped into college by the wicket at eleven-thirty to have a preliminary look round, and the first thing he was aware of was a mild hullabaloo and people tramping through the orchard. And then he heard Deighton-Clerk's voice shouting something about examining the wicket. So he took it matters were badly amiss, cut out of college and came to meet me after Campbell and I had done our first swap. Of course I kept my date for swapping again in the Lane—and that was all."

There was a momentary pause.

"Except that when you got back to college you heard that Umpleby had been murdered?"

"Yes."

"You none of you came forward with your story?"

"We left all that to you." The feeble repartee was absently made; Gott was plainly considering what yet lay ahead.

"Before you go on," Appleby pursued, "there is one particular question. Did any of you in this precious diversion actually succeed in entering Umpleby's study on Tuesday night?"

"Definitely not."

"You were not there, for instance, earlier—when you purported to be in the proctors' office? You were not in the study, conducting any preliminary search?"

"Definitely not."

"Nor Ransome, nor Campbell?"

"Campbell definitely not; Ransome—not if he's not lying."

"You were not there, looking for a safe?"

Gott shook his head. "I had done that much looking long before," he replied.

"You were not there, messing about with a—*candle?*" The word was shot out.

Gott's denial was again absolute, and this time somewhat surprised.

"Mr. Gott, you said just now that the burglary was a foolish proceeding. And the coincidence of the murder was really something rather appalling. What possessed you to persevere in the undertaking the next night?"

"Obstinacy," replied Gott, "and opportunity."

"You mean the fact that you still had one key between you?"

"Exactly. The police had collected nine keys, and we had the tenth. I thought, incidentally, that your knowledge that there was a tenth key somewhere might make you keep up a regular staff of guards. But it didn't. . . . Well, there we were with access to Orchard Ground—and more or less to the study—still. And no one knew. We met yesterday afternoon and arranged the second attempt. It was a perfectly simple plan this time. Ransome had the key and at twelve-fifteen he was to enter Orchard Ground by the wicket. It was risky because, as I say, you might well have had men on guard. But somehow we had got dead keen. . . . He was then to open the west gate on Bishop's and let me into the orchard. And then we were to do what we could.

"It all went well—at any rate, at first. We broke into the study and got the papers from the safe——"

"You knew about the safe? You knew the combination?"

"I knew where there was something—that was all. I had had a sufficient prowl in Umpleby's study, long before, to spot that faked shelf. I guessed there might be a safe——"

"And were confident you could get it open? Even in stories that is surely difficult?"

Gott grinned. "I trusted to my wits. That was why I had to be on the burglary myself. Writing thrillers—and perhaps, as you suggest, my bibliographical training—has given me a certain facility. . . . Anyway, it *was* a safe, and I *did* get it open—didn't I?"

All Gott's simple pleasure in his narrative had returned. Appleby scrapped his official reserves. "My dear man," he said, "in heaven's name *how?* Are you going to tell me you listened with a microphone to the fall of the tumblers—and all that? Perhaps you did. You broke into the study by a next to impossible story-book method—canvas and treacle, heaven preserve us!—and perhaps you got into the safe as absurdly?"

"No," replied Gott modestly, "I didn't listen to anything. I just looked."

"Looked! What at?"

"At the faked shelf—and on evidence of Umpleby's whimsicality of mind. You won't remember the particular dummy books represented on the shelf?"

"Long narrow shelf with about fifty volumes of the British essayists," Appleby responded promptly. His memory was often photographic.

"Exactly. The spines of fifty little volumes all neatly glued on a board. Perhaps you didn't happen to look at the last ten closely?"

"No, I didn't!"

Gott beamed. "I did. And they were out of order. Not actual volumes out of order, remember—but dummies *fixed on* out of order. Something like *49, 43, 46, 41, 47, 42, 50, 45, 48, 44*. In other words, a handily placed record for Umpleby that the combination of his little safe was *9361720584*. Elementary, my dear——"

"—Watson," concluded Appleby, and knocked out his pipe. "And as you say, a trick displaying your late President as a man of whimsical mind." He filled his pipe again and pushed across his tobacco-tin. He was becoming disposed to a good deal of further conversation with the celebrated Mr. Pentreith. . . . "And now," he prompted presently, "we come to a matter of some little delicacy."

Gott pointed to the laundry-basket that still cumbered the lobby. "It was Ransome done it," he said, "and you can't say he hasn't had tit for tat. . . . If it isn't an improper thing to say of a colleague, Ransome is a little pigheaded. He would not go straight out of college with his precious papers; he must come to my room for a drink to celebrate our victory—a victory over a dead man, come to think of it. So out we both came into Bishop's and at the gate he said something about his fixing the lock and my scouting ahead. I went ahead—and gathered afterwards that the silly ass not only left the gate open because it squeaked, but actually left the key in the blasted lock."

Appleby chuckled. "It was a number one size slip and puzzled me rather. I can see that you wouldn't have much confidence in Ransome as a single-handed cracksman. Not that he can't crack a skull with very pretty judgment. But perhaps you were standing by directing?"

"No, I wasn't. It would never occur to me to hit a man on the head—except in fiction. Much too chancey. In Ransome's circumstances I think I should simply have given myself up, or thought of a plausible lie. But he seems to have acted pretty smartly. He found his way of escape guarded, hovered around until he got on your tracks—and you lost the key again."

"I lost a different key."

"Ah, then he made yet another slip. Not much finesse about Ransome, but good in a tight place."

"If it's not a laundry-basket," said Appleby. And then he added, "But why should Ransome be hanging about in the neighbourhood in that fancy disguise today?"

"I put him in the disguise originally myself," Gott replied. "I'm interested in disguises—how far they can really be made to work and so forth. Ransome had a naïve confidence in the whiskers and when he got a bit scared as a result of having hit a celebrated *agent policier* on top he decided to continue to lie low for a bit where he was. And very comfortable quarters he had taken up—until our young friends found him."

Gott had risen and was prowling about the room. Coming to the bookcase he found himself confronted, as had Appleby the night before, with *Trent's Last Case*. He picked up this bible of his craft and, opening it at random, seemed absorbed for a space of minutes. Then he snapped the book shut and spoke.

"And now do you believe all this, I wonder? I *could*, you

know, make up several tales to fit the facts, quite as quickly as speaking. Do you happen to believe the tale I've told you?"

Appleby puffed at his pipe in silence, pondering. *Appleby's Greatest Case* . . . and *Appleby's Most Irregular Case* as well. He was prompted to take a risk—but only because some final judgment in himself, a judgment in which he had faith, told him that it was no risk at all.

"I believe your tale," he said, *"verbatim et litteratim."*

"And that I've kept nothing up my sleeve?"

"And that you've kept nothing up your sleeve."

"Then," said Gott blandly as in if reward for this profession of confidence, "then it only remains for us to find the real murderer. And now, if I'm truly not under arrest, I will just slip across and fetch a little beer. . . . Mild or bitter, Appleby?"

"Bitter, Gott."

CHAPTER XIII

I

THE reflections in which Appleby indulged as he sat waiting the return of the St. Anthony's burglar and the St. Anthony's beer were of mingled satisfaction and exasperation. The rat had really been a red-herring. Its investigation had resulted in the acquisition possibly of a valuable ally—but was he any farther forward with the case itself? The answer seemed to be that he was, but not so much so as he had hoped.

To begin with there were now certain eliminations. Campbell was out. His alibi at the Chillingworth for the relevant times was absolute. The vision of that eminent mountaineer scaling St. Anthony's in order to murder its President was dispersed. Chalmers-Paton was out: the advanced hour of the murder made his alibi unquestionably hold. Gott was surely out. A man who planned a perfect burglary for midnight would not precede it by an imperfect murder—a murder, that was to say, which on the face of it he might quite easily have committed. Murder before eleven followed by an alibi for twelve made nonsense. And if Dodd or another should say that here was no sufficient ground for counting Gott out—well, Gott would be under pretty close observation.

What held of Gott held, in a way, of Ransome. And yet not altogether so. If Gott had proposed to murder Umpleby the whole burglary plot as he had contrived it would have been pointless—simply a following-up of murder with a risky joke. If Ransome had proposed to murder Umpleby

the burglary plot would have had its place in the scheme—
for it had procured Ransome access to Orchard Ground.
But even so the *inception* of the burglary plot could have
had no point for a Ransome projecting murder: it could
have become a factor only after the changing of the locks.
. . . Appleby permitted himself to record an impression
that Ransome would prove to be out, but this time it was
an impression to which he could not with confidence attach
any weight. Ransome's movements on the fatal night, his
movements in the period before he met Gott with the
intelligence of his alleged interrupted reconnaissance at
eleven-thirty, would have to be scrutinized. There was no
physical reason why Ransome might not have entered the
college and murdered Umpleby.

Entered the college. . . . In Ransome's known ability
to do this lay the real progress that had been made through
the elucidation of the red herring. Ransome had had the
tenth key. And with the tenth key *placed* came the most
significant elimination of all. The element of the wholly
unknown was now excluded. Umpleby had been murdered
by, or through the connivance of one or more of a known
group of people. Who?

"Who killed Umpleby?" It was Gott who spoke. Laden
with considerable quantities of refreshment, he had just
closed the outer door and was negotiating the laundry-
basket. He appeared innocently to be seeking information.

"Umpleby," Appleby reiterated aloud, "was murdered
by, or through the connivance of one or more of a known
group of people. On the face of it, the people who may
have murdered him are Deighton-Clerk, Haveland, Empson, Pownall, Ransome, the head-porter, yourself. Any one
of these might also have connived at his murder—made it
possible, I mean, by providing some other person with a
key. The people who, without themselves seemingly being

in a position to commit the murder, might have conspired towards it in the same way are Titlow and Lambrick. And Slotwiner must be considered."

"What of Mr. X the locksmith?" Gott offered.

"Sufficiently eliminated."

"Eliminate locksmith. Eliminate, for purposes of useful discussion between you and me, Gott. Eliminate the head-porter, who will have an alibi—and who didn't murder Umpleby anyway, nor connive and conspire. Eliminate Slotwiner; one should always eliminate the servants early, I think. The shadowy suspicious butler is inevitably a bore——"

"But have you any reason for eliminating Slotwiner apart from these dramatic proprieties?"

"Well, in his restrained way Slotwiner was quite devoted to Umpleby and most unlikely to plot his murder. But I don't see why you say he must be considered. He had no key himself and he doesn't seem to have had a chance to smuggle a confederate out through the Lodging."

Appleby nodded. "All right. Say I was wrong to include him among the possibles—on the face of it."

Gott showed that he was not unaware of the significant reiterated phrase. But for the moment he pursued his own theme. "Eliminate Slotwiner *pro tem*. And that leaves us with seven suspects—quite enough. And a good mystic number at the same time. Come to think of it, not a bad title. *Seven Suspects*. They need handling, though, when one runs as many as that. And they're bound some of them to remain a bit dim."

Gott's hobby-horsical vein lasted only until he had apportioned the beer and settled himself down opposite Appleby with a pencil and a sheet of foolscap. Murder and mysterious crime were associated in his mind with recreation and amusement: now he seemed to turn to them a mind as serious and concentrated as that which he was accustomed to give to the problems of the sixteenth-century printing-house.

"This business of conspiracy," he said, "of *A* giving his key to *B*. On the probabilities, that is really a second line of investigation, is it not? Deighton-Clerk here or Lambrick at home handing a key to a hired assassin . . . ?"

Appleby took up the implied unlikelihood. "Yes," he said. "I agree. It brings in a sort of First Murderer in a very unlikely way. Not that the whole affair is not unlikely enough."

Gott smiled. "So Deighton-Clerk has impressed on me—and on you too, no doubt. He sees me as the spiritual father of the crime. Like the painter who invents an improbable type of beauty—and sees it appear in the flesh in the next generation. . . . But after all such things *do* happen. There was a most horrid murder in this very college in 1483."

"A precedent," said Appleby, "is comforting, no doubt. But to stick to the probabilities of conspiracy: obviously the securing of an alibi for oneself would be as nothing against the risk of plotting with anyone who could be conceived as a ruffian hired for the purpose. But what of a conspiracy between colleagues here, based on the fact that colleague *A* has a key and colleague *B* not? The murder is committed the very day the keys are changed—in other words the keys are deliberately *thrust* into prominence. Say then that *A* gives his key to *B*, who murders Umpleby. *A* has an alibi and we have practically to prove the conspiracy before we can demonstrate that *B* had access to the crime."

Gott shook his head. "In *any* murder a two-man show is less likely than a one-man show. And here surely a conspiracy-theory strains psychological probability very far indeed. A two-man murder is a very different thing, after all, from a three-man burglary."

Appleby nodded. "Yes," he said, "again I really agree. It will be sound methodology not to cast about for a two-man effort until we are baffled on the one-man level."

"Which leaves *five* suspects—Deighton-Clerk, Haveland, Empson, Pownall, Ransome. We're getting on."

"On the face of it, five; actually, it may still mean seven."

There was a minute's silence while Gott, again presented with this theme, thought it out. And then he went straight to it. "Umpleby wasn't killed when we thought he was?"

"Exactly. Umpleby was killed some time between half-past ten and eleven, in Orchard Ground or perhaps actually inside Little Fellows'."

"You can prove that?"

"No—far from it. But there's a fresh blade of grass sticking to a bath-chair."

Again Gott was on it instantly. "Empson's old bath-chair—a good quiet hearse!" There was a moment's silence and then he added his complete comprehension. "Titlow's hearse too, maybe."

"Or Slotwiner's—if you weren't so sure about his devotion. Imagine it. Slotwiner takes those drinks into Umpleby's study at half-past ten as usual. He gives a faked message: Haveland's or Pownall's compliments and would the President step over to Little Fellows' to see or do this or that? Out goes Umpleby with Slotwiner presently after him, and the shot is fired somewhere outside Little Fellows' at a moment when something really noisy is roaring down Schools Street. Slotwiner collects the bones, collects the bath-chair, collects Barocho's stray gown—you don't know about that—and pushes back to the study with the lot. He returns the bath-chair—but forgets about the gown: he will be in a hurry by this time, with eleven o'clock and Titlow's usual visit drawing near. He fixes the pistol with some gadget of wire or string in the study and gives a tug just as he is talking with Titlow at the door. And he has a chance to pocket his pistol and string in the confusion after the finding of the body. Or one can, of course, produce a very similar reconstruction for Titlow."

"I should favour Titlow," said Gott instantly.

"You think Titlow a likely murderer?"

Appleby had dropped the question casually but deliberately; the really unfair thing was to shirk being a policeman. And Gott's charity seemed to recognize this even while he stepped back from the trap. "I shouldn't have talked at large about Slotwiner's sentiments—because I'm not going to talk about anybody else's. We can consider the facts, but we can hardly start tipping each other for the gallows. All I meant was that if Slotwiner had given such a message to Umpleby he could hardly have come up *in front* of him in the orchard and shot him, as he was apparently shot, through the forehead. But Titlow—or almost anyone else—could."

For a few minutes the two men smoked in thoughtful silence. And then Appleby continued. "Do you think, then, simply considering the facts, that we have a special line on Titlow?"

"Far from it. Titlow and Slotwiner merely come in again —that is all. We have nothing more than the suggestion that someone wanted to make Umpleby's death appear to have occurred at a different time and place from that at which it actually did occur. And any of the remaining suspects might have had reason for wishing that: there is no justification for confining the motive of such a thing to Slotwiner or Titlow. Why, for instance, suppose the manœuvre necessarily intended to establish the murderer's own alibi? Why should it not be intended to destroy somebody else's?"

"Yes," said Appleby, "I've got as far as that, though it

took me longer than it has taken you. I got to somebody saying '*He could prove he didn't do it here and now; but he couldn't prove he didn't do it there and in twenty minutes' time—were some indication left that he was guilty.*'"

"Good," responded Gott, "that takes us to an exact review of times and movements."

"And brings us right up against the psychological probabilities."

"Which—as between this person and that—I don't think I should debate with you. But there are still plenty of facts—the bones, for instance. The bones are your focus at the moment. Within the field demarcated by the gates and keys they are the nearest thing at present to a pointer. What sort of a pointer are they on Haveland, their owner, for example?"

Appleby replied with another question. "Last night in the common-room Haveland, you remember, virtually put forward alternative propositions about the murder: do you think they hold?"

Gott nodded his comprehension. "Haveland in effect said, 'Either I myself murdered Umpleby in circumstances only compatible with my being quite insane, or somebody else has committed the murder and has attempted to father it on me.' Well, I don't see that the proposition really holds. Haveland might have committed the crime and yet be sane enough. That is to say, he might have been laborious enough to frame a frame-up against himself."

"You mean that he might have left his collection of bones beside his victim not crazily and in order to give himself away but to fake the notion that someone was framing him? It seems a bit roundabout, and unnecessarily laborious and risky."

"Risky, yes. Unnecessarily roundabout and laborious, perhaps—but perhaps not. It may have seemed his best way to plant the murder on somebody else."

"Plant the murder on somebody else by means of faking a plant against himself! My dear Gott, isn't that rather too subtle?" But Appleby was obviously weighing the suggestion rather than scoffing.

"Subtle, yes," Gott replied, "but, after all, you know, you've come—back, is it not?—to one of the more subtle parts of England. Of course the theory holds—implications."

"Such as?"

"Well, such as that you've *missed* things. Or not been let run up against them so far."

Appleby smiled. "No doubt I've been missing things. But what exactly are you thinking of?"

"Of the subsequent clues on the false trail—the further indications that Haveland would leave about that he had been framed *by this particular person or that.*"

"For that matter he seemed rather venomously inclined towards Empson. Though I haven't discovered any clues against Empson so far—planted by Haveland or otherwise. As you suggest, I may have missed them. On the other hand it is just possible that I haven't missed them because they're not there—that your theory's wrong, in fact."

Gott protested. "It's not my theory. It's simply one suggestion. But 'missed,' I think, was a mistake. There would be no point in Haveland's leaving clues so tenuous that they *could* reasonably be missed. But they may be yet to come."

Appleby chuckled. He enjoyed Gott. "The second murder, perhaps, that throws some light on the first? And then the third and fourth murders, that eliminate two of the possible perpetrators of the second? Let's try the exact review of times and movements. And we can begin with Haveland." And—much like Inspector Dodd—Appleby produced a sheaf of papers. But at this moment there came the second interruption of the evening. Somebody could be heard negotiating the laundry-basket in the lobby and then there came a knock at the door. It was Haveland himself.

The visitor halted when he saw Gott and addressed himself to Appleby. "I beg your pardon—I thought I might find you free. Perhaps I might come again . . . ?"

"Mr. Gott and I have been discussing—my business here," Appleby replied, and at the same moment Gott rose to go. But Haveland meantime had shut the door and his next remark embraced them both. "Can I usefully place myself at the disposal of so formidable a conference?"

Haveland's should have been an easy and open nature. His physical contours were bland and the effect was enhanced by the pleasing, if somewhat consciously æsthetic negligence of his clothes—the clothes he refused to shed for the sober black and white required by the ritual of the St. Anthony's high-table. But, actually, the personality he presented to the world was stiff, uncoloured and—surely—utterly unspontaneous. He was, apart from the hint of irony which always lurked in the fall of his phrases, impassive, deliberately unmoved, deliberately remote. Appleby suddenly resolved to essay the rousing of him now.

"You come at a useful moment," he said. "We were just beginning an examination of your movements at the time of the murder. Do sit down."

That Haveland might display some indignation, if not against the policeman at least against his colleague, it was reasonable to suppose. But there was no flicker. The visitor obeyed the injunction to be seated and said nothing at all. Any business of his own on which he had come he was indicating as put aside at Appleby's pleasure. It had the effect, somehow, of being a distinct score; Appleby had to plunge ahead at once. And he had to do so without being very certain of his ground. The statements collected by Dodd he had not yet had time to review in the light of the slightly altered hour of the murder. Nevertheless he turned coolly to his relevant scrap of memoranda.

"John Haveland," he read quietly, "fifty-nine. Fellow of the college since 1908. Unmarried. Occupies rooms in Orchard Ground. Can throw no light on the murder or on any of the circumstances attending it.

"*Nine-fifteen:* Left common-room and went to own rooms. Read. *Ten-forty:* Quitted Orchard Ground by east gate and called on Dean in Bishop's. *Ten-fifty:* Returned by east gate, going straight to own rooms. *Eleven-twenty-five:* Discovered there by Inspector Dodd and informed of President's death. Appeared scarcely interested."

Appleby pushed the paper aside. Dodd's final observation made good ground on which to pause. But Haveland challenged it at once. "I heard of the President's death," he said, "most certainly without emotion and without regret."

"And without surprise, Mr. Haveland?"

"I must confess to surprise."

"And curiosity?"

"Curiosity?"

"My colleague's note has something more to add on the further interview he had with you in the morning. You had no information to give—about the bones, for instance. But you yourself asked three questions. You asked if the President had been shot, if the weapon had been found, and if the time of death was determined."

"My dear Haveland," Gott murmured at this point, "such friendly interest in the world is unlike your usual self. You must have been quite upset."

Haveland showed what might have been the shadow of impatience. "With my collection of bones on the man's carpet the time of death was obviously material to me. For that matter, it was obviously material to Deighton-Clerk. Umpleby was apparently shot at exactly eleven o'clock. Either of us therefore could just have done it. But if he had been shot at, say, a quarter of eleven both of us would have been nicely out of it—or up to the neck in a conspiracy together. Why shouldn't I ask questions? I don't want to be hanged, you know."

Appleby gave his information guilelessly. "Umpleby was shot a long time before eleven o'clock. Inspector Dodd hadn't got the facts straight when you interrogated him. And we *have* found the weapon."

Without eagerness Haveland took up the first point. "How long before eleven?"

"Anything up to half an hour."

Haveland was impassive still—but not utterly without betrayal. Coming somewhere from the man was an impression that Appleby was now familiar with in the St. Anthony's case—an impression of rapid calculation. Titlow, Pownall, Haveland—these men thought intensively before they spoke. In all of them it was perhaps merely the intellectual habit that gave the impression. And yet with Haveland, certainly, the impression was that of a man intensely calculating—calculating whether to suggest something, to reveal something, to venture some further question. . . . At length he said flatly, "Then Deighton-Clerk or I might still have done it."

"Deighton-Clerk might have shot Umpleby and left your bones in his study?"

"Yes, or I might."

"When do you think the bones were purloined from your room?"

"Between ten-forty and ten-fifty, I suppose—while I was visiting Deighton-Clerk."

"In that case they couldn't have been taken *by* Deighton-Clerk?"

"No. Not that I really know when they were taken. I only know they were in their cupboard—an unlocked cupboard—in the afternoon."

"Was Deighton-Clerk an enemy of Umpleby's?"

"He hadn't picturesquely wished him rotting in a sepulchre, as I so unfortunately had. But they were not on good terms. Deighton-Clerk had taxed Umpleby publicly with improper conduct towards Ransome, the man now abroad."

"Ransome isn't abroad," interposed Gott easily.

"Indeed?"

"He's probably in bed by now—in this college. Not long ago he was in the laundry-basket you must have encountered coming in."

"Indeed?"

Certainly it was a mask that Haveland presented to the world. Hearing of a colleague being kept in a laundry-basket he showed no flicker of surprise, no flicker of interest. And now he had got to his feet. "I can only interfere with your activities. I look forward to anything your collaboration may produce. Good night." And Haveland withdrew.

Appleby was chuckling. "What do you think he meant by the product of our collaboration, Gott?"

"I suspect him of meaning that we are likely to do best spinning novels together. But why did he come?"

Appleby chuckled again, thoughtfully this time. "He came for information. And he got it, I think—or all the whiff of it he wanted. And you see what we've got to do now?"

"Oh, yes," responded the undefeatable Gott. "We've got to carry out a little practical experimental work with a hearse. And the beer will keep."

II

"The miscreant," reported Horace on returning to David's room after a prolonged reconnaissance, "has been released."

"Released!" exclaimed his friends blankly.

"I'm glad to say," replied Horace, who had apparently been thinking it out, "released. Which means, I suppose, that he didn't do it. Which means, in turn, that we haven't caught a murderer. We never decided, you know, on the morality of dealing with him if we did. We were carried away—or Mike was—by the funny joke of delivering him neatly parcelled and addressed."

"They've really let him go?"

"He's gone to his old rooms, had a bath and an enormous meal and Mrs. Tunk has been summoned by telephone to make and grace his downy couch. Pork Evans has seen it all from his window."

"They may only be giving him rope," suggested Mike.

"They may only be giving *us* rope," retorted Horace. "Don't you think it very probable that we shall all be sent down?"

"Not a chance of it. Can you see Ransome going to Deighton-Clerk and complaining of what has befallen him while skulking round the old *mouseion* in a false nose?"

"Well," said Horace doubtfully, "if that's so we're well out of it."

"Out of it?" It was David who spoke. "Surely, Horace, you are not content to let our investigation *rest*? Didn't I tell you both that in addition to a *notion* I had some *information*? No, no, Horace; thy duty duly is performed, but there's more work."

Horace turned to Mike. "He *is* a bore, you know. I've long suspected it—and there it is."

Mike nodded gloomily. "Yes, one sees it coming. Sir David Pennyfeather Edwards, the celebrated Treasury bore. Pattering round suggesting a committee here and an inquiry there. Poor old David." And Mike applied himself with ostentatious concentration to *Selected Sermons of the Seventeenth Century*. Horace slid to the floor and was enfolded in the mysteries of Miss Milligan in a moment. In Two-six Dr. Umpleby's death had ceased to compel.

But David knew his men. Gently, he talked to the air. And in a couple of minutes his companions were absorbed.

III

The beer had been abandoned. Gott was brewing strong coffee. Appleby had his watch out on the arm of his chair and was regarding it thoughtfully.

"An inconclusive experiment," said Gott. "He might just have managed it, but it would be a tight squeeze."

"Yes; and at either time. The two periods Haveland had are just equal: ten-thirty to ten-forty and then ten-fifty to eleven. Even if you put forward his arrival on the Dean to ten-forty-three or even forty-five you must allow something at the other end for Umpleby's leaving his study and getting up the orchard after Slotwiner had brought in the drinks at ten-thirty. A *very* tight squeeze."

"Ah, well, my picture of Haveland trolleying his own bones plus corpse up the garden path was no doubt, as you suggested, a bit steep. But why did Haveland visit the Dean anyway, and what has the Dean to say about the times?"

"Just a minute," replied Appleby. "We'll go over the other people's movements now and begin with the Dean. Here we are." And he produced the relevant note.

'Deighton-Clerk. . . . *Nine-thirty:* Left the common-room with Dr. Barocho and went to the latter's rooms in

Bishop's. *Ten-thirty-five:* Walked across to his own rooms, accompanied part of the way by Barocho. Visited a few minutes after he got back by Mr. Haveland. *Ten-fifty:* Haveland left to return to his rooms. A few minutes later Deighton-Clerk rang up the porter's lodge on college affairs and then settled down to read. *Eleven-ten:* President's butler, Slotwiner, came across with news of fatality. . . ."

"It corroborates Haveland," commented Gott. "And if that telephone-call to the porter took any time at all it looks like clearing Deighton-Clerk himself."

"Unless," Appleby responded, "he telephoned with one hand, so to speak, and shot Umpleby with the other."

"Any shot would be heard in Bishop's."

"He might have followed Haveland immediately into Orchard Ground, met Umpleby and shot him, telephoned from an empty room in Little Fellows', run out again, chaired corpse and bones, dumped them in the study, fired —for some reason—a second shot at eleven and then beat it for his own rooms."

"Good Lord, Appleby, that's a tighter squeeze still! Can you really imagine Deighton-Clerk skipping about like that? And anyway, was there an empty room in Little Fellows' to telephone from? Haveland was back in his. What of the other three?"

"Just a moment. It *is* another tight squeeze, I admit— probably too tight. And if there was no telephone available of course it breaks down. But before we look at the other three let's take Barocho. His movements link up with the Dean's and perhaps we can get rid of him."

"But Barocho hadn't a key."

"Never mind. Let's look at him. I seem to remember he's out anyway. Yes, he is. 'Walked with Deighton-Clerk to the door of latter's rooms at ten-thirty-five and then went straight to the library, reading there until called out after eleven. . . .' There were a number of undergraduates in the library. Barocho's quite out."

"If you're taking people without keys—what about old Curtis? Has he an alibi?"

Appleby shook his head. "Curtis went to his rooms at nine-thirty. He says he didn't stir out again that night. The Dean had him out of bed a bit before midnight to tell him what had happened. And that's all we know."

"What of Curtis as the dark horse?" Gott asked—and added soberly, "Let's try to sum up to date. The people really in the running are Haveland, Titlow, Empson, Pownall, Ransome, Deighton-Clerk and myself. All these had keys. For the purposes of this discussion, I'm out. Ransome's movements at the material time we have as yet no information on. Haveland would seem to have a tight squeeze. Deighton-Clerk's outness or inness depends on the movements of the remaining three. If he couldn't telephone from one of their rooms he just hadn't time to shoot Umpleby and the rest of it between ten-fifty and eleven. And he couldn't have used Haveland's telephone. So let's have Titlow, Empson and Pownall—whose movements, incidentally, are vital in themselves."

Appleby turned to another paper. "Here's Pownall," he said, "according to the story he gave me this morning. He got back to his rooms in Little Fellows' a little before nine-thirty. He read for twenty minutes. Then he went to bed and was asleep by ten-fifteen. He was disturbed by somebody in his room at ten-forty-two."

"The dickens he was! But that's too early to have been Deighton-Clerk at the telephone. . . . And he didn't leave his room after that?"

"No. He prowled about discovering blood and deciding Umpleby had been murdered. But he sat tight in his rooms all the same." And Appleby gave Gott the gist of Pownall's narrative. Then he turned to Titlow.

"*Nine-twenty:* Returned from common-room and worked until ten-fifty-five, when he set off to visit Umpleby as usual. Passed through the west gate into Bishop's and rang front-door bell of President's Lodging just on eleven."

Appleby paused. "You can help there," he said. "Why should he go round to the front door? Why not knock at the French windows?"

"Point of ceremony, I think," Gott replied. "He always did on those occasions. It was a sort of weekly official visit —and the two men didn't love each other."

Appleby nodded. "Well, that's the story. No corroboration—nor anything against it. But for what it's worth it deprives Deighton-Clerk of the possibility of another telephone. And now, here's Empson. He got back to his rooms at nine-thirty and settled down to work. At ten-forty he went over to the porter's lodge by way of the west gate in order to inquire about a parcel of proofs. He was back within eight or ten minutes and remained undisturbed until the arrival of the police. . . . That's the lot." And Appleby tossed aside his notes.

Gott sighed. "What a scope there seems to be for lying about it all! Do you see how no one of these Little Fellows' people makes contact with any other? But if Empson's story is true it cuts out Deighton-Clerk. Empson was back at ten-fifty—before Deighton-Clerk could use his telephone and avoid being discovered. What do you think?"

"I think that unless Deighton-Clerk telephoned from his own rooms *immediately* Haveland left him, and not as the statement says 'a few minutes later' that he *is* cut out. Indeed, I think he's out in any case. The squeeze is too tight quite apart from the telephone."

"In which case," said Gott, "it's down to the Little Fellows' contingent and to Ransome and myself."

"Exactly. But somehow I suspect the St. Anthony's burglars less and less. The key to the mystery lies—"

"In Little Fellows?"

"In Thomas De Quincey," said Appleby.

CHAPTER XIV

I

As APPLEBY crossed Bishop's a few minutes after Gott's departure he had a sense of making his way to the last important interview in the St. Anthony's case. In Gott he had just left a theoretically-possible suspect; in Ransome there was an unknown quantity yet to be dealt with. But the belief was really growing on him that the mystery of Umpleby's death was somehow hidden in Little Fellows': at least it was on Little Fellows' that his mind was going to concentrate before it wandered further afield. And of the four men lodging there he already had more than a little knowledge of three. Haveland he had just been scrutinizing; Pownall he had interrogated; Titlow had deliberately provided him with a sort of set exhibition of himself. But of Empson he had had no more than a caustic word in hall and common-room—and a revealing glimpse asleep. Perhaps he was already asleep again now. But it was still a feasible hour for a call. . . . Once more Appleby slipped through the west gates into Orchard Ground.

Empson's dry voice answered the knock. Perhaps it was some sense of an unexpected contrast to this dryness that gave a peculiarly vivid quality to the moment at which Appleby entered the room. Empson was sitting by the light of the fire and of a single shaded lamp. The severe library, concentrated so uncompromisingly on the man's own subject of psychology and mental science, had receded into shadow. Its owner, who had discarded his ordinary dinner-jacket for the faded silk of some wine-club of a passed generation, was sitting reading in a high-backed, old-fashioned chair. His stick was between his knees, pale ivory matching the pale ivory of the fingers clasping it. And the ivory complexion, set off by the dead white shirt, was softened by the faded rose and gold of the old silk. . . . Empson had risen punctiliously to his feet and put aside his book—it was Henry James's *The Golden Bowl*, and to Appleby it seemed pleasantly to complete a picture of mellow scientific relaxation.

"I wondered if I might trouble you——?" As Appleby spoke, Empson set a chair; the action was markedly courteous—but it had not the air of being an extra politeness shown to an anomalous policeman. Interviews in St. Anthony's, Appleby felt once more, could be very difficult. And casting round for a suitable opening he decided to take the only matter in which Empson had a demonstrable concern. "I believe that some years ago you were in the habit of using an invalid-chair?"

"That is so. The trouble from which, as you see, I suffer" —and Empson lightly tapped the handle of his stick—"was temporarily aggravated and I was obliged to change rooms for a while with Pownall below. For some months I had to be wheeled to lectures, into hall and so forth."

"You know that the chair is kept in a store-room in this building?"

Empson shook his head. "I know only that it is somewhere in college. May I ask if it has assumed some significance for your investigations?"

"It was used on the night of the President's murder. I believe it was used for the conveyance of the body."

For a moment Empson deliberated—the universal academic deliberation of St. Anthony's. Then he spoke. "The conveyance of the *dead* body? You have concluded, then, that the President was shot elsewhere than in his study?"

"Yes."

Again Empson deliberated; but he might merely have been pausing to take in this new view of things. There was something guarded in his next question. "You have proof of that?"

Appleby was prompted to admit the truth. "Only the fact of the chair's having been used. But I think it almost conclusive." And suddenly Appleby found himself being *searched:* it was as if Empson's every atom of professional expertness were turned upon the endeavour to assess the reliability of what he had heard. But when the psychologist spoke it was without emphasis. "I see," he said. And the eyes that had a moment before been essaying to pierce Appleby's mind turned away to stare thoughtfully into the fire.

It was the consciousness of Empson's vocation that prompted Appleby's next approach. "There is a matter," he said, "on which I wish to ask your opinion—for your opinion, you will understand, as distinct from your knowledge of facts. And it is, of course, not at all necessary that you should answer me. But it is a matter you are peculiarly qualified to speak of—a matter of human behaviour——"

Abruptly, Empson interrupted—and it was a thing so much against both his deliberative habit and his courteous manner that Appleby was almost startled.

"The science of human behaviour is yet in its infancy. We are still far better trusting to the prompting of our experience. And yet experience too will betray us. Science will say of a man, 'It is infinitely unlikely that he should do this': experience will add, 'It is impossible that he should do it'—and then he *will* do it."

In Empson there was always the undertone of bitterness. But in the colour rather than in the wording of this speech

Appleby sensed something different, a quality of response coming not from a set habit but from something like a fresh revelation. Empson was speaking not from an attitude long since adopted; he was speaking, surely, from a sense of recent shock—almost of recent outrage. Was it himself, or was it another, who had violated expectation?

"It is infinitely unlikely—it is impossible," Appleby boldly prompted, "that Umpleby should be murdered *here?*" and at Empson's nod he continued quietly, "Mr. Haveland has been at one time subject to some form of mental disturbance. Do you feel you can properly say anything about that? To be frank, would you connect it with homicidal tendencies? The matter of the bones——"

And once more Empson interrupted. "Haveland did not kill Umpleby. The bones you speak of are an abominable imposture." He spoke quietly, but with an extraordinary intensity in the face of which Appleby's next question seemed almost impertinent. But it was a question which had to be asked.

"Is that the fallible voice of science, or the almost equally fallible voice of experience?"

There was only one reply by which Empson could preserve a fully logical position. Would he make it? Would he say that he spoke neither with the voice of science nor with the voice of experience, but with the voice of knowledge? Somewhere in the room a clock ticked out the moments of silence.

"Science is fallible, but it is not nothing. And it will tell you with great authority that the bones are a damnable plant—a plant by someone ignorant of abnormal psychology. I earnestly entreat you, before rushing into a trap, to have Haveland quietly examined by eminent physicians I can name to you. They will substantiate what I say."

"That Haveland did not murder Umpleby?"

Empson deliberated. And it seemed to Appleby that when he spoke again he spoke as one determined against personal impulse to follow the dry light of knowledge merely. "Science would be very fallible if it claimed to tell you that. Science can only tell you that Haveland did not murder Umpleby and then broadcast the crime by scattering bones. That, I suppose, is conclusive. And to it I add my *conviction* that Haveland is innocent."

"Your conviction—the voice of experience?"

"Just that. Again something fallible but of some authority."

"Haveland, then, is mentally . . . normal?" It was a new question, and Appleby's subtle attempt to introduce it as a tail-piece to what had just been said was a failure. Empson drew back just as Gott had done.

"It is my duty, Mr. Appleby, to declare my personal and professional conviction that the circumstances of the President's death are incompatible with what I believe to be Haveland's mental constitution. But I should do very wrong to go on to discuss his or any other colleague's mental constitution at large. You will have little difficulty in finding psychologists willing to discover something crazy in the whole lot of us." Empson was considerate; the jest softened the rebuke.

"One must be one's own judge of duty," said Appleby. And for the third time Empson interrupted—and this time in some queer flare of passion.

"The most difficult thing in the world!"

II

Appleby had turned to a fresh topic. "You came back here from the common-room at half-past nine, and went out again something over an hour later—at ten-forty to be exact—to collect a parcel from the porter's lodge. That took you eight or ten minutes and thereafter you did not leave your room until the police reached Little Fellows'. I believe that covers your movements?"

Empson inclined his head.

"Did you meet anyone on your way either to or from the porter's lodge?"

"I saw Titlow."

"Will you tell me about that, please—just where you saw him and when? And whether he saw you?"

"I do not think he saw me. He was entering his rooms just as I came out of mine. He had apparently come upstairs and was just turning into his lobby when I opened the door there"—and Empson nodded towards his own sitting-room door—"and noticed him."

"That would be about ten-forty—just, that is to say, when you were setting off to the porter's lodge?"

"Exactly so."

"I must tell you that Mr. Titlow has declared himself not to have stirred from his room until ten-fifty-five. And then he went *downstairs* and straight to the President's front door." And Empson declining to take advantage of Appleby's pause on this the latter added: "There is discrepancy, is there not?"

"Titlow has forgotten—or Titlow is not telling the truth." Deliberately Empson seemed to speak without emphasis; there was suppression even of the customary dryness in his tone. There followed a little silence.

"There was nothing remarkable about your glimpse of him?"

"He seemed to have come upstairs rapidly: I had the momentary but convinced impression that he was panting for breath."

"And that he was agitated?"

"I saw him for a second only, and in that second I had the impression—again the momentary but convinced impression—that he was very much agitated."

With just such damning lack of emphasis, reflected Appleby, might a judge set some fatal point clearly before a jury. And the image prompted him to try the effect of sudden violence—the advocate's jump to the vital point. "You think Titlow guilty?"

No change, he reflected ruthfully a moment later, was to be got from Empson that way. A blank silence sufficiently indicated the latter's sense that his guest had asked an impossible question. But at length he spoke. "I should be glad to see justice done, but I am far from able to accuse Titlow." And then he continued, with something of the air of taking up a subsidiary point in order to rescue Appleby from an embarrassing situation: "There was, for instance, what actually happened—the shot, whether fatal or not, heard while Titlow was in the presence of the butler Slotwiner."

"That," said Appleby, "might have been contrived."

"I suppose it might." Empson stared once more thoughtfully into the fire. "Have you discovered—have you considered how? Is there, I mean, any sign of such a thing?"

Appleby was evasive. "The plan would defeat itself if any sign remained." And abruptly he turned to another matter. "Why, Mr. Empson, did you go over to the porter's lodge at all? You have a telephone here; why did you not ring up to inquire if your parcel had come, and get them to send it across?"

"We do not unnecessarily trouble college servants. It did me no harm to walk."

The reply was not exactly a snub, but it was conclusive. And Appleby felt he had only one more set of questions to ask. "And throughout the rest of the evening—from nine-thirty to ten-forty and then from ten-fifty onwards—you were here and quite undisturbed?"

"Quite undisturbed."

"No one called?"

"No one."

"And no one rang up?"

"No one."

Vain persistence, thought Appleby, and was rising to take his leave when something, the echo perhaps of a faintly perceptible tension in the last word spoken, prompted him to add one last query.

"And you yourself rang up no one?"

The pause ensuing was but a fraction of a second; the increased pressure of the fingers on the ivory stick might have been something fancied rather than actual. And yet Appleby had a sudden impulse of overwhelming excitement. In the mind with which he was grappling he sensed, in this moment, calculation more intense than he had hitherto had any feeling of. *Empson was debating his reply: Yes or No.* And the moment, Appleby's temporarily ungoverned intuition asserted, was the cardinal moment in the St. Anthony's case . . .

Empson spoke quietly as ever. "I rang up Umpleby a little after ten. The matter was of no consequence."

III

Tantripp, the head porter, had been in the service of St. Anthony's since a boy. He was an intelligent man and appeared to realize that he must give all the help he could. But the feeling that with policemen ferreting about among the Fellows of the college the end of the world had come was plainly strong upon him. And so Appleby began with an impersonal point. "I should like you," he said, to explain the telephone system of the college."

It turned out to be a subject on which Tantripp was inclined to enlarge. The telephone had arrived in St. Antnony's long after he had, and the innovation was one of which he was disposed to be critical. Moreover, there had recently been innovation upon innovation—and of this he was very critical indeed. There was a telephone in the outer lodge for undergraduates, a telephone in the manciple's office and another in the kitchens, a telephone in the President's Lodging with an extension to his study, and a telephone in the rooms of each Fellow of the college. Originally all calls had gone through a switchboard in the porter's lodge. This system had worked well enough, but putting through calls had required the fairly constant attention of the porter on duty. Recently, therefore, a dialling system had been introduced with the object of rendering automatic all calls within the college. To send a call out of college the caller must dial the porter's lodge; but any instrument within the college could be rung from any other by dialling the appropriate symbol. Unfortunately, when first put into operation, the dialling system had not proved thoroughly efficient and as a result it had not immediately, as Tantripp put it, "caught on." Partly owing to this reason, partly to academic conservatism and partly to academic absent-mindedness, Fellows of the college were still liable to put their intra-college calls through the manual switchboard in the lodge.

"Did Professor Empson," Appleby boldly asked, "put his call through that way on the night of the President's murder?"

"Yes, sir," replied Tantripp—uncomfortably but not unreadily—"he did. He rang through here about ten o'clock."

"You remember what he said?"

"He said, 'Put me through to the President, Tantripp, please.'"

"And he could have got through automatically?"

"Certainly. He had only to dial 01. But he's one that never would use the automatic."

"You are certain it was Professor Empson? You are certain the call came from his room?"

Tantripp appeared perplexed. "Well, sir, I expect it came from his room. I know at once by the switchboard lights, of course, if so happen I think of it. But usually I'm only conscious of the connexion wanted. It was Professor Empson's voice but, come to think of it, he might have been speaking from anywhere—anywhere else in college, I mean. And it was him all right, because I mentioned the call to him afterwards."

"Mentioned it?"

"Yes, sir. His parcel had been here all evening and when he came across for it at a quarter to eleven it struck me I ought to have mentioned its arrival when he rang up earlier. So I said I was sorry I hadn't told him about it when he rang through to the President."

"And what did he say?"

"He just waved his hand and said, 'All right, Tantripp' —or something of the sort—and went out."

"What other calls went through your switchboard that night, can you remember?"

"Only two, sir. The President put through an outside call. Of course, I don't know to whom: I just connected him with the city exchange."

"What time was that—can you be certain?"

"Just before half-past ten."

"And the other call?"

"That was from the Dean, sir, about some gentlemen

who had been gated. And I remember that he finished speaking to me just as my clock there was on five minutes to eleven."

For a few minutes Appleby interrogated Tantripp as to his own movements. Gott had been right about his having an alibi: Tantripp would have no difficulty in proving that he had been in his lodge during the period of the murder. And the Dean was now certainly out. But it was of Empson that Appleby was still thinking—and of whom he continued to think as he strolled through the dark courts a few minutes later. It was abundantly clear why Empson had not been able to deny having telephoned to Umpleby. Not only had he used the manual exchange, thus making himself known to the porter—he had tacitly admitted to the call when Tantripp had chanced to mention it later. And yet for a split second he had meditated denying it to Appleby, meditated a denial which would be inevitably exposed. And this though Empson's brain was not the sort to meditate even for a split second a course merely foolish. . . . But could there, after all, have been anything sinister about the whole incident? For a sinister telephone call why not the secrecy of the dialling apparatus? And yet Appleby could not rid himself of the prejudice that he had arrived somehow at the heart of the case. . . .

It was after eleven o'clock and he had turned automatically towards his rooms for the night, the second night of his sojourn in the college. But the thought of his rooms suggested Gott and with the thought of Gott came Gott's whimsical recommendation to lose no time in eliminating the servants. The head porter he had just disposed of. . . . Once more Appleby let himself through the west gate into Orchard Ground.

The violated windows of the President's study had been secured by a padlock to which he had a key; he let himself in, drew the curtains and turned on the light. The gloomy room, the litter of bones, the dead ashes in the hearth and, above, the grotesquely chalked emblems of mortality: it was all ugly, dreary rather than eerie now, flat, stale, absurd—but mysterious still. Appleby wasted no time. He turned out the main lights, turned on the single standard lamp, settled himself in Umpleby's armchair and rang the bell. Within half a minute Slotwiner had appeared, as normally, as imperturbably as if his master were still alive to summon him. But this time he made Appleby a bow as to one whose status within the college had been recognized. He was, Appleby reflected, a cool card—certainly not one to be rattled by hearing a bell ring in a dead man's room. And Appleby decided to try a disconcerting opening. "Slotwiner," he said, "we have had to consider you as a suspect."

"You must explore every avenue, sir."

"It has become obvious that the shot heard by Mr. Titlow and yourself was a fake."

"Yes, sir. I have always had that possibility in mind."

"Indeed! In that case you must understand the reason for which the fake might have been arranged?"

"I can imagine more than one, sir. But one would be to provide an alibi for Mr. Titlow or myself—presuming one of us guilty. I trust the whole matter will be gone into with minute exactness."

Slotwiner, his colloquial style apart, came well out of these exchanges. Appleby proceeded to a frank statement. "If the President was not killed by the shot which you and Mr. Titlow heard he must have been killed not in this study but some way up Orchard Ground, where the noise of traffic might drown the report. I have to calculate times on that basis. Now, can you tell me anything helpful about yourself?"

Slotwiner considered thoughtfully. "I see what you mean, sir. And I think I have at least a partial alibi. I think I may take it that to follow the President through the study and up the orchard and later to return with—with the body and the bones would take seven or eight minutes?"

Appleby agreed. Actually, he knew, a longer time would be involved—time to cover a journey back to Little Fellows' with the bath-chair.

"Well, sir, I was not, I think, alone for so long a period after ten-thirty. Mrs. Hugg, the cook, was engaged as it happened upon the elucidation of a puzzle in the kitchen. And she several times ventured upstairs to the pantry to ask my advice. Beasts of seven letters beginning with 'P' and that sort of thing, sir. I suggest that you question her closely. But for the period before ten-thirty—supposing, that is, that the President was no longer alive when I affected to take in his refreshment—I fear I am quite uncovered."

"Don't worry," said Appleby quietly. He was coming to have a good deal of confidence in Slotwiner. "Don't worry. I know that the President was alive just before ten-thirty: he made a telephone call. You heard nothing of that?"

Slotwiner unstiffened a little. "I am, if I may say so, sir, distinctly relieved. But I heard nothing of the telephone call: the President's extension was operating and he could make a call without my being aware of it. He always spoke very quietly into the instrument and in my pantry at the end of the passage the sound would be quite inaudible. Indeed, when working there I am often unconscious of any conversation from this room. But I have to tell you of something which I did hear. It has come back to me since our previous interview. I believe I heard the bones."

"Heard the bones?"

"Yes, sir. Some time before Mr. Titlow's arrival I happened to emerge from my pantry into the hall. And I remember becoming aware of a curious noise from the study. It was not like the President moving books or chairs, and I could not quite place it. May I venture, sir——?" And at Appleby's nod the dignified Slotwiner bounded into activity. In a moment he had glided over the floor and collected the major portion of the scattered bones. Bundling them into a newspaper, he handed the bundle to Appleby. "Now, sir, if you would be so good——?" And Slotwiner vanished out of the room, shutting the door after him. Appleby was interested and amused. He waited until he heard a distant shout and then, tilting the newspaper, he let the bones tumble to the floor. They made a surprising clatter. And in a moment Slotwiner was back in the study—positively animated. "That, sir," he said, "was precisely it!"

Appleby asked the vital question. "Can you time it?"

"With fair confidence, sir—to within five minutes. It would be between a quarter and ten to eleven."

Appleby allowed himself a moment to place the implications of this as exactly as was momentarily possible, and then he turned to a further interrogation of Slotwiner. But the man had heard nothing further, had no further light to throw on the events of the fatal night. And questioned in more general terms as to the relations of Umpleby with the various Fellows of the college, he became reserved. It was an uncomfortable line of inquiry but in a matter of the sort Appleby never allowed the luxury of nice feelings to interfere. And presently his persistence was rewarded. Slotwiner, admitting to a pretty accurate awareness of the disquiets that had troubled St. Anthony's of recent years, came at length to recount one particular scene of which he had been a witness not long before. Umpleby had been holding some sort of meeting in his study with Titlow and

Pownall. Whether it had been a protractedly acrimonious meeting Slotwiner could not say. But he had been summoned in the course of it by the President—who was always apparently a punctilious host—to bring in afternoon tea. He had considered the atmosphere strained—although (or perhaps partly because) almost nothing had been said while he was in the room. But opening the door a little later with the intention of replenishing the supply of buttered toast he had heard Pownall speaking with an emphasis which had made him pause. And in the pause he had heard Pownall make a remarkable declaration: "Mr. President, you may rejoice that it takes two to make a murder— for you are a most capital murderee!" After which Slotwiner had retired to his pantry—with the buttered toast.

Appleby wondered if he had eaten it.

CHAPTER XV

I

On the second and last morning of his sojourn in St. Anthony's Appleby was greeted, as on the previous day, by an early visit from Dodd. The burglars were safely under lock and key, having been caught in a masterly ambush in the small hours of the morning. As a consequence, Dodd was in strange and boisterous mood. He affected solicitude for Appleby's personal safety during the night, searched round the room to see if any of his belongings had been stolen and then, switching to another topic, inquired after the progress of his studies—what the lectures were like, and when he would be taking his degree? And finally he asked, after a great deal of chuckling over all this—who had killed Dr. Umpleby?

Appleby was cautious. "Well," he said, "it might have been Ransome."

"Ransome!"

"Oh, yes. Ransome has been hovering round us in false whiskers these many days. In fact it was he who downed me t'other night."

"There!" said Dodd emphatically, "what did I say about their saying he was in Asia? They're a deep lot!"

"On the other hand it might have been Titlow; it might very well have been Titlow, you know."

Dodd had heard enough on the previous evening to have his understanding of this. "The pistol-shot being engineered?"

"Exactly."

Dodd stood in front of Appleby's fire. He seemed to expand. "It's just possible," he said, "that we can give a little help."

Appleby smiled. "You've been doing some more of the rough work, as you put it?"

"Kellett has. A conscientious fellow, Kellett. He's been having another hunt round this morning."

"Ah! Again while I was still heavily asleep. And what has Kellett found this time?"

"Kellett," Dodd replied very seriously, "thought he would have a look at the drains. It's wonderful how often, one way or another, the drains come in. Well, he was having a poke down some sort of ventilator or such-like in Orchard Ground when he found this." And Dodd produced from his pocket a twisted length of stiff wire.

"Kellett found it twisted up like this?"

Dodd nodded affirmatively and Appleby after a moment took up the unspoken train of thought. "It hardly seems long enough to be useful. I don't really see——"

"One can imagine some sort of gadget—weights and so forth——?" Dodd tentatively prompted.

"One can imagine," Appleby sceptically responded, "a plumber clearing a pipe or drain."

"*Leaving* it down the drain?"

"Plumbers are always leaving things," Appleby replied with rather feeble humour—his thoughts seemed to be far away. But presently he added: "I rather agree that a plumber wouldn't leave it down a drain—twisted up like this."

"What about sending it to Scotland Yard to be photographed?"

Appleby started, and then chuckled. "I wonder if your sad sergeant will bring us any news? Meantime you and I will go and have a heavy talk with young False Whiskers."

"Asia, indeed!" said Inspector Dodd.

Mr. Ransome was found in his regular rooms in Surrey, in the middle of a perplexed telephone conversation with the proprietor of the Three Doves. That he was the guest who had left in such unseemly circumstances the night before; that he was really Mr. Ransome of St. Anthony's College; that it was quite all right; that nothing serious had occurred; that it was all a matter of a bet; that he wanted his luggage sent on—this was Ransome's side of the exchange. But the mention of the momentarily notorious St. Anthony's in conjunction with such a thin story obviously caused alarm at the other end of the line. Ransome was pink and snorting by the time he turned to receive his official visitors. But he calmed himself at once and spoke up with what seemed an oddly guileless cordiality.

"Oh, I say, you know, do sit down! I'm most frightfully sorry about the other night—should really have apologized yesterday evening. But honestly that basket-thing was so dashed uncomfortable that I was quite *furious*—and just before dinner, too! Did I hurt you too terribly? Dreadful thing to have done, I'm afraid. I suppose you will have to prosecute me? Really dreadful—I'm so sorry. But then one has to go all lengths for one's work, don't you think? Well, not all lengths—not murdering and things—but when it's just a matter of knocking a man out—well, don't you think, really? If you would put yourself in my place, I mean?"

This ingenuous, haphazard appeal seemed to come genuinely from Ransome. He was a sandy, egg-headed, prematurely-bald young man, given to gestures as vague and rambling as his speech. That such an absent person had hit Appleby on the head with just the right amount of force must have been the merest luck, and he was certainly not one to engineer an efficient burglary on his own. A very pretty specimen of the remote and temperamental scholar in the making, consciously capitalizing, perhaps, the advantages of being a "character"—such was Ransome. Or such, Appleby cautiously put it to himself, was the appearance which Ransome presented to the world. And now, feeling that Dodd was about to offer some minatory speech in this matter of an assault upon a colleague, he quickly interposed.

"We needn't discuss the minor incident now, Mr. Ransome. Our concern is with the death of Dr. Umpleby. I am sure you realize that your position is unfortunate. You were confessedly in the vicinity of the college secretly and in disguise, at the time of the murder. And you were on anything but friendly terms with the murdered man."

Ransome looked his dismay. "But hasn't Gott told you all about it—our burglary, and the alibis and the rest of it? And isn't it all square and above board—or above the board you say *you're* concerned with, so to speak—what?"

"The situation is quite simple, Mr. Ransome. You have to account for your movements between half-past ten and eleven o'clock on Tuesday night if you are to be absolved from the possibility of suspicion. And so has Mr. Gott—and everybody else."

"Bless me!" exclaimed Ransome with what seemed all but impossible ingenuousness, "I thought it was clear it was going to be poor old Haveland, scattering bones and what-not——?"

"You must endeavour to satisfy us about your movements—or, at least, it will be prudent and reasonable for you to do so. Inspector Dodd here will take down any statement you may think proper to offer. And I have to tell you that any statement you may make can legally be used as evidence against you."

"Oh, I say! I must have time to recollect, mustn't I?" Ransome looked round the room in a distracted but still easily vague manner. "Don't you think you or your colleague might just ask questions? Way of sticking to the point, you know?"

"Very well. You came in from the Three Doves, I take it, on Tuesday night?"

"Oh, yes, rather. After dinner. Bus from the lane-end—got in just on half-past ten."

"And what did you do in the succeeding hour, before you attempted to reconnoitre the college at eleven-thirty?"

Ransome's reply was prompt but disconcerting: "I tried to work out the Euboic talent!"

Heavy breathing from Dodd seemed to indicate a feeling that the majesty of the law was being trifled with. But Appleby was perfectly patient. "The Euboic talent, Mr. Ransome?"

"Yes. Quite off my line, of course—but I suddenly got an idea about it in the bus. Boeckh, you remember, puts the ratio to the later Attic talent as 100 to 72, and it struck me that——" But here Ransome broke off doubtfully. "I say, though—I don't know if you'd really be interested——?"

"I should be interested to know just *where* you indulged in these speculations."

"Where! Oh, I say—is that important? But, yes, of course it is. I'm most frightfully sorry, but I really don't remember. I was rather absorbed, you see—so absorbed that I almost forgot all about the burglary business. And that of course was enormously important. I remember I had to run. That shows you it was pretty absorbing, because I was awfully keen to get my stuff back from that old beast. . . . Now I wonder where I could have been?"

"Do you remember, perhaps, any method you adopted in working on your problem; sitting down, for instance, to write?"

Ransome suddenly jumped up in childish glee. "To be sure," he cried, "a sort of menu-card; I scribbled down figures on that. Yes, I went straight to a tea-shop—that place in Archer Street that is open till midnight. And I was there all the time, right up till about twenty past eleven. Isn't that splendid? What luck!"

"Do you think they would remember you there?"

"I'm sure they would, whiskers and all. There was a bit of a fuss. They brought me Indian tea. . . . Often in that sort of place they do, you know"—Ransome concluded on a note of warning.

"Well, Mr. Ransome, pending the verification of that, I don't think we need trouble you further. Just one other thing. What put Mr. Haveland in your head as the murderer?"

Ransome was distressed. "I say! Don't think I think Haveland's the murderer. It seems just to be the gossip going round—because he was once a bit rocky, I suppose."

"But that was a long time ago?"

"Oh, yes, rather. Though he had a bit of a relapse when I was home last—but it was soon all right. Good chap, Haveland—knows his Arabia."

"Can you tell me about the relapse you mention?"

"Oh it was a couple of long vacations or so ago. He felt a spot unsteady and went into a sort of rest-home for a bit—place a long way off—a Dr. Goffin near Burford—so nobody knew. Nobody except me, as it happened: I visited him there on the quiet. All blew over."

"I see."

"But I say, Mr. Appleby, there's something I'm most frightfully anxious about. Can I hang on to my stuff—the stuff, I mean, we lifted from the old beast's safe?"

"Mr. Ransome," said Appleby gravely—and to the scandal of the attendant Dodd—"I advise you not to discuss the materials in question with the police until the police discuss them with you. Good morning."

II

"And your remarks on the text," Mr. Gott declared, "are merely a muddle."

"Yes, Gott," said Mike meekly.

"You see, Mike, you haven't any *brain* really."

"No, of course not," said Mike.

"You must just keep to the cackle and write nicely. You write very nicely."

"Yes," said Mike dubiously.

"Keep off thinking things out, and you'll do well. In fact, you'll go far."

Mike's acknowledgments faded into silence and tobacco smoke. The solemn weekly hour that crowns the System was drawing to its close. The essay had been read and faithfully criticized. The remaining ten minutes would be given to pipes and to silence punctuated by desultory conversation. . . .

"It's the fifth of November today," Mike presently offered. And his preceptor plainly failing to find this an interesting observation, he added: "Silly asses, letting off rubbishing fireworks—and all that."

"No doubt."

"Like Chicago during a clean-up. Guns popping."

"Quite."

"D'you remember last year, Gott? Titlow acting as sub-dean while the Dean was away, and Boosey Thompson chucking a Chinese cracker at him, and Titlow wading in and confiscating old Boosey's stinks and bangs?"

"Very unedifying," responded Gott absently. And suddenly he looked hard at his pupil. "Mike, who put you up to that?"

"Put me up——?"

"Mike dear, you're very nice. But as I've just had to point out, you have *no* brain. Who's been stuffing you?"

"Well, as a matter of fact, it was David Edwards that——"

"David Edwards's suggestion," said Gott, "will be conveyed to the proper quarter."

There was silence for some minutes, and then Mike ventured: "There's something more. . . . David thinks it's a pity we haven't been told more of the precise circumstances attending the poor President's death."

"What has the poor President's death got to do with David Edwards?"

"David thinks he might have some useful information—if he only knew, that is, what would *be* useful information."

"I can hardly believe his logic is as rocky as that. But out with what you've been crammed with."

"I think," said Mike mildly and respectfully, "that you're rather rude. But it's like this. On Tuesday night David was working in the library, quite late. Dr. Barocho was there and several other people and David was sitting on top of one of the presses in the north window—you know how people do sit on the presses—and of course it was quite dark outside. But when David was just happening to look out into the darkness there was a sudden beam of light—and he saw somebody."

Gott had laid down his pipe. "*Recognized* somebody, you mean?"

"Yes, recognized somebody. In the light from the President's study. The light just showed for a moment as the person came out——"

"Came out!"

"Yes; came out of the French windows of the study—and

David just made out who it was. He wondered a little afterwards because he doesn't know if this person keeps a key to Orchard Ground and he wondered how he was going to get out if he didn't. But of course it was quite a normal person to be visiting the President, so David didn't know if it would be the least important. As he says, the circumstances of the poor President's death have been kept so dark——"

"What time was this?"

"Oh, just before eleven o'clock."

For a minute Gott was lost in speculation. Then he asked: "Who was it he saw?"

"David won't say. But we have the matter in hand."

"*You* have the matter in hand!"

"Yes, Gott—David and Inspector Bucket and I. You see, David thought it *might* be important. So he investigated. And he discovered one thing about this person whom he had seen. He discovered he had a nice, secret, private way in and out of college——"

Gott sprang up. "Do you mean in and out of Orchard Ground?"

"Oh, no. Just in and out of one of the main buildings here."

"You young lunatics—why haven't you been to the police? Where is David Edwards now?"

"Well, as a matter of fact, he's on the *trail*. And I think if you'll excuse me . . ."

And before Gott could interpose Mr. Michel de Guermantes-Crespigny had gone.

III

It was a positively excited bibliographer who accosted Appleby and Dodd in the court a few minutes later to report on the report of his pupil. Dodd was not inclined to scout the suggestion that St. Anthony's was not a submarine after all; with an attitude of mind that was distinctly to his credit he soberly admitted the possibility of an oversight, and suggested an immediate and even more thorough inspection. But Gott had a preliminary problem to advance.

"Even if it does exist it's difficult to see how it fits in. For according to this precious Edwards it's not in Orchard Ground but somewhere here in the main part of the college. And he saw somebody come out of the French windows about whose possession of a key he was doubtful. But he must know that the four men lodging in Little Fellows' have keys. Somebody other than these four, and somebody who might normally be visiting the President, had therefore to get out of Orchard Ground. How did he do it? The fact of there possibly being a secret exit from somewhere in the main buildings seems irrelevant."

"No doubt it's obscure," said Dodd a little shortly. He did not approve of co-opting a layman—even a favourite author—as a colleague. "I leave the obscurity to Appleby here and intend to test the truth of that young fellow's story."

"Why not wait," Appleby asked, "till the enterprising Edwards comes back from the trail?"

But Dodd would have none of this. And he was just making off in the wake of Gott, who was called away by the demands of the System, when a diversion appeared in the shape of the sad sergeant—in whose dreamy eye some reminiscence of a night in London might still be detected. The sad sergeant had a letter for Appleby and having presented it somewhat hastily withdrew. Appleby poised the official-looking envelope for a moment unopened in his hand. "Well, Dodd—what do you think? There were no finger-prints on my bath-chair handle: will they have had better luck with that pop-gun?"

"No," replied Dodd stolidly. "They will not."

Appleby tore open the letter. There was a moment's pause and then he spoke quietly.

"Pownall's prints."

IV

The sandwich at the Berklay bar, postponed from the previous day, had been duly consumed and Appleby had set out on a solitary walk by the river to think things over. And he began with that formula which he had evolved as he stood mid-way between Pownall's and Haveland's rooms the day before:

He could prove he didn't do it here and now. He couldn't prove he didn't do it there and in twenty minutes' time—were some indication left that he was guilty.

There had been a rider to that, he remembered:

An efficient man: he reloaded and let the revolver be found showing one shot.

And there had been a query:

Second bullet?

Mentally, Appleby deleted the query now and altered the rider:

No reloading; no second shot; a suitable squib.

But a moment later an echo of the first rider came back:

An efficient man: he . . . let the revolver be found . . .

There was the rub. Or there, so to speak, was the absence of the rub—a good brisk rub that would have removed the last traces of finger-prints from the weapon. Pownall was a clumsy man—physically. And here, perhaps, after much ingenuity, had been some answering and fatal clumsiness of mind. It might be that he had done something to obliterate the prints but had not been careful enough. The chemists could almost work magic nowadays: Appleby remembered the authentic report he had given to Deighton-Clerk of the German criminologists who were getting finger-prints through gloves. . . .

Would everything fit? First Haveland's times. Haveland was with Deighton-Clerk from ten-forty to ten-fifty. That would be the period that wouldn't do (*he could prove he didn't do it here and now*). Could Pownall have been certain of Haveland's leaving the Dean—being without an alibi (*he couldn't prove he didn't do it . . .*)—by eleven o'clock? Surely there was a way by which he could have been quite certain. To begin with, he might easily know that Haveland had dropped in on the Dean for *a short time*. Suppose Pownall knew *that,* and had shot Umpleby in his own room in Little Fellows' at ten-forty. . . .

And then Appleby improved on that. Even with traffic near by no one, surely, would risk a shot right in the building. At ten-forty Pownall had shot Umpleby in Orchard Ground—and had known: *Haveland is now with the Dean.* He had got the bath-chair from the store-room, put the body in it, stolen Haveland's bones and put them in the chair too—and wheeled the whole lot into his own room. All perhaps by ten-forty-five. And then he had waited. And while he waited, from Umpleby's body, head lolling over the side of the chair, he had suddenly become aware of a drip, drip on the carpet. . . . Appleby was striding along obliviously now. Was it going to fit? Next there was Barocho's gown—if only it could be proved that its owner had left it in Pownall's room! Pownall would have snatched it up to swathe the head and its little trickling wound. And then, a few minutes after ten-fifty, he had heard Haveland return to his own rooms opposite, had slipped to his door, maybe, to make certain he was unaccompanied—defenceless in the matter of an alibi. A minute later he would set off with his grim cargo on the hazardous journey to Umpleby's study. And then at once the unloading of bones and body; the "big bang" or whatever the particular pyrotechnic might be let off at the right moment; the swift return with the empty chair to the storeroom; the revolver, too-hastily wiped, thrown down where Haveland in his recklessness or unbalance might easily have thrown it.

What else fitted? Pownall's own story, offered to explain away the fatal doctoring of the carpet, had possessed one significant element: it had contrived to point at Haveland even while it cleared Pownall himself. Haveland—such had been the suggestion—killed Umpleby, became aware that he had failed in a scheme to incriminate his neighbour and then by some sudden freak of mind abandoned concealment and virtually signed his own name to the murder by leaving the bones. And two other facts fitted. It was Pownall who along with Empson had known of Haveland's wishing the President "immured in a grisly sepulchre." It was Pownall who, in an outburst of his own, had addressed Umpleby as "a most capital murderee."

And now, what did *not* fit? Here Appleby gave himself a caution. Everything needn't fit—there lay the difference between his activities and Gott's. In a sound story everything *worried over* in the course of the narrative must finally cohere. But in life there were always loose ends, minor puzzles that were never cleared up, details that never found their place. And particularly was this so, Appleby had found, of *impressions*: things at one time felt as significant in the course of a case simply faded out. And yet . . . Appleby liked his smallest detail to fit, his impressions stage by stage to demonstrate themselves as having been in line with the facts.

First among the elements that didn't fit was Slotwiner's statement that he had heard the arrival of the bones between a quarter and ten to eleven. That was a little too early if Pownall were to set out only after he was sure of Haveland's having got back from Deighton-Clerk's. But on a matter of two or three minutes, too much emphasis must not be laid. Next was this still obscure story of Gott's pupil. Was it another red herring? If he had it accurately (but it had come to him in too roundabout a way for much confidence as to this) it seemed too closely linked to the case to be something incidental and insignificant. Someone, not a dweller in Little Fellows', had come out of the study *just before eleven*. And that somebody possessed a secret means of getting in and out of St. Anthony's. It was an unsettling complication and the sooner young Mr. Edwards was interrogated the better.

There was another element that didn't fit. It was Titlow and not Pownall whom this same undergraduate recollected as having, just a year ago, impounded Boosey Somebody's fireworks. But there was nothing very significant in this: the whole firework theory was unnecessary, represented indeed no more than an ingenious guess in the dark. There was no real reason to exclude two genuine revolver shots, even two revolvers. The more Appleby reviewed his facts the less substantial opposition did they seem to present to the reconstruction he had just built up. Apart from what might well prove a mere undergraduate joke, there was really *no* solid material objection. It was certain impressions merely, difficult to assign a just weight to, that continued to cause obstinate misgivings. Until these—or the more assertive of these—were fitted into place, the case, although it might *do,* would leave Appleby uneasy.

But often, he reiterated to himself, he had been obliged to discount mere impressions towards the end of an investigation: why was he so reluctant to do so now? And presently he believed himself to have penetrated to the source of his doubts. More vividly than usual, he had been impressed at St. Anthony's by a number of personalities and he was reluctant to lose sight of any of them. The picture of Pownall plotting against Haveland did not, on this plane of impressions, take in nearly enough: it ignored sundry moments in his contacts with this man and that in which he had sensed himself as at the end of *some* thread leading to the heart of the case. Most vividly before him now was that fraction of a second in which Empson had hung mysteriously suspended between a "yes" and "no"— mysteriously, because in a matter in which he had proved to be without power to prevaricate. And there had been similar moments with Titlow—even with Slotwiner. . . . Slotwiner startled by the mention of candles. The spot of grease. The *Deipnosophists*. A length of wire. Something noticed about the revolver. . . . With these things Appleby's mind had come back to material factors: material factors which, without positively being obstacles, yet did not *fit in.*

He had been pacing the river's bank in deep abstraction. But something suddenly made him aware of his surroundings—the rhythmical but laborious passage of an eight up the stream. It might, he idly speculated, be the St. Anthony's boat, and in relief from his absorption he gave a critical eye to the oarsmanship. The crew seemed near the end of a longish spell; the boat was rolling slightly; the cox, a shrill and improperly plump little person, was doing his best to hold things together. "Drive . . . drive . . . drive; *in* . . . out, *in* . . . out, *in* . . . out. . . ." And the next moment a deeper voice shouted startlingly close to Appleby's ear; it was the coach darting past on a bicycle. "Eyes in the boat, Two. *Late,* Six. *Late,* Six. One . . . two . . . three . . . four . . . five . . . six . . . seven . . . eight . . . nine . . . ten. . . . *Drop* them, Six!"

Drop them, Six! That was another moment that stood out: Pownall's curious insistence on beginning his story with an almost detailed account of a dream. How could he feel such a thing significant, if he were innocent? What purpose could it be meant to serve, if he were guilty? If he were guilty. . . . And here Appleby found himself confronted by the real crux. Why should this rather dim ancient historian shoot Umpleby? Why should he commit the unspeakable crime of fastening the deed on an innocent man? Those psychological probabilities which Gott had very properly refused to discuss—they made the really baffling feature of the case. There was only one reasonably probable core to the thing—and the facts would not fit it. Unless . . . unless a key lay, as he had mockingly hinted to Gott, in De Quincey's anecdote of Kant—that queer pointer given him by Titlow. . . .

Presently he had left the river and struck into winding country lanes. He liked nothing better than to do his thinking during a lonely ramble. And the thought of his solitude striking him now, he remembered Dodd's facetious injunction to avoid being hit on the head again in the course of a woodland walk. It hardly seemed a very likely contingency; Appleby's eye roved whimsically and appreciatively over the peaceful countryside around him. And in doing so it became aware of a succession of interesting circumstances.

The first was an old gentleman pedalling past on a bicycle—not a likely assailant, but an object of some curiosity as soon as Appleby had recognized a Fellow of St. Anthony's. It was the venerable Professor Curtis, looking so absent that Appleby marvelled that he did not pedal placidly into the ditch. Perhaps he was meditating some interesting detail in the curious legend of the bones of Klattau. Conceivably he was pondering the equally curious fact of the bones of Haveland's aborigines. But if he looked absent he also it occurred to Appleby, looked curiously expectant—a happy expectancy rather like that of a small child going to a party.

Curtis had pedalled about a hundred yards ahead, oblivious of Appleby, when the latter, happening to glance behind him, observed a car just coming into view round a bend in the lane. Appleby slipped into the hedge to observe, for to a policeman at least there is something singular in a powerful car doing a resolute eight miles an hour. It was a reticently magnificent De Dion; it contained three intent youths of vaguely familiar appearance; and it was keeping laboriously in the wake of the gently bicycling professor. The procession represented, it sufficiently appeared, Gott's pupil and Gott's pupil's friends "on the trail." It was a trail which Appleby could follow too. Letting the De Dion get a little way ahead, he fell in behind at a brisk walking pace. The November afternoon was chilly, with a light but keen wind blowing: what might be important business and what was certainly beneficial exercise had come conveniently together.

But the walk was scarcely stretching. In something over a mile Appleby came up with the car, abandoned by the side of the road. Proceeding some fifty yards further, he came upon a cottage standing some way back from the lane in the seclusion of a sizable, trimly-hedged garden. Moving to the gate, Appleby could see Curtis's bicycle standing by the front door and Curtis's trackers crouching picturesquely by one of the windows. But even as this sight presented itself to him the young men scrambled up and began to beat a retreat—not precipitately as if they had been discovered, but rapidly nevertheless as if in some discomfiture. Reaching the gate they fairly bolted into Appleby's arms. Mr. Bucket exclaimed distractedly: "It's the detective!" The detective's eye ran critically over the trio and singled out his man. "Mr. Edwards?" he asked crisply.

"I'm Edwards." The young man as he replied edged a little further away from the garden gate.

Appleby went straight to the point. "Mr. Edwards, do you assert that you saw Professor Curtis leave Dr. Umpleby's study about eleven o'clock on Tuesday night?"

Mr. Edwards answered readily, as on a resolution taken long ago. "Yes, I did."

"You are certain?" Again Mr. Edwards was ready—and intelligent. "Quite certain. It was long chances seeing anything and very long recognizing. But I did."

"And now what is happening here?" Appleby's gesture indicated the cottage.

But this time Mr. Edwards, like his companions, was uncommonly confused. "Something that I'm awfully afraid is none of our business. . . . As a matter of fact, sir, I think it's what might be called the lady in the case."

Appleby, without superfluous delicacy, strode up the garden-path to the window. It gave upon a scene of domestic felicity. Professor Curtis was consuming tea before a large fire; perched on the arm of his chair and plying him with muffins was a youthfully mature lady—the sole glimpse of femininity that the St. Anthony's mystery affords.

V

"It was quite true," Dodd greeted Appleby on the latter's return to college, "it was quite true; I should have spotted it."

"Spotted Curtis's bolt-hole?"

Dodd stared. "You've found out?"

"I know who was the owner, but not quite what he owned: tell me."

"Well," said Dodd, "it was pretty tricky, but I oughtn't to have guaranteed St. Anthony's as watertight all the same. Curtis's rooms look out on a little blind-alley off St. Ernulphus' Lane. His windows are barred like all the rest —but if you go out there you'll find, just next door to them, a sort of coal-hole in the wall. It's quite firmly bolted on the inside. And then when you come into the court to investigate you find that the cellar is the breadth of the building, and that the door to the court is securely locked. The porter has the key. But when I thought that there was an end to the matter I didn't reckon with the queer way these places are often built. What has Curtis, whose rooms are next door, got, if you please, but a door of his own opening straight into the cellar—so that he can help himself, no doubt, to a lump of coal when he wants it? Not that there is any coal kept there now, incidentally; it's just a nice, clean, empty space. And all that old reprobate had to do was to slip in there, unbolt the outer door, and amble quietly away."

Appleby laughed. "I don't know yet that he's exactly an old reprobate—but I suspect he has some interesting information to give."

"You've seen him?"

"I came across him in the course of my walk. He was a bit occupied, but I've arranged to see him in his rooms presently. Any further news here?"

Dodd nodded. "Gott's out." He spoke half-regretfully, as if the drama of having the celebrated Pentreith really implicated in a murder were something to be abandoned with reluctance. "A perfectly flat and simple piece of routine work has ousted him. A certain Mrs. Preston cleans the proctors' office, usually between seven and nine in the morning. But her daughter was to be married on Wednesday, so she did some of the cleaning late on Tuesday night instead—taking care not to be seen by the gentlemen. But *she* saw *them*. And she was aware of Gott off and on from the time he arrived till the time he went out again after the return of the Senior Proctor."

"Unexciting but conclusive," Appleby agreed. "And Ransome?"

"Ransome was in the bun-shop all right. Made a great fuss, it seems, about his tea—and forgot to drink it when he got it. He sat scribbling until a bit after a quarter past eleven and then suddenly rushed out as if he had remembered something. It all squares. And now, what's to be done next?"

"Done next, Dodd? Nothing more—except a chat with Curtis and a lot of thinking. We shan't get any more evidence, you know."

"No more evidence?"

"I think not. As I see it, I don't know what further evidence—Curtis apart—there can be."

"Well," said Dodd doubtfully, "as long, of course, as you *see* it——"

At this moment there came a knock at the door and a junior porter brought in a telegram. Appleby tore it open—and for Dodd his expression became a gratifying study.

"The revolver," he said. "It has Empson's prints too."

CHAPTER XVI

I

"It has always appeared to me," began Professor Curtis, "that on retiring from my Fellowship here I could not do better than settle down. Actually, as you see, my marriage, although it is of recent date, has preceded that retirement."

Professor Curtis placidly stroked his beard and looked with mild and luminous intelligence upon his guest. With just such a lucid little proem would he begin expounding the mysteries of the papal chancellery to his pupils.

"You may think it in some degree singular, Mr. Appleby, that I have not communicated the intelligence of this domestic event to my colleagues. But to begin with I may—may I not?—plead precedent. Of course you remember dear old Lethaby, who was Dean of Plumchester Cathedral? He was an honorary Fellow here and a regular member of our common-room for ten or twelve years, coming up every week. But it was only when he died and Umpleby went down to attend his funeral that we became aware that he was a married man. He had not mentioned it.

"In my own case I saw distinct inconveniences, which I need not particularize, as likely to be attendant upon a public announcement. And for the remainder of my time—which is now merely a matter of a few terms—I determined, therefore, on reticence."

"Mrs. Curtis," Appleby smoothly interposed, "of course agreeing."

"My wife, as you say, agreeing. She is a most meritorious female, Mr. Appleby, and I am happy that she had the pleasure of meeting you today. But all this—save in one particular—is really irrelevant to the distressing and confounding circumstances to which I must presently come. Let me mention this particular at once: you will see later how it gained significance. Attendant upon keeping my marriage clandestine there were certain difficulties which you will no doubt apprehend. But these have been minimized by the fact that I happen to possess, adjacent to this room, a convenient and private means of egress from the college."

"Yes," said Appleby, "I know: the coal-hole."

"Exactly so. That is no doubt the purpose for which it is actually intended. For a long time, as I think I told your colleague, I have been without a key to the college, and this emergency exit"—and Curtis beamed at his little joke—"has been most useful. By leaving the door—aperture perhaps I should say—that gives on the little blind-alley unbolted at night I have on occasion been able to slip in that way. And now," continued Professor Curtis with great complacency, "I approach the agitating portion of my narrative."

Appleby produced notebook and pencil. "I shall ask you to sign your statement," he said, "and I have to warn you——"

Curtis nodded amiably. "Yes, Mr. Appleby, yes—and I believe I have got, as they say, on the wrong side of the law. But so bewildering—so very bewildering—has everything been, that I have paused during these last two days in order to watch the turn of the event. I think that expresses it: to watch the turn of the event."

"The event might have turned more quickly if you had come forward at once with such information as you possess."

"That is no doubt a just observation, Mr. Appleby. And

—well, *here goes.*" And Professor Curtis, after an appreciative pause over the dashing colloquialism, really went, if somewhat parenthetically, ahead.

"That I have the knowledge—if knowledge such a confused concatenation of impressions may be termed—of events on Tuesday night that I do have is purely fortuitous. It results from my having resolved, I suppose a little after ten o'clock, to pay a visit to Titlow. It was not a merely social call. A vexed point in a Carlovingian manuscript had been worrying me for some time and it suddenly occurred to me that Titlow might help. He is not, of course, in *any* sense a palæographer, but then he *is*—is he not?—an epigrapher and I thought he *might* help. The notion was most exciting and I put the document in my pocket and went straight across. Or rather I did *not* go straight across—and that no doubt was the trouble.

"I had entered Orchard Ground when it occurred to me to consult Umpleby. I did not"—Professor Curtis continued with some severity—"*approve* of our late President: for some years, it had seemed to me, he had turned controversy into dispute—always an unbecoming thing, Mr. Appleby, in a scholar. But Umpleby was really remarkably intelligent. And being distinctly excited over my problem and seeing a light in his study, I tapped at the French windows—rather familiarly, I fear, considering our by no means intimate relations—and, in short, I stepped in and consulted him. He was very civil and immediately interested—it must be said of our late President that he was a man generously eager for the furtherance of learning—and I suppose we spent some ten minutes over the document."

"That would take you," Appleby interposed, "to about ten-twenty-five?"

"Until about ten-twenty-five. Umpleby made one or two

interesting points and then I left him in order to consult Titlow as I had originally proposed. I left, as I had come, by the French windows, and that"—added Curtis as if with some memory from Pentreith's fictions of the proper formula for such matters—"was the last occasion on which I saw Umpleby alive.

"Well, I went straight to Titlow's. Or rather—you must excuse my lack of lucidity—I did *not* go straight to Titlow's. For it occurred to me half-way to Little Fellows' that in addition to the document in debate I might advantageously have brought certain other documents showing analogous problems. So I struck over the orchard in the dark, intending to return to my rooms by way of the east gate and get what I wanted. I had quite forgotten, of course, the vexatious business of these gates being locked at ten-fifteen. I came up against the closed gate with such unexpectedness, indeed, that injury might well have resulted. Upon that, I turned back to Little Fellows': if the further documents proved necessary, Titlow, who had a key, could come over with me to my own rooms. And it was just as I was approaching Little Fellows' once more that I received the first great shock."

"Can you fix the time," Appleby gravely inquired, "of the first great shock?"

"I believe I can. I was presently to be very much *aware*, and that awareness, by some retrospective operation of the mind, seems to include anterior events as well. I remember that the half-hour struck a moment before I came up so abruptly with the east gate. And in the dark it would take me three minutes—would it not?—to arrive at Little Fellows'.

"And then, Mr. Appleby, I became aware of Haveland. He was standing just outside the doorway of Little Fellows' and the light from the lobby illuminated him, if not clearly, yet sufficiently. I believe I must have discerned, and been much struck with his expression: I cannot otherwise account for the fact that I pulled up immediately. For it was distinctly a second afterwards that I became aware of what he was holding. He was holding a pistol—rather delicately in both hands. And he was examining it, it seemed to me, with something like fascination. But he had paused for a moment only; the next second he vanished into the darkness, only to return almost immediately and disappear into Little Fellows'.

"Haveland, as you know, was at one time afflicted by a nervous ailment and my first thought was that he was about to make some attempt upon his own life. In that persuasion I was about to rush into the building after him when I became aware of a disconcerting, indeed of a horrible impression. *I had the distinct impression that I had already heard a shot.* It had lodged itself in my unsuspicious mind as some noise incident to the abominable traffic by which the university has come to be afflicted. But now it came back to me as a *shot*. I could not tell *when* I heard it: it might have been any time after leaving the President's study.

"And then, Mr. Appleby, I did what I believe was a weak thing. I ought, I know, to have accosted Haveland at once—or alternately to have sought other assistance. But some unreadiness of nature supervened and I took a turn in the darkness of the orchard to reflect. I was already perplexed: how much more of perplexity was to come!"

Professor Curtis paused at this and smiled comfortably at Appleby. Then he resumed.

"I paced about in great agitation for, I suppose, five minutes——"

"Ten-thirty-nine or forty," said Appleby.

"And at the end of that time I determined to consult Titlow on the whole disturbing incident. Titlow is our

Senior Fellow and a man of brilliant if volatile intelligence: he seemed at once a proper and convenient person in whom to confide. I therefore retraced my steps to Little Fellows'—and for the second time became aware of something *most* untoward. Titlow himself was just emerging, *dragging what was plainly a human body*. He hauled it just out of the circle of light from the doorway, pitched it down, to use a vulgar expression, like a sack of coals, and disappeared once more into Little Fellows'. I was very much shaken.

"I am humiliated to think,' continued Curtis with every appearance of the blandest ease, "that my duty was once more clear and that I again failed in it. Indubitably I should have hurried at once to the victim and rendered what assistance I could. But I was horribly convinced that the body I had momentarily seen was a *dead* body—and I was, moreover, excessively perturbed. I retreated once more into the orchard and it was a few minutes before I was sufficiently calm to take action. Then I saw that my proper course, in circumstances so exceedingly grave, was to go at once to the President. I made the best of my way through the orchard to his study . . . I would remind you, Mr. Appleby, that the horror of these events was exacerbated by the inspissated gloom in which they were enveloped.

"Dr. Umpleby's study was deserted—and it was only on discovering this that I remembered, in my agitation, his having remarked that he was going over to see Empson almost at once. Within a few moments of my leaving him he must have followed me through the windows. I had as yet no suspicion of his fate, but I saw that I had no resource save to return at once to Little Fellows'. I passed out of the window once more and had advanced a few steps on my way when I became aware of a mysterious object advancing upon me through the darkness. I was so unnerved by this time that I at once withdrew from the path and made no sign of my presence. And the object soon revealed itself as some species of conveyance; a moment later it had halted before the windows of Umpleby's study and I became aware of sounds of intense physical effort. Then the curtains were drawn for a moment aside, allowing a vision of yet another appalling spectacle. *Pownall was hauling out of a bath-chair what was plainly the dead body of Umpleby*—and a moment later he had disappeared into the study with his burden.

"I will not pause," said Professor Curtis, who had just paused impressively over this lurid picture, "I will not pause to particularize my feelings. I will merely say that I fled—and again passed some minutes in the darkness of the orchard in great agony of mind. At length I hurried back to Little Fellows' to throw myself for counsel—and I may almost say for protection—upon Empson. In the inferno in which I was trapped—I do not think my expression is too strong—it seemed plain to me that there remained only one sane man. I hurried upstairs to Empson's rooms. He was out. The resource had failed. I disliked the thought of Umpleby's study—but I disliked Little Fellows' yet more. I hastily sought the protection of the orchard once again and there I formed what I believe was the most rational plan open to me. I would wait some minutes to allow Pownall to get clear of the study and would then enter it and call the assistance of the President's servants. Looking at my watch, therefore, I gave myself five minutes. Then I, boldly I hope I may say, approached the study——"

"What time was this?" There was a tremor of excitement in Appleby's voice.

"It was between two and three minutes to eleven o'clock. I stepped straight through the windows and came upon

Umpleby's body laid among a litter of bones. But I came too upon something far more appalling than that. At the far end of the room by one of the revolving bookcases, and so absorbed in some operation of his own that he was quite unaware of my presence, was—Empson!

"I had just volition to slip silently from the room once more—and then, to use a familiar expression, my wits deserted me. I was, as I said before, trapped: my only way out of Orchard Ground was by the President's Lodging, and that was blocked by the presence—the sinister presence I cannot but call it—of Empson. It is really disconcerting, Mr. Appleby, for a retiring scholar to find himself incarcerated in a college court with a congeries of criminal lunatics."

Professor Curtis lost himself for a moment in the placid contemplation of this alliterative effort. And then he continued. "Of my movements during the succeeding half-hour I can really give no coherent account. I was conscious, shortly after leaving the study, of hearing another shot; I have a memory of wandering round the orchard in plain distraction. I came to myself only with the sound of voices and what I took to be a general alarm. I was standing in the farthest corner of the orchard, beside the wicket that gives upon the street—and suddenly I noticed that the wicket was opening. By the light of a street-lamp I discerned a bearded person whom I did not recognize step tentatively into the orchard and check himself at the sound of the shouting. But I had seen my chance and, making a dive for the gate, I caught it just before it shut to and made good my escape. To such an extent was I nervously indisposed that I felt momentarily incapable of any other action. A few minutes later I slipped exhausted into my own rooms here—by means of the coal-hole, as you accurately call it. And since then I have waited, as I expressed it, on the turn of the event—waited for what was most plainly a horrid conspiracy to unmask itself."

"There was no conspiracy," said Appleby.

II

After Curtis, Barocho. And from Barocho came confirmation.

Yes, he had at length recollected where he had mislaid his gown: he had left it in Pownall's rooms. . . . Yes, his embarrassing questions in hall had been aimed at Titlow. It was interesting to see how people reacted—and about Titlow since the murder there had been something provoking experiment.

"But you had heard that it was believed not physically possible for Titlow to have killed the President?"

"No. I had not the particulars. But it is not that. Titlow would not plan a murder."

And then Appleby put the grand question. "The Titlows: would they fake a text?"

And Barocho pondered and understood.

"The Titlows," he replied at length, with a gesture that took in the whole academic world of Appleby's question, "would not fake a text, for a text belongs to a realm of pure knowledge which they would not betray. There can be no question of expediency in that realm. But in the world of affairs, knowledge is not serene: it is often obscured—sometimes by human wickedness, often by human stupidity. In the world, truth may require for its vindication the weapons of the world—and the necessity will justify their use. The Titlows do not think of the world—*your* world perhaps, *Señor*—as very perceptive, as very pertinacious for the truth. They live themselves remote from the world—too remote today. And when the world suddenly thrusts its crisis, its decisions upon them, their response is uncertain, erratic—like that of children. But in intelligence, in pertinacious thought, they regard the world as a child. And so, although they will not fake a text to pass about among themselves, they might, to guide the world . . . put out a simplified edition."

CHAPTER XVII

I

ONCE more the long mahogany table gleamed beneath the candles in their heavy silver candlesticks; once more the firelight flickered on dead and gone scholars round the common-room walls. Once more the ruby and gold of port and sherry, the glitter of glass, the little rainbows of fruit had been swept away untouched. Outside, the courts of St. Anthony's were still hushed in decent quiet, but from the lane beyond and from adjacent colleges came the intermittent splutter and crackle of fireworks: it was the evening of the Fifth of November. . . . And once more Appleby was seated at the head of the table, the Fellows of the college assembled round him. And presently Appleby spoke.

"Mr. Dean and gentlemen, I have to tell you that the circumstances in which your President met his death on Tuesday night are now known. Dr. Umpleby was murdered by one of his colleagues."

The formal announcement had its effect. The stillness was absolute. Only Dr. Barocho, his eye circling speculatively round his companions' faces, and Professor Curtis, whose dim absorption might have been directed to Bohemian legends or Carlovingian documents, were without a uniform strained rigidity of attention.

"In a moment," Appleby continued, "I am going to call for a number of statements which will make the facts clear. But I believe you will find these facts less disturbing than they otherwise would be if you will allow me to make one preliminary point.

"We speak of murder as the most shocking of crimes. It is just that. Nothing stands out more clearly in my sort of experience than the surprising effects upon human behaviour which the shock of murder can have. Faced by the sudden fact of wilful killing, called upon for action and decision, a man will do what he might never think to do were he merely coolly imagining himself in the same circumstances. For murder goes along with fear, and when we are controlled by fear we are controlled by a more primitive self. In such a condition our reason may for a time become a slave—something used merely to give colour to unreasonable things. And should murder suddenly erupt in such a quiet and securely ordered society as yours, this shock may be very severe indeed: it may master a temperamental man not for minutes merely but for hours or even days—and particularly is this so if the fear is substantial and real, the product of a danger which even the rational mind must realize. And on Tuesday night, as you will learn, danger took a strange course through St. Anthony's. . . . But though shock and danger may drive us out of ourselves for a time, sooner or later the normal asserts itself. We test our actions by normal standards—and find perhaps that we have to confess a brief madness. I cannot usefully say more and I will ask for the first statement. . . . Mr. Titlow."

II

"I was convinced from the first," began Titlow, "that Pownall had murdered Umpleby. And very soon I was to believe that, in order to escape the consequences of his guilt, he had attempted to fasten the crime upon myself. But for the horror and, as Mr. Appleby has truly put it, fear arising from that second belief I would no doubt more quickly have seen the truth about the first. The truth is that I had *almost* conclusive evidence of Pownall's guilt— but only almost. As soon as I realized this—as I did in conversation with Mr. Appleby in the early hours of yesterday morning—I realized that I must narrate what I had done. When I dispatched such a narration to him this afternoon I had arrived, he would say, at judging my conduct once more by normal standards.

"Here is my story. I returned from the common-room on Tuesday night at about half-past nine and settled down to read until it should be time to make my usual call on the President. I became interested in my book to the extent of letting two important things happen: I let my fire get low and I lost an exact sense of time. As a result of the one I felt chilly and got up to close a window on the orchard side; as a result of the other, I vaguely felt myself to have heard ten strike a minute or so before, whereas I must actually have heard half-past. I leaned out of the window for a moment to see if it was raining, wondering if I should need an umbrella to visit the President. And at that moment I became aware of the President himself just coming into the circle of light from the lobby. He was about to enter Little Fellows' when he was stopped by somebody calling to him from the darkness of the orchard. I was just able to hear; it was Pownall's voice, speaking urgently but at a low pitch. 'President,' he had called out, 'is that you?' And Umpleby replied, 'Yes, I'm going in to see Empson.' I was startled at the response: 'Empson is here, President. He has had a fall: will you help?' At that, Umpleby at once turned round and vanished into the darkness. I was on the point of calling out and hurrying down to assist when it occurred to me that the President and Pownall could do all that was required and that there was nothing that Empson would like less than a fuss. And so

I returned to my book. But I retained an uncomfortable impression that the thing was a little odd: it was odd that Empson should have been walking in the darkness of the orchard. And after a time it struck me as disturbing that nobody had come upstairs; I was afraid that Empson was too badly hurt to be brought up to his room. And on that I decided to go and investigate.

"I stepped out to the landing—and received a distinct shock. *Empson was moving about in his room.* Nobody, I knew, had come upstairs—and yet I could not be mistaken. Empson has a polished floor with rugs and you will understand that the sound of his footsteps and stick together make a pattern with which I am perfectly familiar. For a moment I stood dumbfounded—and then I realized that Pownall must have made a mistake, calling out prematurely that the injured person he had discovered was Empson. I ran downstairs—and I think the natural thing would have been to knock at Pownall's door. I do not know what growing sense of strangeness and alarm sent me straight into the orchard, to light upon the body of Umpleby—a revolver lying beside him.

"The shock, as Mr. Appleby has charitably argued, was very great; for a moment after I had distinguished that quite conclusive wound I could only stand and tremble. Then I looked at my watch. It was ten-forty. Actually, that would seem to have been only some eight minutes after the committing of the crime. But I did not realize that: I had believed it to be just after ten when I rose to close my window and in the succeeding interval my sense of time had remained confused. Well, I had only one opinion—certain knowledge rather—from the first. Pownall, under cover of calling Umpleby to Empson's assistance, had lured him into the orchard and done this unspeakable thing. There came back to me with tremendous force a scene at which I had been present only a few days before, a scene in which Pownall had told Umpleby that he was 'born to be murdered'—or some such phrase. And already I was aware of the vital fact. I was the only witness to what had occurred—either in the orchard that night or on the occasion of Pownall's using the words I have just quoted. . . .

"Almost without knowing what I was about, I had begun half to drag and half to carry Umpleby's body towards Little Fellows'. And there, I suppose with some idea of confronting the criminal with his crime, I hauled it direct into Pownall's sitting-room. The place was in darkness and I switched on the light. I crossed over to the bedroom: if Pownall was there I was going to have him out. And he was there—asleep. It was the horror of that, I think, that finally determined my actions: less than an hour after doing this thing the miscreant was asleep!

"I stood and thought for what seemed a long time—perhaps it was only sixty seconds all told. Pownall had killed Umpleby, and Pownall had got away with it. On that revolver there would, I knew, be nothing; and for evidence there were only my stories—the story of a sinister phrase spoken, the story of uncertain observations made from an upper window in the dark. . . . And at that moment my eye turned to the body and I was aware that something immensely significant had happened. The wound was bleeding upon the carpet. *And the blood represented evidence.*"

The gathering round the long table was listening in a consternation which was turning to horror. Deighton-Clerk voiced the dawning understanding: "You resolved to *incriminate* Pownall?"

Titlow continued unheeding. "I referred Mr. Appleby to a contention of Kant's. Kant maintained that in no conceivable circumstance could it be justifiable to lie—not even to mislead an intending murderer as to the whereabouts of his victim. Standing there over Umpleby's body I seemed to see quite a different imperative. If the cunning of a murderer could only be defeated by a lie, then a lie must be told—or acted. I saw a moral dilemma——"

For a moment the Dean's voice rang out in passionate refutation: in the pause that followed the sporadic explosions outside reverberated as from a battle-field. And coldly Titlow continued. "Deighton-Clerk is right. And Mr. Appleby too is right: a brief madness, no doubt, was upon me. I saw myself in an utterly strange situation and called on for an instant decision. And what dominated me was this: were I not to act, the thing was over—in the next room was a murderer who could never be touched. But were I to act—act on the plan the blood-stained carpet had suggested to me—then nothing final and irrevocable would have been done. If a shadow of doubt should later come to me, if reflection should dictate it, I could cancel the effect of action by a single word. I did not think I should be afraid to do so—nor have I. But that is unimportant. I acted. I tore a couple of pages from Umpleby's diary and left them, burnt but for a fragment of his writing, in an ash-tray. I dragged the body out into the orchard again—that was obviously necessary. And then I returned with the revolver."

Titlow paused. And in the pause there was a touch of the histrionic, as if a flash of his ungoverned imaginative sense had come to ease for a moment the situation in which he found himself. "I had remembered a vital fact. During the alarm of fire we had some years ago, Pownall had revealed himself as an exceptionally heavy sleeper. That gave my plan, I thought, a substantial chance. I returned with the revolver, held by the barrel in my handkerchief, and went into the bedroom. Pownall was fast asleep, his arms outside the coverlet. I took his right wrist with infinite caution and lightly pressed the pistol-butt to his thumb. He stirred in his sleep but I had slipped from the room, as I thought, without his being roused. I tossed the revolver into the store-room, where it would certainly be found, and then retreated upstairs to my own rooms. But that is only half my story. And if I needed confirmation of Pownall's guilt the other half brought it—and with a shock. For Pownall turned the tables on me."

There was a stir round the common-room—a furtive shifting of limbs, here and there a cough. Dr. Barocho was providently rolling himself a stock of cigarettes. Lambrick thought to lower the tension by turning with unconvincing heartiness to throw a log on the fire. Curtis was looking with vague interest at Appleby, as if trying to place an uncertain acquaintance. Titlow continued.

"I determined that I had better do what I had always done—go over, I mean, at eleven o'clock to visit Umpleby. When he was found to have disappeared from his study I could give something like an alarm—and perhaps manage to direct the search to Pownall's rooms. . . . So I presented myself on the stroke of the hour at Umpleby's front door. I had hardly spoken to the butler when we heard the shot from the study. We both rushed in. I could do nothing else, but I knew at once that some devilry was afoot."

"That some devilry was afoot!" It was the Dean speaking, a fascinated eye on his colleague.

"And there the body lay, in the litter of bones. I knew at once that I must have awakened Pownall and that he had contrived some plot. On the face of it it was a plot against Haveland—a plant. But I was wary enough to send Slotwiner to the telephone and hunt feverishly around. There was of course a smell of gun-powder in the room, but there was a smell too of something else—a badly snuffed candle. And then I saw: Pownall had contrived a plot against *me*. . . . It was fiendishly clever, and if I had not penetrated to the farther end of the room it would have caught me. He had arranged a simple demonstration that I had both killed Umpleby and attempted to incriminate someone else and secure an unshakable alibi for myself. He had reasoned like this. If a shot heard by Slotwiner and myself had killed Umpleby neither Slotwiner nor I could have killed him. From that it followed that if such a shot were heard and then proved to be a *fake* it must have been faked to provide an alibi for Slotwiner or myself. If in the faking of that shot there were used something that could be identified with me then the case against me would be clear —or clear enough to give me a very bad time. And that was what he contrived. On the top of a revolving bookcase in a bay at the farther end of the study, concealed behind a few books, he had arranged just such an apparatus as I might have used to engineer that shot. It was an arrangement of a candle-stub and a burnt-out squib—just such a one as they are letting off around us now and just such a one as I was known to have impounded from an unruly undergraduate a year ago tonight. With a little practice such an arrangement could have been quite accurately timed by a person wanting to suggest an alibi in that way. And if I had not discovered it you see what would have been said: that I had not had the opportunity on which I had counted for removing the traces of my plot. As it was, I had time to thrust squib and candle into my pocket and the books back on their shelf before Slotwiner returned. My escape had been a very narrow one."

Titlow's extraordinary narrative was concluded. And Appleby allowed no pause. "Professor Empson," he said crisply.

III

"I knew," Empson began, "that Titlow had murdered Umpleby."

The common-room was passing beyond sensation. Deighton-Clerk looked as if he had shot his bolt of indignation; Ransome had plainly taken refuge behind further calculations on the Euboic talent; Curtis was asleep; Titlow himself was immobile in face of the accusation.

"I knew," said Empson, "that Titlow had murdered Umpleby and that he had contrived a diabolical plot to incriminate an innocent man. And I knew that I was in some danger myself. The simple knowledge of Titlow's guilt would not have moved me to act as I did—nor, I believe, would the knowledge of my own peril. But when I saw dastardly advantage taken of another man's misfortune in order to send that man in his innocence to the gallows, I acted without a qualm. Titlow has always seemed to me unbalanced, and that impression enabled me to get hold of the situation more quickly than I otherwise should have done. For I could not see—and I still cannot see—any rational motive which Titlow could have had for murdering Umpleby and attempting to incriminate Haveland and possibly myself. . . . But that is what I saw him to have planned.

"It is remarkable what, in a familiar and secure environment, one can witness without question or alarm. On Tuesday night I actually saw Titlow dragging Umpleby's body through Orchard Ground—*and I suspected nothing*. It seems incredible. But it is true—and this is how it happened. About ten-forty I decided to go over to the porter's lodge in search of a parcel of proofs. They were of my new book and the expectation of them put me in mind of certain passages about which I felt misgiving: the thought of these no doubt served to preoccupy my mind as I went out of Little Fellows'. But I was not so oblivious as not to see Titlow, and not to see what he was doing. He was a little way off in the orchard—not far, because the light behind me was sufficient to illuminate what he was about: he was dragging an inert human body towards Little Fellows'. And, as I say, I thought very little of it. To be exact, my mind distorted the image of what I had seen sufficiently to allow of a facile and quasi-normal explanation. Titlow, I thought, had found somebody almost dead drunk in the orchard and was charitably assisting him to his own rooms. A moment's reflection shows that that would be surprising in itself and the fact of my inventing and accepting such an interpretation rather than let myself be arrested by something positively disconcerting makes an interesting, but by no means extraordinary scientific observation. I half-resolved to look in and see if I could help on my return. And then I simply walked on to the porter's lodge, my mind wholly given to those sections of my book about which I was dubious.

"What occurred next has, I think, real scientific interest. The porter, who as you know is a most accurate man, happened to imply that I had recently put through a telephone-call to the President—which was not the case. Normally, I would simply have assumed that he had made a mistake: I might have taken the trouble to trace the source of the error; more probably, being sufficiently absorbed in a train of thought of my own, I should have let the matter slide. But on this occasion I was instantly *alarmed*—almost wildly alarmed. It was an extraordinary reaction. And a moment's—I suppose professional—introspection enabled me to connect my alarm *with what I had just seen in Orchard Ground*. Two slightly disturbing facts had made contact—and produced not disturbance but extreme agitation. And at once that distorted image of what I had seen corrected itself. I saw Titlow as doing what he really had been doing: furtively dragging a dead body through the orchard. And instantly an equal impression of the sinister communicated itself to the odd business of the telephone. A blind instinct of caution prompted me to offer no denial to the porter. I hurried out of the lodge with my head in a whirl. It had come to me overpoweringly that in this quiet college, in which I had spent the greater part of an uneventful life, danger was suddenly lurking. It was a fantastic notion. But its fantasticality was something of which I was merely intellectually aware; its *reality* was immediate and overpowering—something felt like ice in the veins.

"It would be hard to say what made me do as I then did. I suppose I had recognized *whom* Titlow was dragging, and that the recognition had sunk instantly into the subconscious. Be that as it may, in making my way back mechanically to Little Fellows' I tapped at the President's French windows—and looked in. And there my eyes met substantial horror enough. Umpleby was lying on the floor, his head queerly muffled in a gown. I went straight to him and felt his heart: he was dead. And as I straightened up I became aware of the grim scrawls of chalk, and of the bones. . . .

"Such a situation would make a dull man's brain move fast. I thought it out, I suppose, in something under thirty seconds. Titlow with Umpleby's body; no alarm; this tableau with what I knew to be Haveland's bones—the series could mean only one thing. Titlow was attempting to incriminate Haveland. He was turning a weakness of Haveland's—long all but forgotten—to what was wellnigh the foulest use conceivable by man. But he had acted in psychological ignorance. I knew as a fact of science that Haveland could never murder Umpleby and deliberately give himself away after that fashion. Even had I not detected Titlow in the midst of his crime I could not have been deceived. . . . But facts of science are too often not facts at law.

"And then my mind came back to the false telephone call—as it now obviously was. That too could have only one meaning: I was implicated in some manner myself. And I realized just how urgent the danger was. If a man of Titlow's ability had contrived such a crazy thing he would have contrived it well. What further hidden strokes he had planned, what other crushing evidence he had contrived, I had no means of knowing. I knew only that discovery might be a matter of minutes. Within those minutes I had to act. And a moment's reflection showed me that there was only one certain way of escape. The crime must be brought convincingly home to the wretch who had committed it."

Empson, who was now speaking in his dryest manner, paused for a moment. And Deighton-Clerk managed to exclaim: "Empson, you *too* are going to tell us——?"

"That I did what you would have done yourself," Empson replied, "if you had managed to think of it. Consider my position. I had stumbled by the merest accident upon a very subtle plot in which Haveland and myself—in whatever relation or proportion—were plainly to be incriminated. I had no reason to suppose that by merely giving an alarm at that point I could foil Titlow. And that the police would get to the bottom of an elaborate piece of ingenuity planned by such a man I had very little hope. Nobody, I think, could have predicted the arrival of an officer of Mr. Appleby's perspicacity.

"Well, I hit on a plan—just the plan which Titlow fathered upon Pownall in the very ingenious story he has just told us. *It must be made immediately obvious that Titlow had killed Umpleby:* that was the postulate with which I began. And if I could not actually show Titlow murdering Umpleby I could, I thought, show him as *avoiding* being so shown. I could show him faking an alibi. I relied on his continuing to act normally and making his usual call on Umpleby at eleven o'clock. If I could fake Umpleby's murder for the moment at which Titlow would be in the hall with the butler *and arrange matters so that the fake would then certainly reveal itself* I should have achieved my object.

"And then I remembered an incident that had happened just a year ago today. Titlow had been acting as sub-Dean and had had occasion to purloin certain fireworks from an undergraduate. And these fireworks I had reason to believe were still in a drawer in his room. . . . A couple of seconds after I had realized that my plan was formed.

"I slipped out of the study, let myself through the gate and into the deserted common-room here: I took a candle-end from one of the candlesticks on this table. And with that I hurried back to my own rooms and, leaving the door open so that I could hear Titlow's movements opposite, waited. Presently, as I had hoped, he came out: he was plainly going to make a show of visiting Umpleby as usual. As soon as he had passed the turn of the stairs I entered his room and in a moment had found what I wanted: a firework of a simple explosive kind. Then I hurried after Titlow and was back in the study before he could have got as far as the west gate. That gave me about a minute and a half. I went swiftly to the far end of the study, lit my candle, affixed it to the top of a revolving bookcase in one of the bays and hid it behind a few volumes taken hastily from the shelf. Then I simply waited until I heard the butler open the front door, ignited the touch-paper of the squib at the candle—which was later to suggest, of course, some primitive but practicable fuse—laid the squib too behind the books, and hurried as fast as my legs would let me from the room.... I do not know that I made any mistake."

"Mr. Pownall," said Appleby.

IV

"My action on Tuesday night," said Pownall, "was dictated solely by my knowledge that Haveland had murdered Umpleby and attempted to lay the crime upon me."

Deighton-Clerk almost groaned; Barocho gave an approving nod; Curtis woke up and took snuff. And slowly and curiously gently, his head dropped characteristically sideways and his hands lightly clasped, Pownall told his story.

"Empson, in his appalling mixed-up version of the affair, has mentioned how one can come across something odd without—if one is unsuspecting—thinking much of it. That was how my own adventures on Tuesday night began. As everybody here knows, I have the habit of going to bed exceptionally early—often at about half-past nine. I was a little later than usual on Tuesday: it must have been just on ten o'clock that I stepped out of my room to fetch some hot water from the pantry. As I did so I heard somebody making a telephone call from Haveland's room opposite. All I heard was a voice saying 'Is that you, President?' and then I passed on. But the voice had been Empson's and I was vaguely surprised that he should be telephoning from Haveland's room. I suppose I was thirty seconds in the pantry, and I had a view of the lobby all the time. I heard no more on my return, for the door of Haveland's room had been pushed to. But I saw something that I immediately thought puzzling—that I ought to have realized as very curious indeed. Glancing upstairs as I passed into my room I saw Empson himself. He was making his way to the little landing half-way down—apparently to get a lump of coal from the locker there. I wondered how he could have got back upstairs without my noticing—but I failed to wonder long or vigorously enough to see that his having done so was a physical impossibility.

"I went straight to bed and, as my habit is, fell asleep at once. But the curious incident was still on my mind and I believe it entered my dreams. I dreamt of somebody speaking in an odd, unnatural voice, and into the same dream was woven what I now believe to have been the sound of the shot that killed Umpleby. And I dreamt yet further of somebody or something clinging to my wrists. And with that I woke up, knowing, as I have explained to Mr. Appleby, that somebody had been in my room.

"The story we have heard from Titlow I cannot attempt to explain, but the things he has mentioned—the bloodstains and the diary pages—I presently found in my room. And then, hurrying outside, I found the body of the President. . . . You know with what vividness one can sometimes recall a voice? In that moment there came back to me exactly what I had heard earlier that night and I recognized it with complete certainty as being not Empson's voice but Haveland's voice imitating Empson's. Under cover of that disguise, it was clear, Haveland had lured Umpleby over from his study to Orchard Ground. And having lured him there he had shot him and was plotting, by what variety of means I could not tell, to incriminate me.

"Haveland was a murderer. Upon that, there came to me an illuminating thing that had been told me by Empson. We all heard it the other night: It was the crazy sentiment Haveland had uttered to Umpleby about wishing to see him immured in one of his own grisly sepulchres. That gave me my idea: I saw how I might escape and at the same time see justice done.

"I ran to Haveland's rooms. He was out. I secured the bones, ran with them into the store-room and stowed them at the bottom of the bath-chair. Then I pushed the chair into the orchard, hoisted in the body, wrapped Barocho's gown round the head and retreated with the whole thing into my own sitting-room. I was just in time. A few seconds later I heard Haveland returning. As soon as he had closed his door I was out again and hurrying, chair and all, to the President's study. The rest you can guess. Within six minutes of finding Umpleby's body and the plot against myself I had arranged in his study a very tolerable version of what had been his real murderer's expressed wish when he had talked of grisly sepulchres. I thought it would be conclusive."

Again there was silence in the common-room; it was broken by the Dean. "Mr. Appleby, what light have you to throw on this mass of contradiction? And where is Haveland? He is not at our meeting." Automatically, everybody looked towards the foot of the table where Haveland had sat facing Appleby two evenings before. But his place was now occupied by Ransome—who gave an alarmed "Oh, I say!" at the sudden concerted scrutiny. . . . Quietly Appleby took up Deighton-Clerk's questions.

"There is no contradiction, Mr. Dean. We have heard— as far as each man's actions are concerned—nothing but the truth. It so happened that on Tuesday night a certain member of the college who chanced to be present in Orchard Ground was witness of a series of transactions which tally exactly with what has been said. It was the information given me by that gentleman which put me in a position to elicit the narratives you have just heard.

"These, Mr. Dean, are the facts. I repeat that everybody

has at length told the truth as they knew it. But everybody acted from contradictory beliefs as to what had really happened—contrary beliefs which proceeded first from the design of the murderer and secondly from the first fatal assumption of Mr. Titlow. . . . You ask for Mr. Haveland. Haveland, the murderer of your President, killed himself while resisting arrest this evening."

v

"Haveland killed Umpleby," Appleby continued, "but he was far from intending to set his signature on the deed. That he would not do such a thing Professor Empson was prepared to state with all the authority of his science. But Professor Empson, although passionately concerned at what he conceived as a dastardly plot against Haveland, was unprepared to discuss the question of Haveland's normality in general terms: such a discussion, he plainly felt, would distract the lay mind from the one piece of scientific knowledge he felt as relevant—*Haveland was not the sort who would deliberately give himself away*. But that was not after all the basic fact. The basic fact was this: Haveland had that sort of abnormality which never loses at least its tenuous connexions with reason. Take his motive. He was, as I learnt from you, Mr. Dean, a likely candidate for the Presidency—and so, as I learnt from a remark of Professor Curtis's passed on to me by Inspector Dodd, is Professor Empson. When Haveland proposed to kill Umpleby and let the blame fall on Empson (for that was the original plot) he was acting with just that combination of moral imbecility and logical sense which characterizes his type.

"He had a remarkable power of mimicry: in this room a couple of evenings ago he shocked you by a momentary imitation of Mr. Deighton-Clerk—and it was deftly enough done to strike a mind interested in such things. . . . He rang up Umpleby, then, at ten o'clock, in Empson's voice and using the porter's manual exchange so that the call would be remarked. Umpleby came over to Little Fellows'—to keep an appointment with Empson, as he thought—just after half-past ten. Haveland's plan was perfectly simple. He lurked in the orchard until the appearance of the President and again used the ruse of an assumed voice—Pownall's this time—to lure him into the darkness. And under cover of the roar of traffic in Schools Street he shot him dead, leaving the revolver beside the body. On that revolver, as I can demonstrate, he had secured and contrived to preserve Empson's finger-prints. Having done so much he went straight to the Dean, paying him an ordinary visit of some ten minutes. And thereafter he went straight back to his rooms. That concluded his activities. The strength of his plan was, I say, in its complete simplicity.

"Mr. Titlow found the body at ten-forty and unfortunately concluded that Mr. Pownall was the murderer Thereupon he took the extraordinary course he did to ensure that Pownall should not escape. But in doing so he roused Pownall from sleep. And the latter, discovering the murder, concluded first and rightly that Haveland was the perpetrator, and secondly and incorrectly that it was Haveland who had attempted to incriminate him, Pownall. He guessed correctly, that is to say, the implications of the telephone-call he had overheard, but he had no suspicion of Titlow's interposition in the matter. Acting rapidly on the plan he thereupon formed, he had body and bones arranged in the study before ten-fifty—and just in time to be discovered by Professor Empson. And Empson, having seen Titlow hauling the body into Little Fellows' and alarmed by his discovery of the spurious telephone-call, concluded that Titlow had murdered Umpleby and was plotting to involve Haveland, and possibly himself, in ruin. He therefore evolved his plan to reincriminate Titlow—who however on bursting into the President's study discovered the device of the faked shot in time to obliterate almost every trace of it.

"And the result of all these subtleties, gentlemen," Appleby dryly concluded, "has been an investigation of some complexity. The double inquest will reveal the insanity which brought about Dr. Umpleby's death. . . . Nothing more, I think, falls to be said."

There was the longest silence that had yet been. Then Deighton-Clerk nodded to Titlow and Titlow pressed a bell. The door of the inner common-room opened.

"Coffee is served!"

CHAPTER XVIII

IT was late. The yellow Bentley—dispatched as a gesture of official recognition in response to a brief announcement of success—waited at the gates. Appleby, already overcoated, Dodd, still faintly bewildered, and Gott, largely appreciative, were consuming liqueur brandy from enormous rummers in the latter's rooms. And Appleby was summing up.

"Umpleby was murdered pat upon the changing of the Orchard Ground keys—in other words under conditions which made access to him possible only to a small group of people. There were various possible explanations of that obtrusive point. One was that the conditions of access were not as they seemed: that the murderer had some hidden means of access and was utilizing the surface conditions to mislead. Another was that he had arranged things as he did for fun: that he was one of the group indicated by the conditions and was giving us a fair start that way. And yet another was that he was one member of the group wishing to *plant* the crime on another member and taking a first step by limiting the possible suspects to the group. And the theory of planted murder proved of course to be the key to the case. Everything that turned up fell in with it—only far too *much* turned up.

"First came the strong suggestions of a plant against Haveland. And soon I came to couple with that idea the name of Pownall. Pownall was concerned to *point* at Haveland: he had pointed at Haveland during a scene which subsequently turned out to have made manifest the pattern of the whole affair; and he pointed at Haveland later

269

when putting up a story to explain his own strange conduct. It seemed reasonable to suspect that in that story Pownall was ingeniously turning the facts upside down. According to his version, Haveland had murdered Umpleby and attempted to plant the murder on him, only setting his own signature to it with the bones in a fit of craziness after his plan had been foiled. In reality (I conjectured), Pownall had murdered Umpleby and planted the crime on Haveland. When it became apparent that both the time and place of the murder had been fudged I was able to see a likely motive for both deceptions. By fudging the time Pownall was making sure of Haveland's having no alibi; by fudging the place he was contriving a particularly striking fulfilment of the rash wish that Haveland had once expressed.

"I allowed this more or less simple case against Pownall a long run. But it didn't seem good enough. For one thing the revolver had significantly given itself the trouble to turn up and I had been prepared to find 't faked in some way to represent another link in the chain against Haveland. On the contrary it had Pownall's prints; if Pownall had shot Umpleby with it he seemed to have been almost unbelievably careless. Again, I had a very distinct impression about the interview I had had with Pownall—the impression that his story had been a complicated mixture of truth and falsehood. This complication, and much else that I felt as having a place in the case, my theory so far failed to cover.

"I was, for instance, convinced that in some way or another both Titlow and Empson came in. With both these I had had what I felt were significant interviews. Titlow, an erratic person it appeared at all times, was strung up *to believe some specific person guilty*. He had it all curiously involved with a philosophy of history—was obviously in a state of unwonted intellectual confusion—but it came down to this: if there was anything incredible about the idea of X having murdered Umpleby then he, Titlow, had some duty before him. . . . And then he gave me the strange reference to Kant: I was to turn upside down the contention that the duty of truthfulness overrides the duty to protect society from murder.

"There was something here which any theory of the crime must elucidate and incorporate. And that consideration held also of the results of my interview with Empson. Empson too had an X in his mind; was shocked that, contrary to the expectations of science and experience, X should have murdered Umpleby—that, at least, was what I read into his attitude. And his X was, of course, not Haveland; there was something like passion in his assertion of Haveland's innocence. And there were two other points. When the possibility came up that the shot heard from the study might have been faked he was anxious to know if any trace of a contrivance for effecting such a fake had been discovered: he was inquiring, in fact, for what would be evidence against Titlow. The last point was his hesitation over the telephone call. That was enigmatical until the revolver was revealed as bearing Empson's prints as well as Pownall's. That revelation brought, of course, the suggestion of a plant against Empson and a faked telephone call fell into place as another attempted piece of evidence against him. Why had Empson *almost* denied making that call, when he knew the porter would seem to expose such a denial? And the answer came: because he knew such a call had been planted on him and he had been on the verge of taking the line of saying so. . . . At the same time I saw how Empson's finger-prints at least might have been got on the revolver. I remembered that the revolver had tried to tell me something, so to speak, the moment I saw it. It was a slight little weapon with a slim curved ivory handle—uncommonly like the handle of Empson's stick. I could imagine it tied to some actual stick and thrust into Empson's hand for a moment in one of those dark lobbies before being withdrawn with an apology for the mistake. The result, almost certainly, would be the slightest and most imperfect of prints—more imperfect even than the prints cautiously got by Titlow from the sleeping Pownall. But very poor prints—the impress of quite a dry finger on an indifferent surface—can be made susceptible of identification nowadays. Here we had an instance of a technical advance in criminology being exploited not once but *twice* in the same case. Which is as good as a word of warning, perhaps, in the field of 'scientific' detection.

"Then came the twisted wire found by Kellett thrust down a drain. You might have guessed that, Dodd. It was the crumpled cousin to the wire contraption you had seen me make to protect possible finger-prints on the revolver! Enclosed in a little cage like that, the revolver could be handled and fired readily enough without obliterating or marring previous prints.

"By that time there was a most embarrassing wealth of clues of the possibly or probably planted sort. Against Haveland: the bones. Against Empson: finger-prints and a faked telephone call. Against Pownall (accepting some truth in his story): the bloodstains, the diary pages and—again—finger-prints. Against Titlow alone of the Little Fellows' group there seemed to be nothing planted. So I tried him out for a bit as sole villain. I toyed with the idea of his trying to incriminate all three of his Little Fellows' colleagues. Then, taking it another way, I tried to see him concerned to establish his own alibi. I brought in Edwards's suggestion of the fireworks and my own observations of the candle-grease on the bookcase there. But I didn't much like it and presently—I suppose for the sake of schematic completeness—I began to explore the possibility of the candle-grease being the sole remaining evidence of a plant against Titlow. I got as far, in fact, as seeing the possibilities of the planted faked shot as an instrument for incriminating him. But there I knew I was on very speculative ground.

"What I had got was the four Little Fellows' men involved in some queer chain of events. I began to search for a *direction* to it. A minute ago I said that, quite early on, Pownall had pointed at Haveland. That was in the common-room on my first night. But more had happened on that occasion. It would not be too much to say that the air had been heavy with insinuation. And an analysis of what had been said or hinted produced this: Pownall had pointed at Haveland, Haveland had pointed at Empson, Empson had pointed at Titlow, and Titlow had pointed at Pownall. Nothing could well be more schematic than that: it gave what was certainly a chain, and it gave a direction in which the chain went. Could I find any start to it all? Was there any correspondence between the way the pointing went and anything known or suspected as to the direction of the planted clues? I could get at only one correspondence: Haveland's insinuations were against Empson—and I had some reason to regard Haveland both as the likely imitator of Empson's voice (he had a talent for it) and as the person who had planted Empson's prints on the revolver (he had been concerned to know if the revolver had been found).

"So I made another tentative start there. *Haveland killed Umpleby and attempted to lay the blame on Empson.* That turned out to be correct. But I went on from it to another guess which turned out to be wrong. *Titlow had suspected Haveland's guilt and had arranged the bones as a means of bringing the crime home to him*—and he was now very properly worried over the morality of such a procedure and was anxious as to the certainty of his belief. But presently I had to discard that—for Titlow's insinuations had been directed against not *Haveland* but *Pownall*. . . .

"But what I was not immediately prepared to abandon —having got so far—was Haveland's guilt. For, paradoxically enough, the notion of somebody's faking a case against Haveland now removed the chief obstacle to seeing Haveland as really guilty. A case faked against Haveland was really protecting him—because it was *unconvincingly* faked: Haveland, as Empson knew, was not the man to sign his deed in the way suggested.

"And Haveland had always been the likely murderer. In searching for a murderer amid any group of people every detective knows the importance of a history of mental unbalance. In real life murderers are not, on the whole, found among the chief constables and Cabinet Ministers: they are found among the less normal portion of humanity. Anyone may behave more or less fantastically in the face of murder, but the commission of murder is—well—specialist's work. Deighton-Clerk, I believe, had recognized Haveland as the murderer and had instantly blanketed the fact in his own mind in a manner—as Empson would say —full of scientific interest. The first *spontaneous* remark Deighton-Clerk made to me showed the subconscious run of his thought. Between Umpleby and Haveland there had been detestation. . . .

"At that point I had pretty well shot my bolt. By following up the chain: Haveland—Empson—Titlow—Pownall— Haveland, I might get things a little clearer in my own mind; might even arrive at a position from which I could begin to extract a little unvarnished truth from people. But of one thing I was almost convinced. I should never see either Haveland or anybody else in the dock. Whatever these four people had been up to they had between them produced a mass of complications which no defending counsel could muff."

Appleby rose and set down his rummer. "Titlow's story I was half counting on, but my anonymous observer in Orchard Ground was the simple bit of luck that enabled me to dictate explanations after all. And Haveland's choosing the way out he did has been a crowning blessing all round. It cuts down the scandal here; and if it deprives Treasury Counsel of considerable fees it spares a harassed policeman a good many sleepless nights."

Appleby clapped Dodd on the shoulder and moved towards the door. Then he turned and smiled at Gott. "We shall meet again, I hope. And meantime I have a parting present for you."

"What's that?"

"A title for the book you may never be able to write: *Seven Suspects.*"

Visit Penguin on the Internet
and browse at your leisure

- preview sample extracts of our forthcoming books
- read about your favourite authors
- investigate over 10,000 titles
- enter one of our literary quizzes
- win some fantastic prizes in our competitions
- e-mail us with your comments and book reviews
- instantly order any Penguin book

and masses more!

'To be recommended without reservation ... a rich and rewarding on-line experience' – Internet Magazine

www.penguin.co.uk

READ MORE IN PENGUIN

In every corner of the world, on every subject under the sun, Penguin represents quality and variety – the very best in publishing today.

For complete information about books available from Penguin – including Puffins, Penguin Classics and Arkana – and how to order them, write to us at the appropriate address below. Please note that for copyright reasons the selection of books varies from country to country.

In the United Kingdom: Please write to *Dept. EP, Penguin Books Ltd, Bath Road, Harmondsworth, West Drayton, Middlesex UB7 0DA*

In the United States: Please write to *Consumer Sales, Penguin Putnam Inc., P.O. Box 12289 Dept. B, Newark, New Jersey 07101-5289*. VISA and MasterCard holders call 1-800-788-6262 to order Penguin titles

In Canada: Please write to *Penguin Books Canada Ltd, 10 Alcorn Avenue, Suite 300, Toronto, Ontario M4V 3B2*

In Australia: Please write to *Penguin Books Australia Ltd, P.O. Box 257, Ringwood, Victoria 3134*

In New Zealand: Please write to *Penguin Books (NZ) Ltd, Private Bag 102902, North Shore Mail Centre, Auckland 10*

In India: Please write to *Penguin Books India Pvt Ltd, 11 Community Centre, Panchsheel Park, New Delhi 110017*

In the Netherlands: Please write to *Penguin Books Netherlands bv, Postbus 3507, NL-1001 AH Amsterdam*

In Germany: Please write to *Penguin Books Deutschland GmbH, Metzlerstrasse 26, 60594 Frankfurt am Main*

In Spain: Please write to *Penguin Books S. A., Bravo Murillo 19, 1° B, 28015 Madrid*

In Italy: Please write to *Penguin Italia s.r.l., Via Benedetto Croce 2, 20094 Corsico, Milano*

In France: Please write to *Penguin France, Le Carré Wilson, 62 rue Benjamin Baillaud, 31500 Toulouse*

In Japan: Please write to *Penguin Books Japan Ltd, Kaneko Building, 2-3-25 Koraku, Bunkyo-Ku, Tokyo 112*

In South Africa: Please write to *Penguin Books South Africa (Pty) Ltd, Private Bag X14, Parkview, 2122 Johannesburg*

BY THE SAME AUTHOR

Hamlet, Revenge!

The murder was planned, deliberately and at obvious risk, to take place bang in the middle of a private performance of *Hamlet*. Behind the scenes there were thirty-one suspects. In the select and distinguished audience twenty-seven. 'Suspions,' said Appleby, 'crowd thick and fast upon us.'

The Daffodil Affair

While Inspector Appleby's aunt assigns her favourite cab-horse to Scotland Yard's missing persons file, Mrs Rideout is equally distressed at the loss of her daughter. Appleby, mystified by the motive for stealing Daffodil, a half-witted horse with exceptional numerical skills, travels to Harrogate to learn more. Meanwhile Hudspith, also of the Yard, is hot on the trail of Lucy Rideout. The enigmatic young girl seems to have been magicked away to an unknown isle by a foreign gentleman.

Appleby's End

The Raven family of Long Dream Manor were distinguished by their noses and their shabby plumage – relics of happier times when Great-uncle Ranulph Raven wrote his thrillingly Gothic stories and made Victorian England shudder. Unhappily, Gothic *frisson* is now out of fashion and the family are forced to look to other means of survival. In the circumstances John Appleby can't help wondering why they have invited him to stay.

also published:

From *London* Far
The Journeying Boy
Operation Pax
The Man from the Sea

Death at the Chase
An Awkward Lie
Appleby's Other Story